NOWHERE LEFT TO FALL

KAT MIZERA

Copyright © 2019 by Kat Mizera

All rights reserved.

No part of this book may be reproduced in any form or by any electronic or mechanical means, including information storage and retrieval systems, without written permission from the author, except for the use of brief quotations in a book review.

Cover Art: Dar Albert

Cover Photography: Wander Aguiar

Cover Model: Pat Tansky

ALSO BY KAT MIZERA

Las Vegas Sidewinders Series:
Dominic
Cody's Christmas Surprise
Drake
Karl
Anatoli
Zakk
Toli & Tessa
Brock
Vladimir
Royce
Nate
Sidewinders: Ever After
Jared
Ian (2020)

Inferno Series:
Salvation's Inferno
Temptation's Inferno
Redemption's Inferno
Tropical Inferno (formerly "Tropical Ice")

Romancing Europe Series:
Adonis in Athens
Smitten in Santorini
Lucky in Lugano

Alaska Blizzard Series:
Defending Dani
Holding Hailey

Winning Whitney

Losing Laurel

Saving Sarah (TBD)

The Nowhere Trilogy:

Nowhere Left to Fall

Nowhere Left to Run

Nowhere Left to Hide

Other Books:

Special Forces: Operation Alpha: Protecting Bobbi (Susan Stoker's Special Forces World)

Special Forces: Operation Alpha: Protecting Delilah (Susan Stoker's Special Forces World)

Brotherhood Protectors: Catching Lana (Elle James's Brotherhood Protectors World)

For Lisa Sealey
For being there from the beginning...

1

Casey

"Thank you, Las Vegas—see you next tour! Good night!"

Wrapping our arms around each other, the members of my band and I took our final bow of the tour before turning to head backstage. Viktim of Prey was one of the hottest rock bands in the world right now, and some nights it felt like we couldn't get any more successful.

I grabbed a towel from my guitar tech and wrapped it around my neck. I was drenched in sweat and high on adrenaline, like always after a big show, but tonight was different. We'd been on tour nonstop for nearly three years now, and the idea of actually taking a break was daunting. Though I could tour forever, the rest of the band had begged for a break, and if I was honest with myself, we all needed it. We'd been playing, traveling, and partying for too long. It was time to regroup, plan the next album, unwind a little. Not that I had any idea what to do with myself if I wasn't playing music.

"I need to talk to you guys." Nick Kingsley, our bass player, as well as my best friend with benefits, spoke in such a somber tone it made the hair on the back of my neck stand up.

"I just want to go home and sleep for a week," Jade Simkowski, our lead singer, moaned, her long red hair fanning out behind her as she walked behind Nick towards our waiting tour bus.

"It won't take long," Nick said, bypassing a few fans with backstage passes and our road crew.

Jade and I exchanged a look but followed him, our drummer, BJ, pulling up the rear.

Nick climbed into the tour bus and collapsed on one of the lounge chairs, grabbing a bottle of water.

"What's going on?" I asked, settling next to him.

"I don't want to do another album," Nick said quietly.

"What?" I gaped at him.

"Tabby and I are having a baby," BJ blurted out, referring to his wife.

"Really, you guys?" Jade made a face, shaking her head.

"My dad wants me to work at the hotel," Nick spoke softly, not meeting my eyes. "And the truth is that I'm not really good enough to do this. The only reason I'm here is because you asked me to be in the band. I'm a mediocre bass player who doesn't write music. You'd be better off with someone who can pull their weight."

"And I'm tired," BJ admitted. "It's been fun, but I'm ready to stay put for a while, be a husband, a dad." BJ was the oldest member of the band at thirty, while I was twenty-two, Nick was twenty-three, and Jade was twenty-four.

"That's a cop-out," Jade said. "I'm a mom, and I've been on tour on and off for four years."

"Your daughter is older," BJ pointed out. "She wasn't a newborn when we started. She also has a father who's happy to split parenting duties."

"She's seven," Jade responded testily. "Still really young, but this is how I afford to give her nice things, make sure she's taken care of."

"Okay, let's take a deep breath." I needed to take control of the situation sooner rather than later, because this band was my life, and Nick was essentially talking about ending it. "We should all go home, get some sleep, relax a little. We can have a meeting next week, take some time to digest and—"

Nick reached out and took my hand, cutting me off. "I'm not going to change my mind, Casey. I did this because you wanted it so much, and we got so big so fast…but being a rock star was never on my radar."

I bit my lip to keep from saying something that would end a lifetime of friendship.

"I know you're mad." Nick sighed, squeezing my hand. "Go ahead and say what you want to say."

"What is there to say?" I muttered, looking away. "Without you and BJ, Jade and I can't do this."

Nick reached for me, forcing me to look at him. "Casey, you're going to find another band, another group of people to share your gift with. It's wasted with me. I don't have your talent or your drive. Besides, our agreement was one album and one tour. It's been two albums and a huge, multi-year tour. Even if I wanted to keep doing this, we all need a break right now."

"He's right about needing a break," Jade added softly. "I need to be at home with Alyssa for a while, doing mommy things. I love music, but my kid needs me, too, and Kirk shouldn't be raising her alone, even if we're not together anymore."

I sighed, nodding. They were right. I hated it, but we were all tired.

"I have to get going," Jade said, standing up and pulling me into a hug. "I'm taking the red-eye home so I can be there to surprise Alyssa when she wakes up in the morning. I'll call you in a couple of days and we'll regroup, okay?" She turned to the guys and smiled. "I love you guys, even if you're pains in my ass." She hugged them both, grabbed the backpack she always traveled with, and got off the bus.

"Tabby's waiting to take me home," BJ said, getting to his feet. He leaned over and kissed my cheek. "Love you, Casey. Don't be mad." He high-fived Nick and went in the direction Jade had gone.

"Are you going home?" Nick asked, his blue eyes finding mine in the semidarkness.

"Where else would I go?" I asked, frowning at him. "Tour is over, and we live here."

"You could come home with me if—"

"Come on, don't." I shook my head at him. "It's not like we're a couple. And, frankly, I need a break."

"From me?" Nick actually looked hurt, and I managed to stop myself from rolling my eyes.

"From you, from music, from everything. As much as I love being on the road, now that we're home, I need some normal too. I want to hang out with my parents and see some friends. Hibernate for a while."

"You can't stand hibernating," Nick said, eyeing me suspiciously. "That's your least favorite thing. If you're not in the spotlight, on the go, guitar in hand, you're miserable."

"Maybe you don't know everything about me," I shot back, annoyed that he knew me so well.

"But maybe I do." He reached out and tugged a lock of my hair. "Come on, don't be mad. Wanna share a cab?"

I gathered a few of my things and threw my bag over my shoulder. "After your little bombshell, I honestly need some time to myself." I leaned up and pressed my lips to his cheek. "I'll call you in a couple of days."

"You're pretty mad, huh?"

"I'm not mad, Nick." I paused and turned to look over my shoulder at him. "I'm lost."

2

E*rik*

MEETINGS WITH THE ROYAL FAMILY WENT ON FOREVER. AS SIXTH IN LINE TO the throne of Limaj, I'd never understood why I had to be at these meetings every six months, but my father and uncle both seemed to think it was necessary. There was a weird vibe today, though, and as I strode through the halls of my country's Parliament House, no one was making eye contact. The idea that I was in trouble briefly flitted across my mind, but I shook it off. My position within the family was mostly that of an ambassador, with no real duties to speak of since almost everything I did included getting the world's best education and making appearances at this charity or that sporting event. I showed up at dinner parties I was told to attend, went out with women who would make good potential wives, and generally kept to myself.

I spotted my best friend/cousin, companion and bodyguard, Sandor, and breathed a sigh of relief. I joined him by the doors that led to the royal family's private conference room and leaned against the wall.

"What the hell is going on here today?" I muttered under my breath. "Did someone die?"

He grimaced. "No, but apparently your sister has everyone on a tear."

"*Fuck*. What did she do?"

"She's getting a divorce."

"A divorce?" I stared at him as if I'd never heard the word before. "But..."

"Yeah, I know." His eyes met mine, and sudden understanding washed over me.

"Sonofabitch. Did he hurt her?"

Sandor nodded. "She's in the hospital. He did a number on her."

I whirled around, searching the hallway. "Where's my father? For that matter, where's the king?"

"Calm down, my friend." Sandor tried to grab my arm, but I was already moving, heading toward the king's office, even though he rarely used it. If nothing else, his assistant would be there to tell me where he was.

"Erik." My father's voice froze me in my tracks, and I turned, gearing up for an argument.

"He hit her? Omar fucking put her in the hospital?" I was pissed and didn't care who heard me.

"Calm down," my father replied, eyeing me with a warning look.

I didn't back down, though, meeting his gaze without flinching. "Where is he?"

"At home, I assume."

"I'm going to kill him." I turned, but my father grabbed my arm and held fast.

"You'll do nothing. The council is about to meet, and we'll decide what to do as a whole."

"Seriously? The council? With their antiquated legalities and old-school morality, they'll probably pat him on the back!" I didn't have much power, but I had a voice, and while I rarely spoke up when it came to matters of state, this was my sister.

"Nice to know you think so highly of your old uncle." My father's brother, King Isak, gave me a fond but wry smile as he approached us.

I respected him but rarely agreed with the policies of our country. One of many reasons I hated these meetings. "I apologize, Your Majesty, but you know how I feel about this topic."

"Indeed, I do. Believe it or not, I agree with you. But we have rules of law we must follow and a process that's been in place—"

"For so many years no one even remembers how it works anymore." I refused to look away, even when everyone around us averted their eyes.

"Let's continue this discussion in the conference room, shall we?" This time his look was more meaningful, and I nodded, understanding that these types of conversations needed to be held in private, no matter how upset I was.

We filed into the conference room where a veritable breakfast feast had been set up, and everyone made their way to the food. I held back, going to the coffee bar instead and having the barista my uncle employed for these meetings make me a cappuccino. I took it and sank into my usual place next to my father, who sat on the king's left side. We always sat in the same places, with my father, me, my cousins Daniil, Sandor and Vardan to the king's left. The king's sons—my cousins Anwar, Yusef, and Rafael—sat to his right, in order of their birth. It was usually a bunch of bureaucratic bullshit, but something was different today. I exchanged a look with my dad, who didn't look happy.

"Good morning." King Isak didn't stand on ceremony at these meetings. We were all immediate heirs of the royal family and since nothing much ever happened when we met, most of the time we shot the shit for a while, went over our official duty schedule for the next six months, and then discussed random laws and other boring matters of state. At some point, they brought in a fabulous lunch, and if we were lucky, we'd be out on the golf course by five. Sometimes, it was more like three.

"We'll start today's meeting by discussing the situation with Skye." King Isak looked down at some papers and made a face. "Our laws allow for a husband to punish his wife, so we'll have to tread carefully if we're interested in filing any charges."

Anwar, the king's oldest son and heir to the throne, rolled his eyes. "She probably deserved it."

I tensed, but my father gripped my forearm under the table, the force telling me he would handle this.

"Anwar, you disappoint me." My father, Prince Benjamin al-Hassani, spoke in a bland, almost bored voice. "This is the twenty-first century, not the Middle Ages. Is this how you plan to treat your wife?"

"My wife will know her place. You've lived in America so long you've forgotten that we still enforce boundaries here."

"I've got a boundary that keeps me from kicking your ass into the middle of next week," I responded with a smirk, since I'd done it before. "You want to try me?"

Anwar narrowed his eyes. "Remember who you're talking to, cousin."

"That's the only reason you're not on the floor." I wasn't a big fighter, but Anwar had always been an asshole. Because of my position, I'd been trained in the martial arts, boxing, and wrestling. Friendly competition among the cousins always went wrong for Anwar, no matter how hard he tried. There were six years between us, his thirty to my twenty-four, but I'd been taking him on since I was fifteen. And winning.

Anwar seemed ready to get out of his seat, but his father grunted something under his breath and Anwar settled back down. I wanted to laugh, but that would just piss off my father, so I held it in and smirked instead. I got along with all of my other cousins, but the heir to the throne had a stick up his ass, and I figured someone had skipped over the lube.

"It's time to move beyond laws of the past," King Isak was saying in his stately voice. "Our country has sat precariously balanced between the east and the west, Europe and Asia, old and new, for too long. We must, for the sake of our people and our future, move into the modern world."

"We have some of the best technology and infrastructure in the world," Anwar protested. "Fiber optics, satellites—"

"Yet we do not have respect, prestigious universities, or even much tourist trade other than a bit in summer," his father interrupted him. "We remain firmly seated in the past while much of the world moves on without us. We cannot continue to focus on the old ways when it leaves us looking weak."

"Weak?" Anwar scowled at him. "Our military is strong, our weapons growing, and the scientists say we're within three years of nuclear—"

"Nuclear!" Uncle Isak pounded his fist on the table, making all of our dishes bounce slightly. "This, above all, will destroy us. Our history, our people, our children's futures. Have you learned nothing from me, Anwar?"

"How can you not see that the world has gained so much freedom, so much power, it's imploding on itself!" Anwar shot back, leaning forward.

"And it's up to small, rich countries like ours to do what's right and help guide it back to where it should be."

"You're a foolish old man!"

"And you're an insolent embarrassment." Uncle Isak shook his head. "To think you will someday replace me worries me, my son."

Anwar threw up his hands. "Because I follow the old ways? Because I believe our ancestors had it right?"

"Our ancestors would have you living in a tent in the desert," his father snapped. "I don't see you giving up your Ferrari or your condo in the city."

"All right, enough." Dad spoke up quietly, though the authority in his voice was hard to miss. Technically, he was the firstborn son of the previous king and should have succeeded him, but he'd fallen in love with a commoner from Sweden and had abdicated the throne to be with her. Though his brother, the current king, had allowed him to keep the title of prince, he and his heirs no longer had any power in the bloodline. I was sixth in line on paper--merely because of the DNA running through my veins--but barring a horrific tragedy that eliminated all of my male cousins, I would never ascend the throne, and I'd always preferred it that way. Anwar was a terrible human being and no matter how many times I told myself he would grow up, change, it hadn't happened. At thirty, I didn't think it would, and it scared me.

"You have no right—" Anwar began.

"He has every right behind these doors," Uncle Isak said sharply. "Were it not for him, you would be a powerless cousin relegated to ambassador duties."

It went on for another hour. I got up twice to refill my coffee, once to get some food, and another time to use the bathroom. By eleven thirty they'd made no decisions about Skye other than to remove her from the country, no plans to finalize their schedule of appearances for the next six months, and Anwar was as petulant as a three-year-old who didn't want to take a nap.

"I'm fucking done," I muttered to my father as servants served lunch. "What's wrong with everyone today?"

My father sighed, glancing in his brother's direction. "There's a lot going on. The country is at a crucial point in our history, on the verge of civil war."

"We've been saying that for years," I protested.

"Yes, but it's coming to fruition, and Isak is struggling with how to deal with it."

"What of Skye?"

"I've got a plan in motion. As soon as it's safe to move her, I'm having her airlifted to Las Vegas. She can recover with her mother and me there. Once she's physically able, she can decide where she wants to go, what she wants to do."

"She'll just go back to him."

"I don't think so. Not this time. At least, I hope not."

"He's done this before?" My mouth fell open, but I was so shocked I didn't care.

"Not this badly, but yes, he's hit her before. This time, he broke her nose, her collarbone, and two of her fingers. I think her eyes are finally open."

"Why didn't you tell me?"

"Because you'd be in prison on a murder charge, which wouldn't help anyone. Trust me, I'm on top of this."

I wanted to strangle him, and her, but since I couldn't, I cut a piece of steak and stuck it in my mouth. Maybe a good meal would improve my mood. Probably not, but there was always a chance.

"So, are you in?"

"In?" I looked at him in confusion. "In what?"

"The rescue mission, of course. Omar's not going to agree to a divorce without a fight, so he'll try to stop us from taking her out of the country."

"Sure." What the hell else was there to say?

3

Casey

AFTER TWO DAYS OF SLEEP, EATING MY FAVORITE MEALS, AND ONLINE SHOPPING, I was ready to get out of my condo. Nick hadn't been right about much the other night, but he'd been right about me not being good at staying still. That's why I loved touring so much. Without it, I didn't know what to do with myself. I'd been playing music my whole life. My father was a legendary rock guitarist from the eighties and nineties, and I'd had a guitar in my hand since I was two years old. I played a little bass, a lot of piano, a touch of drums, and even some saxophone. But guitar was my heart, my soul, my passion. A day didn't go by that I didn't at least pick up my acoustic and strum a few melodies. Songwriting was my second passion, and I was constantly scribbling notes on pads, napkins, or the Notes app on my phone. Except the last two days.

I hadn't picked up my guitar, hadn't written any song lyrics, hadn't even thought about it. Instead, I'd given myself a few days to wallow in self-pity. I was done, though, and on my way to my parents' house to let my mom give me some love and my dad give me some insight on what to do next. I was twenty-two years old, independently wealthy, and had zero idea what I wanted to do now that Viktim of Prey was no longer a band.

I got to my parents' suburban McMansion and used my remote to open the gate. I hadn't lived at home for a few years, but I still had a key and my own room. As I rounded the corner, a familiar limousine was parked on the side of the house, and I sighed impatiently. Just once, I wanted my parents all to myself, but as always, they had company. Uncle Ben and Aunt Kari were my parents' closest friends, and they were together constantly. Usually, I didn't care because I adored them—I'd known them my whole life—but today I wanted to sit on the couch with my dad and talk about music while eating something my mom baked and listening to her make fun of us.

Taking a deep breath, I opened the kitchen door and walked in, calling out to my mother. "Mom?"

"Casey!" My mother was still a stunner at fifty-two, and she came into the kitchen in cut-off denim shorts and a tank top that said "I love rock 'n' roll." "What are you doing here?"

"I came by to hang out, but I didn't realize you had company."

"Ben and Kari are family." She hugged me tightly. "Are you hungry?"

"I could eat."

"Go say hi to your father, and I'll make you something. Scrambled eggs with feta cheese sound good?"

"Sounds amazing. Thanks, Mom." I grinned and hurried into the living room where my father, Lucas Hart, was playing cards with Prince Ben al-Hassani, or Uncle Ben, as I'd always called him.

"Hey, baby girl." Dad gave me a lopsided grin, unlit cigarette hanging out of his mouth as he put his cards down. "Full house," he told Uncle Ben.

"Asshole." Uncle Ben tossed his cards down and turned to me. "Come give your old uncle a hug."

I hugged both of them, happy to be back in my family's fold. I craved music, but my family grounded me, even when they were far away.

"Casey!" Aunt Kari came down out of the guest bathroom and immediately held out her arms.

"Hi!" I hugged her too.

"You're pale," Aunt Kari announced, frowning. "You need sun. We should fly to Hawaii for a week."

I laughed. Kari's solution to everything was a trip to a beach.

"We'll see," I told her.

"Eggs are ready," Mom called from the kitchen.

"Go eat." Aunt Kari smiled at me. "We'll catch up after."

I walked back into the kitchen and was just about to sit down when the door opened, and the man of my dreams came in. Prince Tariq al-Hassani, or Erik as we'd always called him. I nearly stumbled, staring at him in surprise. What was he doing here? I hadn't seen my teenage crush in two years, and seeing him in my parents' kitchen left me flustered, which almost never happened.

"Hello, Casey." His soft, well-modulated voice and faint British accent always did things to my treacherous insides, but I managed a quirky smile.

"Hello, Your Greatness. What brings you to our dusty desert oasis?" He'd always hated Las Vegas when we were kids, and I'd always mocked the way most people greeted him as "Your Highness."

"My sister's getting divorced, so I came to offer a little support."

I arched a brow and laughed. "How's that going?" Skye and I disliked each other, and Erik had never been all that close to her, either, from what I'd heard. In fact, no one really liked her.

"About how you'd expect."

"Awesome." I sank down and dug into the meal my mother had prepared.

"I'm going back to the living room," my mother said softly, squeezing my shoulder. "You two can join us when you're ready."

"Thanks, Mom."

"You look sad," Erik said gently. "Are you okay?"

"The band is breaking up, and I guess I'm at a crossroads in life."

"I'm sorry. I hadn't heard. Why?"

"Nick doesn't want to be a rock star, and BJ is going to be a father."

"You and Jade could pull together another group, no?"

"I suppose." I looked at him with a sad smile. "But it won't be the same, and I think Jade wants to spend more time with her daughter too. I don't know right now. I'm a little lost."

"I understand."

"Do you?"

"You think it's easy being a prince with no real role? My entire life is education, raising money for charities, and being told how to behave."

"I thought you loved all that."

"Not even a little."

This was news to me.

"What would you do if you weren't a prince?"

He frowned. "I don't know. It's never been an option, so I never thought about it. I think professionally I'd like to be involved in corporate law, international finance, that sort of thing. Big business."

"And personally?"

He met my gaze with a look I'd never seen before. Was he flirting with me? Holy shit, he was checking me out, and I didn't know what to do. Prince Tariq al-Hassani, though the son of my parents' best friends, had always been off-limits to me. He was a few years older and had gone to boarding school and university in Great Britain. We'd hung out on occasion, and I had the biggest crush on him, but he always left too soon and didn't seem that interested. He was smokin' hot, and I was just a regular girl, so it didn't surprise me. It didn't stop me from wanting him in the worst way, though.

"I think I'd find a beautiful woman to love and have a family with."

"Can't you...do that anyway?" I wasn't sure why my breath felt a little short.

"I'm not interested in the women my family thinks are appropriate for me." He looked away. "But that's a conversation for another time and another place."

"Okay?" I wasn't sure how to respond so I just kept eating.

Erik was gorgeous, and I was having a hard time believing he was single. He had his father's dark hair and green eyes and his mother's incredible features—long eyelashes, a full mouth, and a straight nose. There was a cleft in his strong, square chin, and I'd always fantasized about licking it.

"So, what are you going to do now?" His question brought me out of my fantasy.

"Drink," I replied with a smile. "I'm going to go underground with some of my rock and roll friends and drink until I can't feel any of the disappointment or confusion about my future. Then I'm going to hit the recording studio and start writing some new songs. I always come up with great lyrics when I'm depressed."

He chuckled. "Amazing how that works, isn't it?"

"Yeah." I got up and grabbed a bottle of water out of the fridge. "What happened with Skye?" That was a much safer subject than my life.

"Omar hit her."

"He hit her?" My eyes widened. "Holy shit. What happened?"

"She won't tell us the details, but I guess she learned that Omar is a lot more old-school than she thought, and she was nothing more than a vessel to produce his future offspring. She simultaneously discovered his mistress."

"Shit."

"When she told him she wouldn't tolerate infidelity, he hit her hard enough to break her nose, a couple of fingers and a few other things."

I grimaced. "Why would she marry someone like that?"

"I don't know," he said with obvious confusion. "I asked her if she ever really loved him, and she told me that wasn't why people in our position married."

I shook my head. "I've never understood her."

"I thought I did until she married Omar, but she seems to have her own agenda now."

"Omar is the one with the agenda," Uncle Ben said, coming in to put some plates in the sink. It always struck me as odd that a man of his wealth and bloodline did such menial tasks, but he always did when he was at my parents' house.

"What does that mean?" I asked him.

"I wish I knew," Uncle Ben admitted, looking at me. "I hope I'm wrong about him, but his interest in Skye always bothered me. We always kept her under the radar, raising her out of Limaj and away from arranged marriages and the like. He appeared out of nowhere, courting her and getting her to agree to marry him and move home to a country she'd never lived in other than for a handful of extended visits. I did a little digging and he's not a good man, the type that would kick a puppy just because he wanted to. I could never prove it, but it always felt like he wanted something."

"What could he possibly want?" I asked. "I thought he was wealthy in his own right."

"I don't think it's about money," Ben said tentatively. "If anything, it's about power."

"He doesn't think he's going to be king, does he?"

"Not hardly," Erik snorted.

"Well, whatever he intended, hopefully, that's behind us now," Uncle Ben said, changing the subject. "And you, my dear, are you terribly depressed following the break-up of the band?"

"Terribly hungry, it seems." I laughed, cleaning my dish and getting up in search of more.

"Well, then, I will leave you two to chat and go comfort my wife who is determined to become a grandmother before she turns fifty so she can have the energy to play with them. Either that, or we're going to have another one of our own. For which I'm going to suggest we start practicing immediately."

Erik rolled his eyes as his laughing father left the room. "I don't know which of them is worse."

"I think your parents are adorable."

"They're uncouth sometimes, that's for sure."

"Uncouth?" I asked, surprised.

"That's not the type of thing you say in front of others. At least not to me."

Oh, there it was, his snooty royal side showing up. It came and went in my experience, and it always annoyed me when he switched from casual and relaxed to uptight and snobby. Especially when his mere presence made my palms sweat a little and parts of me tingle that shouldn't. "Why do you think being royalty means being a snob?"

He looked at me in surprise. "You think I'm a snob?"

I shrugged. "Well, your sister is a snob and then some, and you're a borderline snob. Or, at the very least, decidedly stuffy."

"Stuffy?" He gaped at me. "What does that mean?"

"When was the last time you were drunk? When was the last time you acted silly? Do you tell dirty jokes? Hell, do you tell jokes at all?"

"Because I take my position and family reputation seriously, that makes me stuffy?"

"No one who's serious all the time is any fun—and you've always been this way—even as a teenager."

He paused. "So, you think being serious is a negative?"

"I think being serious all the time is sad. I don't ever remember seeing you laugh or have fun, even though your parents are tons of fun."

"And what way am I?" he asked dryly.

I didn't like where this conversation was going or why I'd suddenly started picking on him, but I was having a hard time thinking about anything except his gorgeous green eyes or the little tuft of chest hair I saw peeking out from his dress shirt. My childhood crush had grown into six-feet-two-inches of hunky royal temptation, and that would only get me into trouble. "Serious…isn't that what we've been talking about?"

"You really dislike me, don't you?"

"Not at all. I don't have much of any relationship with you." I self-consciously wiped my mouth, wondering how good of a liar I was. "And I probably never will because you have no concept of my life, my career, or even how to have fun."

"I have fun," he protested.

"Oh, yeah? When? Playing golf a few times a year with your father and cousins?"

"Well, that's fun, yes."

"Okay. And?"

"I go to the races when I'm in England and—"

"I almost feel sorry for you. You're too good-looking to be this boring. I bet you don't even have exciting sex."

4

E*rik*

I managed not to turn red, but I had to take a long drink of water before I was able to answer her.

"My sex life is private, thank you," I said slowly. "But I believe I do know how to please a woman."

"And who's going to tell you otherwise?" She laughed. "I can't see some poor girl who thinks she has the chance to marry into the royal family telling you you're no good in bed."

I stared at her. "I'm fairly certain I can tell when a woman is faking."

"If you say so." She got up and put her dishes in the sink, keeping her back turned as she rinsed them.

As frustrated as I was with the turn the conversation had taken, I was enjoying sparring with her. She was gorgeous, with long blond hair and the biggest, bluest eyes I'd ever seen on a woman. Her legs were long and lean, sitting beneath the most luscious backside I'd ever wanted to sink my teeth into. Regardless of what she thought, I had a healthy, abundant sex life, and the women I'd slept with most certainly enjoyed themselves. I wasn't sure how to convince her of that though. Well, I knew how I wanted to convince her, but that didn't appear to be in the cards.

"Do you really think I'm stuffy and boring?" I asked instead. "I was raised as a proper royal, so I've always had a set of rules to follow, a way of doing things outsiders don't understand."

"You're right, and I understand that part of it." She closed the dishwasher and turned, leaning against the counter. "Look, I don't want to argue. I was just pointing out how different we are and why we don't have any kind of relationship. I didn't mean to be rude."

"What would I have to do to prove to you that I'm not a bad guy?" I didn't know where that came from, but I was suddenly pissed off and intent on showing her I wasn't stuffy and certainly not a snob.

"I never said you were a bad guy." She laughed. "But, anyway, why do you care what I think? You're going back to Limaj, or wherever you spend your time, and I'm positive you won't give me a second thought once you go."

"How do you know what I think about?" I demanded. "You just admitted you barely know me. So, I'll ask you again…what would it take for you to believe I'm not all bad?"

"And I'll tell you again, I never said you were bad. I just said we're very, very different."

"You didn't answer my question." I stood up, towering over her, fixing a gaze on her that seemed to surprise her based on the way she took a hesitant step back. "What would I have to do to prove to you I'm not truly stuffy, that I know how to have fun, and that I care about people? Maybe even you."

She stared at me, squinting slightly as she tried to come up with a response. Finally, she shrugged. "Come to New York with me. I'm going on a rock 'n' roll drinking and partying fest. I'm going to see old friends, get drunk, and forget all about this debacle with my band. If you truly want to be my friend, come with me to make sure I don't get into too much trouble."

"Fine."

"But you can't sit there like a stick in the mud."

"All right."

"And you have to lose your bodyguards."

"That's not possible," he said. "My father wouldn't allow it."

She pursed her lips. "All right, but just your personal guard, Sandor, and he has to dress like us, act like us, and hang out with us. He can wear his gun under a jacket or something, but he can't tell anyone who he is or who you are."

"And a car with my personal driver to follow us discreetly, just in case."

"As long as they stay far away, and the only way they come anywhere near us is if they see something that looks dangerous."

"Done."

She gave me a funny look. "I'm heading to the airport in the morning."

"We can take the family plane. Mother and Dad aren't planning to travel any time soon."

"Hmmm, now that's downright useful." She chuckled. "I'd like to be out of here by around ten if that's okay with you."

"I'll arrange it."

"Perfect. See you later."

I watched in frustrated astonishment as she blew me a kiss and strolled into the living room to join the others without giving me a backward glance. What the hell had just happened, and what had I gotten myself into?

I'd always had a hard-on for the bright-eyed blonde, but she was two years younger than me, and I'd never spent more than a few weeks at a time in Las Vegas growing up. Between boarding schools, summer camps, and official family visits to Limaj, I'd worshipped her from afar. Watching the insanely talented and sexy woman she'd turned into had me jerking off in the shower more often than I wanted to admit, but I'd never dared let her or anyone else know just how much I wanted her.

Up until recently, I'd believed I would marry the woman chosen for me and go about my life the way everyone expected me to. After the last meeting of the royal family, something sour had settled in my gut. I enjoyed life as a royal, but with virtually no chance of taking the throne due to my father's abdication, I was content to be a bit of a playboy, enjoying all that life and my position had to offer, though I was always discreet. Recent events, however, had shown me that things were changing in my country. As part of the royal family, I couldn't sit back and allow things to happen the way they always had.

Limaj sat in a unique position both geographically and politically. Settled between Europe, Asia, and the Middle East, it was what I'd once thought was the perfect balance of old and new. East of Turkey, bordering Iraq and Iran, with Georgia to the north, we were a tiny blip that essentially spanned three regions. Limaj had always represented the best of all those worlds to me with the food and summer tourism of Turkey and the rest of eastern Europe, the pride and history of Asia, and the oil of the Middle East. We had wealth, freedom, and decent weather. There were some antiquated laws, like giving men almost complete control of their wives, but spousal rape was no longer allowed, and women had the freedom to work, get an education, drive, and most other rights.

As in most things in life, Limaj wasn't perfect. Families still believed in arranged marriages, winters in the northern part of the country could be brutal, and some of the newer politicians had radically old-fashioned ideas, suggesting longer hem lengths for women's clothing and less freedoms for citizens, in general. Thus far, they'd been shut down by the general assembly of senators and the king himself, but the fact that they kept popping up bothered me. Anwar seemed to be aligning himself with that faction of the government, and though King Isak made noises about not approving, he hadn't removed him as next in line to the throne either.

All of this had been a quiet nagging in the back of my mind, and since I'd finished my master's degree, I'd been paying a lot more attention to what was going on. My father had abdicated the throne before I was born so I'd never thought about being king and it seemed like a huge hassle anyway. I preferred my much less demanding life and had brought up getting a job more than once. But the family always shot me down, leaving me far too much time to think. And every time Anwar said something stupid, something deep inside of me burned with a need to find a way to take my rightful place as heir to the throne.

I'd never said these things aloud, of course. My father probably wouldn't be happy, and my uncle would have a heart attack, but what else was there for me to do? My role as an ambassador was boring, I'd had enough parties and polo matches to last a lifetime, and sex with giggling debutantes and ladder-climbing socialites had begun to bore me in ways I didn't understand. In fact, until running into Casey today, I'd given up on women altogether. Just sparring with her earlier had gotten my dick hard, and I wanted her more than ever.

Unfortunately, she didn't seem to like me very much, though she'd been polite at first. It had always been that way, with her politely avoiding me since our teens. She'd started calling me "Your Greatness" instead of my appropriate title, and though I never knew why, it always made me laugh. Hearing it today had sent blood flowing to regions I'd thought were dormant, so that undoubtedly had played a role in my deciding to go to New York with her.

"Erik?" My mother's voice brought me out of my reverie, and I looked up at her with a smile.

"Hi."

"I'm so glad you decided to come with us. When was the last time you saw Uncle Lucas and Aunt Teal?"

"Too long," I admitted.

"Did you and Casey have a nice chat?"

I snorted. "She mocked me for a while and called me stuffy, to which I promptly invited myself along on her upcoming trip to New York."

My mother bit her lip, the twinkle in her eyes belying her attempt to not laugh. "I see."

"Go ahead and laugh. She doesn't like me."

"Oh, she likes you." She ran a gentle hand along my cheek. "I think she feels you're out of her league, so she covers it with sarcasm and snide remarks. Take the time to get to know her, my love. She's a smart, talented, strong young woman who's still finding her way. I think the two of you would be good for each other."

"How so?" I asked curiously.

"She needs someone to guide her through adulthood now that she's at a crossroads professionally, and you need someone to show you how to let go of everything you can't have." Her words were filled with hidden meaning, and I searched her face, trying to grasp what she wasn't willing to spell out.

"Mom, I just—"

"I know. You're troubled, unsure of your place in the world... Trust me when I tell you I know what you need better than you do."

I sighed. She was probably right—she always was.

"Go to New York and let yourself get lost in fun. You've always been the perfect son, well-behaved and loyal, intelligent and cognizant of your role within the royal family. But that's not your life, so why not enjoy the one you have instead of the one you feel was taken from you?"

Damn. How did she always do this to me? It was like she read my mind. It pissed me off sometimes, but not today. Today, it made sense because I was making myself crazy watching things out of my control go sideways. Whatever happened in Limaj, in the government, with Anwar, had very little to do with me, and I'd be so much happier not worrying about it. At least in theory.

"Thanks, Mom." I rested my head against her side, and she gently stroked my hair.

"My daughter has never taken a single piece of advice I've given her," she whispered. "And look where she is now. So, do me a favor and be the child who does."

"Okay." I nodded, and for the first time in many years, I was genuinely excited about something. Whether it was Casey or merely the freedom to be myself for once, I couldn't tell, but whatever it was, I was ready. Consequences be damned.

5

Casey

I DIDN'T USUALLY DO THINGS THAT WOULD LEAD TO HEARTBREAK, BUT apparently, I wasn't firing on all cylinders right now. Inviting Erik to come to New York with me had been stupid, and as I finished fixing my face for a night out, I stared in the mirror self-consciously.

I was a rock and roller through and through, from my collection of leather jackets to my custom Harley-Davidson to my penchant for Jack Daniel's Tennessee Fire, but I often found myself struggling with that label. I had no interest in drugs, though I smoked a little weed once in a while, and I longed to get a bachelor's degree in music even though I'd probably never need it. I liked ball gowns and makeup just as much as leather pants and worn jeans, and though I didn't get to travel for fun very often, one of my goals was to visit every corner of the earth.

I didn't fit into any mold and had always liked that about myself, but with Erik tagging along now, I wondered if he had any idea who I really was. The thought of rejection made me wince a little on the inside, but it wasn't like I lacked male attention. Men came out of the woodwork anywhere I went, even though most didn't interest me at all. Touring with Nick meant I'd had a convenient, sexy lover available whenever I wanted so there hadn't been any need to date. Except now I had the opportunity to spend time with

Erik and that was all I'd thought about all day. Hell, I'd been thinking about it on and off since I was about twelve.

A knock on the door forced me to step into my black high heels and grab my purse.

When I opened the door, Erik nearly took my breath away. How was it possible he was even hotter in ripped black jeans and biker boots than he was in a suit? I was in so much trouble.

"Ready for New York?" he asked with a grin.

"The question is, are *you* ready?" I laughed, hoping my attraction wasn't somehow tattooed on my forehead.

"I think so."

"Don't worry, I'll be gentle."

His eyes smoldered, and I pretended to be checking my purse for my room key to avoid staring into them too long. I had too much to do and too many plans to make to allow myself to act on whatever was going on between us, but I really wanted to. It was just a few days of fun, though, right? We were adults and would be able to handle something casual and brief. Then, when it was over, I would dive into a few projects I'd had on the back burner for a while now. My dad was in the process of opening a recording studio; I wanted to produce solo albums for myself and for Jade, and then I would use the studio as a way to discover and mentor new talent.

"You looked so serious all of a sudden," he said gently. "Are you okay?"

"I'm fine." I shut off the light behind me. "Let's go."

WE TOOK THE BLACK SUV ERIK HAD RENTED TO A STUDIO I WAS PLANNING TO visit. Friends of mine were playing a showcase for the press and a bunch of their record company's executives, and I was hoping to surprise them. It would be a little odd showing up with Erik and Sandor, but since Erik had said his bodyguard and a driver weren't negotiable, I wasn't going to worry about it. My goal was to hang out with my musician friends tonight, get drunk, and maybe seduce the object of my fantasies. He'd probably use me and leave me, but you only lived once, right?

"What is this place?" Sandor asked as we pulled up.

"It's a recording studio that friends of mine booked for a private event," I said, getting out of the car before our driver, Aziz, or Erik could help me.

We were on the upper west side, at a studio I'd never been to before, and I was pleasantly surprised when we got inside. The room was set up for a combination performance, interviews with the press, and a meet-and-greet for contest winners who'd been invited. An incredible buffet was laid out, including everything from lobster tail to baked Alaska, and champagne flowed from some sort of ice sculpture formed in the shape of a tiger, which was the band's logo. Tables were set with candles, fresh flowers, and immaculate linens. The band's music played on the loudspeakers, but other than that, we might have been attending a wedding or a meeting of a board of directors somewhere.

"Remember," I reminded Erik. "You're friends of mine from the U.K., and you're definitely not royalty."

"Yes, Your Highness."

I laughed since I refused to call him that, and now he was throwing it in my face.

"Behave," I said, looking around for my friends as I headed to the bar. I spotted them on the other side of the room and waved as I ordered a Jack Daniel's Tennessee Fire with one ice cube.

Keegan Ryan and Tyler Thompson came running to the bar, lifting me in big bear hugs and spinning me around. Their band, No Intent, had opened for us for all of our New York area shows and we'd gotten to know them pretty well. Their bass player, Tyler, was incredibly talented and it had occurred to me that he would make a great replacement for Nick, but stealing him from his current band would be a shitty thing to do to the rest of the guys. Besides, Tyler was barely eighteen, so he needed a little time to grow up. I didn't want to be anyone's mom on tour.

"You didn't tell us you were coming," Keegan said, shaking his head. "How'd you get in?"

I laughed. "Really?" The guy at the door had almost genuflected when he recognized me.

"Dumb question." Tyler nudged his buddy. "So what's shakin'? How long are you in town? You wanna party?"

"You're not old enough to party," I pointed out.

"You weren't old enough to party when you first went on tour," he shot back, his eyes twinkling with mirth.

"Do as I say, not as I do," I teased, laughing.

In my peripheral vision, I caught Erik staring at me and motioned him over.

"Come meet my friends," I called, holding out my hand to him.

The sexy bastard approached us with a smile that did things to my heart. Damn, was he teasing me or was I just completely in love?

"Gin and tonic, please," he said to the bartender. "Twist of lime."

"Erik, this is Tyler Thompson and Keegan Ryan, with No Intent. This is their first album, and my dad co-wrote one of the songs."

"Nice to meet you." Erik smiled lazily, and then he gave me a once-over that made it very clear I belonged to him. What the hell was that about?

"This is my friend Sandor," he continued.

"Where are you from?" Keegan asked, his eyes already glassy from one too many glasses of champagne. "The U.K.?"

"I just finished my master's in business at Oxford," Erik responded casually. "I guess I picked up a bit of an accent."

"New boyfriend?" Tyler murmured under his breath.

"None of your business," I whispered back.

"We gotta warm up," Keegan said. "Nice to meet you guys—we'll see you after, Casey."

"Break a leg," I called after them.

"They look young," Erik commented.

"Keegan's twenty-two and Tyler's eighteen. He was still seventeen when they opened for us earlier this year. He turned eighteen while we were in Boston, and we had a huge party for him. I invited his parents and everything. It was great."

"That was nice of you."

"I'm actually pretty nice."

"Are you?" His eyes met mine again and it took all of my self-control not to kiss him. Except he was looking at me like he wanted me to and suddenly, I didn't care. Why shouldn't I throw caution to the wind? What was the worst thing that could happen?

Before I could change my mind, I raised myself up on my tiptoes and pressed a light kiss right on his lips. Nothing prepared me for how soft they were. Or how much I liked it. I was in so much trouble.

6

E*rik*

Holy fuck.

Casey freakin' Hart just kissed me. Her lips sent a shockwave rocketing through me that made me want to do unthinkable things to her. I wanted to grab her by the ass, yank her against me, and stick my tongue down her throat. She'd already stepped back, though, her eyes twinkling as she waited for my reaction. Damn, she was beautiful, and mischievous, and everything I never realized I wanted in a woman. How did the wrong woman feel so incredibly right? I'd always wanted her because she was beautiful and talented, but she wasn't the kind of girl a guy like me could marry. She was a rock star, for god's sake, and the thought of her dressing in conservative suits and hosting tea parties was almost laughable.

Except I was never going to be king, and there was no reason to follow the rules anymore. All that had gotten me was frustrated. Maybe it was time to take my mother's advice, push back against tradition and pursue a woman I wanted simply because my entire being reacted whenever she was near me. There wasn't anything to lose, and now that I'd had a taste, I wasn't as willing to repress my attraction as I'd been before.

"You shouldn't tease a man," was all I could think to say.

"Who's teasing?" She winked and moved off toward a group of people that had come in.

I watched her with a private smile, wondering just what mischief she would lead me into on this trip. The look on Sandor's face told me he was already horrified, but as an official guard to the royal family, he felt duty-bound to follow me to the ends of the earth. We'd enjoyed some interesting evenings while we'd been students at Oxford. That was one of the fringe benefits of being a protector of the royal family, as well as a cousin; my father insisted that Sandor be just as educated as I was. So, although Sandor was a couple of years older than me, he'd dutifully waited until I was ready for college before attending himself. However, what we'd thought was adventurous in those days was probably nothing compared to what Casey had in store for us.

One part of me was excited. I'd been infatuated with her for years, and she'd barely given me the time of day. Now, I was going to be in her company for an undetermined length of time, without Nick—whom I knew she dated on and off—or anyone else to distract her. I wasn't worried about her music industry friends; had there been anyone of any romantic interest to her in those circles I would've heard about it. All I really had to worry about was my own perception that I'd never be the kind of man she wanted. Not that I had any idea what kind of man that was, but could a sexy, successful woman like her truly be attracted to a man she'd already called stuffy and boring?

I liked to think I was a mature, educated, respectable man who had a lifetime of public service in my future, but when it came to Casey, I felt like an inexperienced teenager with sweaty palms and knocking knees. I wanted to throw convention to the wind and marry her. Today. My parents had long since given their blessing if such an occasion ever arose, which was weird and heartwarming at the same time, and I had a gut feeling this was going to be my one and only chance to win her over. The question was how to do it. Sandor would be no help, and if given a choice, I would've preferred Sandor not come along at all. Hopefully, a few glasses of whiskey would put Sandor in a mellow enough mood to leave us alone.

As the evening wore on, I watched Casey make frequent visits to the bar. Each time she would down a shot of that Tennessee Fire she loved so much, and then walk away with a whiskey and Coke that she would sip as she mingled. She seemed to know everyone, from the publicity people to the band's managers to their girlfriends and parents. She charmed the record company executives, made small talk with Keegan's girlfriend, and unobtrusively picked up a piece of lobster dipped in butter and seductively popped it in her mouth. Every man in the room was watching her, and she knew it. I had to admit, I'd never seen this side of her before, and it fascinated me. I'd seen her perform live a bunch of times, and I'd seen her rare television appearances, but I'd never seen her so alive. She was a star, she knew it, and she had a room full of people practically salivating to get close to her.

"I must admit," Sandor said as he came up behind me and glanced in Casey's direction. "She's never been my type, but she's a very sexy woman."

I smiled. "She's always been my type, and it's taking all my self-control not to go over there and throw myself at her feet."

We were still chuckling as Casey approached, for the first time a bit unsteady on her feet. She gave us a smile and cocked her head. "You're talking about me again."

"Busted." I smiled down at her.

"If you two are going to exchange drool, I'm leaving," Sandor muttered.

Casey laughed, linking her arm through mine.

"So, what do you think?" she was asking me. "Did you like the music?"

I nodded. "Not bad. I'm more a jazz fan though."

"Why am I not surprised?" She shook her head. "Come on, let's do a shot."

"Casey, I—"

"You what?" She leaned against me. "You want to play without paying first? No way. If you're not as drunk as I am by the time we leave here, you're sleeping alone tonight."

I met her gaze directly, my green eyes boring into her blue ones. On the inside, my stomach had begun to churn, but I refused to let her see what she was doing to me. "I can match you shot for shot."

"I'm about six up on you right now, so you've got a lot of catching up to do!" She turned and took a step toward the bar. Then she paused. "Coming?"

"Soon, I hope."

I followed her as Sandor muttered, "You're insane."

"Casey!" a loud male voice shouted from across the room, and I turned to see an extraordinarily tall man with glasses and a blond ponytail open his arms. Casey ran into them, and he scooped her up in a huge hug, spinning her around until they were both laughing. They kissed, but it was without passion, and I forced myself not to react.

"Lance! What are you doing here? And you're late!"

"I'm always late," he chuckled. "But I was working, so I have a good excuse."

"Likely story."

"I'm glad to see you though."

"So am I." She turned then, seeking me out. "I want you to meet my friends, Erik and Sandor."

Lance frowned slightly and looked in our direction almost suspiciously. "Erik!"

She was calling to me, and I had no choice but to join them.

"I want you to meet Lance Baker," she said. "He's been our tour manager since our first headlining tour, and he's like family."

"Nice to meet you." I shook his hand and was surprised to find it firm and dry. Lance was probably close to seven feet tall, and his glasses redefined the analogy of Coke-bottle lenses. However, upon closer inspection, every inch of the man was steel, and his voice was deep and sincere.

"Likewise. Casey running you ragged?"

"She's trying," I laughed.

"Well, then, let's do a shot." Lance turned toward the bartender and automatically ordered a round of Tennessee Fire.

"We're going to die," Sandor muttered under his breath.

My hopes that the party was dying down were dashed even though the release party was coming to an end, but the band had invited everyone to a club in Greenwich Village, and more than a dozen of the guests filed out to find taxis. Lance joined us in the SUV though.

"Casey, you really need to do a solo album and tour," he was saying.

"I want to," Casey agreed. She was pressed up against my side and seemed perfectly content there. I knew she was drunk, and that she might not be flirting with me like this if she hadn't been, but tonight I didn't care. "I'm not ready to think about the future yet."

"Gonna let loose for a while?"

"That's the plan." Casey turned those gorgeous blue eyes to me and leaned in, letting her lips hover millimeters from mine.

"Oh, bother," Sandor muttered, staring out the window.

"Kinda sucky to be the third wheel, ain't it?" Lance asked him. "I hate it, too, but since I rarely get to hang with Casey, I guess I'm willing to put up with it."

To my surprise, Sandor laughed. "I suppose, in an odd way, I feel the same way since I rarely get to spend quality time with my favorite cousin."

"Oh, you guys are cousins?" Lance began talking a mile a minute about his own cousins, and Casey looked over at me.

"What?" I asked softly.

"Just kind of surreal that we're here like this."

"You're beautiful," I whispered. I desperately wanted to kiss her—really kiss her—but this was neither the time nor the place. Not yet.

"Not yet," she said, echoing my thoughts. "Later—there's time." She looked out the window and let out a yell. "We're here. You guys are going to love this place," she cried, hopping out of the car before I could grab her. She linked her arm through Lance's and called over her shoulder to Sandor and me. "Come on, slowpokes!"

It was past midnight now, but Casey didn't seem to be tired at all. She immediately headed for the bar with Lance in tow, and Sandor and I found a table in the back of the private room the band had reserved. Unlike the recording studio where we'd been earlier, this was a nightclub where bands played, music blared, and couples found dark corners in which to make out, dance, or do any number of other things I didn't want to think about. Casey and Lance arrived carrying a tray with shots for all of us.

"If we die," Sandor whispered to me, "I'm going to follow you straight to hell and kick your ass."

"At least we'll be together," was my response as the liquid burned its way down my throat.

"Casey, dance with me!" Keegan had appeared, and Casey was whisked off in his arms as he spun her around a raised dance floor.

For a hard rock musician, he could move, and I watched in irritation. Casey was also an excellent dancer, and they were the center of attention as Keegan dipped her over and over.

"Don't worry about Keegan," Lance spoke behind me. "He's all but married, quite happily. But his girl is pregnant, so she went home. Casey's the reason their band got discovered, so they love her—and they're good guys. Besides, she scares the hell out of them."

"She scares the hell out of me sometimes too," I chuckled, starting to relax.

"How long have you known each other?" Lance asked.

I sighed. "Most of our lives, actually. My family lives in Las Vegas most of the year, but I went to school in England so I wasn't around much."

"And she was probably hooking up with Nick."

"Absolutely."

"Look, I don't know you or what your story is, but Casey's like a sister to me. She's kind of vulnerable right now—don't hurt her, okay?"

"Believe me, that's the last thing on my mind."

"Good." Lance nodded at me and then strode out to the dance floor where he tapped Keegan on the shoulder and cut in on the dance. Lance, however, could not dance, and soon he and Casey were laughing too hard to move.

A rock ballad filtered through the sound system and that was my cue. "It's my turn," I announced, nudging Lance.

"Cool." Lance inclined his head and moved toward the bar.

Casey let me take her hand, and we moved into each other's arms easily. I'd never enjoyed a dance as much as this one, and we swayed in silence for a while before Casey put her head on my chest. "You smell yummy," was all she said.

"You look yummy," I responded. Her mouth was inches from mine, and she smiled invitingly, but then she was yanked away from me.

7

Casey

"CASEY!" A TALL BLACK WOMAN WAS CALLING MY NAME, AND I SWUNG AROUND in frustration. "Girlfriend, what are you doing here?!"

"Vicki!" I was overjoyed to see my old friend, though her timing couldn't have been worse. I felt Erik's sigh and I squeezed his hand before letting Vicki yank me into a hug.

That was my last chance to be in Erik's arms for the rest of the night. By the time the club closed at three in the morning, I felt like I'd played a full set with a dozen encores. It seemed like every musician I knew had shown up, and I spent hours moving from one group to the next, talking, drinking, and dancing. I kept my hand in Erik's, though, hopefully letting him know I wanted him just as much as I thought he wanted me.

When the club closed, a group of us moved the party to an after-hours club where there was more drinking, more dancing, and a lot more sexual tension between Erik and me. Sandor gave in to exhaustion and dozed in a chair against the wall sometime close to dawn, and it was around that time that Vicki and her husband, Ice, snuck out. Lance, Erik, and I did our final round of shots at six in the morning, and Lance carried me out to the waiting SUV while Erik nudged Sandor awake.

We dropped Lance off at Penn Station so he could take the train home to his Long Island apartment, and we arrived back at our hotel around seven. Sandor did his perfunctory check of our adjoining rooms, assured himself we were safe, and then promptly fell on his bed and into a deep sleep, fully dressed.

"You look tired," Erik whispered, standing in the doorway of my room.

"I gotta pee," I whispered. I went into the bathroom to freshen up and give my pounding heart a few minutes to settle down. He wanted me, and I wanted him, so I didn't know why I was so nervous, but it was now or never. I pulled off my dress and slowly walked back into the room in nothing but my matching bra and panties.

"Let's get you to bed," he said with a gentle smile.

"Will you come with me?" I whispered, leaning against his strong chest.

"I will, but nothing is going to happen when you're in this condition. If and when I make love to you, you're going to be completely sober."

"How chivalrous," I murmured.

"I try." He tugged me toward the bed, and we crawled under the cool sheets. He'd removed his shirt at some point, so the warmth of his torso seared my skin as he pulled me close. This, I thought as I drifted off to sleep, was heaven.

I CAME AWAKE SLOWLY, ACUTELY AWARE OF MY ACHING HEAD AND THE ERECTION pressed against my butt. Oh, god. There was no way I was wasting this opportunity, the chance to be intimate with the man I'd been thinking about for years. I moaned with desire as last night's events came rushing back and Erik's arms tightened around me. The clock on the nightstand told me it was only noon, and though my mind screamed with exhaustion, my libido had a mind of its own. The muscular body draped around me was too hard to resist, and I turned over to face him. He was still wearing pants, and I fumbled with his zipper in frustration.

"Casey, what—" He spoke sleepily, slowly opening his eyes.

"I want you," I breathed.

"Sweetheart..."

I silenced any protest with my mouth, softly kissing his lips. I reached out to touch his face, stroke the line of his jaw, mesmerized by the powerful man that he was. I had no delusions about the future, but the present was overpowering all sense of reason. And that dip in his chin was all mine for the touching. Or licking. Or both.

His body reacted to my touch, and he managed to slide his jeans down without breaking contact. Then he dug his fingers into my hair and pulled me to him, kissing me like no one ever had before. His tongue stroked mine with delicious precision, each flick igniting a tiny flame inside of me I'd never known existed. His mouth was a veritable feast, taking pull after pull, all while giving me a taste of delirium. I'd never been kissed like this, with such intimate perfection, and I raked my fingers down his back, desperate to have him closer.

"Easy," he whispered against my mouth.

"Erik, please..." I moaned his name, lifting my hips as he tugged at my panties and pulled them free of my legs. My legs fell open of their own volition and then he was there, his cock thick and heavy against my thigh.

"Oh, god, yes."

He slid into me, and I didn't remember anything being so natural. We'd barely touched, had barely done anything at all, yet I was wet, needy, practically on the verge of orgasm the second he was inside me. I wrapped one leg around the back of his thighs as he kissed me, our bodies moving together in a frantic rush. I'd never done anything like this before, and the orgasm that ripped through me caught me off guard.

"Shit, I'm sorry," he groaned, jerking inside of me.

"Holy shit." I was breathless and confused, but utterly helpless to stop whatever was happening, the intensity almost bringing me to tears.

"Are you all right?" he whispered against my hair, holding me tightly.

"I think so." My eyes were closed but I was smiling.

"What just happened?" His fingers found mine.

"Do they not teach this kind of thing to the royal family in Limaj?"

"Not like this." He shifted so he could look at me. "Do you know how long I've been waiting for this?"

"As long as I have?" My eyes met his in the semidarkness.

"I thought I was stuffy?" he asked, leaning forward and nipping my lower lip.

"I see that you're not all that stuffy when you're naked." I grinned, wrapping my arms around his neck. "In fact, you're not stuffy at all when you're naked."

He finally pulled out and a strange look crossed his face as he did.

"What's wrong?" I asked.

He blew out a slow breath. "Honey, we didn't use protection."

Oh, shit. I blinked and looked down at our naked bodies, as if that would somehow affirm or negate what we'd just done. Without protection. Boy, when I got stupid, I didn't hold back.

"Are you..." He looked as shocked as I felt.

"No." I swallowed. "I'm sorry. I don't know what came over me. One minute I was asleep and then we were..."

"Naked," he sighed. "It's my fault. I seduced you."

"We're both responsible, but I swear to you, I don't have any diseases. That was my first time not using a condom. *Ever.*"

I looked at him. "Me too."

"Are you upset?"

I stared at him. "How could I be upset? When I woke up and realized you were beside me, all I could think about was touching you...*being* with you."

"Really?" He looked so surprised I couldn't help a small laugh.

"I've been waiting a long time, too, you know."

"How did we not know we felt this way?"

"I didn't think I was good enough for you."

"That's ridiculous."

"And I always wanted a chance to get to know you."

"You're getting to know me now."

My heart was pounding, some sixth sense warning me that if I walked away, I'd never see him again. How had our first time become a disaster? Was it a disaster? And why was I more worried about losing him than the possibility of being pregnant?

8

E*rik*

THE INSECURITY IN HER EYES STARTLED ME, AND I RAN A FINGER ALONG HER lips, kissing her lightly, playfully. I sought out her tongue and toyed with it for a moment, until our lips locked together, and she softened against me. I had to have her again, to show her I wasn't going anywhere, that our passion had been more than a fluke. I'd been telling the truth that I'd never gone without a condom before, and it truly hadn't crossed my mind until it was over. Being inside of her was as natural as breathing, as though we were meant to be together, and I had to make sure she understood that my feelings for her went much deeper than sex.

We went into the bathroom together to clean up and this new intimacy between us was actually sexy. I liked the way she made me feel, both physically and emotionally, which was something new for me. When we stepped into the shower, she leaned against my chest and trailed her fingers lightly down my back, bringing on goose bumps. She continued down over my ass, my thighs, and around front to my hips. Her touch made me shiver even though the last thing I was feeling right now was cold.

I brushed her hair back from her face and looked into those beautiful eyes I'd been mesmerized by for years. I couldn't explain all these weird feelings, because they were wonderful, but I didn't want to push her. Being with her was better than anything I'd dreamed of so I wouldn't do anything to scare her off.

"I need to taste you," she whispered.

I groaned in anticipation. "Well, you do what makes you happy, baby."

She slowly slid down my body, her lips trailing across my torso with soft, wet kisses. The water sluiced over her but she was oblivious, kissing the crease of my leg as she wrapped her hand around my erection. She glanced up at me, meeting my eyes with an impish smiled just before she practically swallowed me whole.

"Sweet fucking hell..." I groaned. "Jesus, baby, how do you..." My voice trailed off as my cock hit the back of her throat and she swallowed. Damn, she didn't do anything halfway. She had me pumping in and out now, practically bottoming out each time and she never flinched. With her eyes closed and her lips and tongue working in tandem, I'd never seen anything as erotic as me fucking her mouth. She loved it too, because she hummed around me, lightly squeezing my balls with one hand and working me into a frenzy.

I'd had blow jobs before, but nothing like this. If I'd ever doubted a woman could enjoy doing this, I never would again. She worked me like a magician, sucking me so hard and deep I was only going to last about ten more seconds. Much as I hated to get off this quickly, I also preferred to be buried deep inside her pussy when I came, so this would allow me maximum staying power for when I was.

I growled out my release, watching her swallow every last drop and then lick me clean. God damn, she was the sexiest fucking woman on earth.

She slowly stood up again, her body against mine. "Now that's what I call breakfast."

"Jesus, will you marry me?"

Shit. The look on her face told me I'd just pushed her too far. I'd said it in jest, but obviously it freaked her out a little.

"It was a joke," I said softly, kissing the side of her face.

"Erik, what are we doing?"

"Everything. Anything." I wound my fingers in her long hair and held her head so I could look at her. "I want you. I've always wanted you. And now that I've had you, the real thing is better than anything I imagined. Stay with me, Casey. Let me show you how good it can be between us."

"I want you so much it hurts," she admitted.

I turned off the water and grabbed one of the towels, wrapping both of us in it. I didn't wait to dry off, though, and carried her back into the bedroom.

"I want you more," I said as I set her on the bed.

Her answer was to arch her face towards mine, until our lips were fused again, her breath hot against mine.

"Take me," she whispered.

"Condoms," I murmured, fumbling around to find my wallet.

"Princes keep condoms in their wallets?" she giggled, watching me.

"Horny, virile men who enjoy sex do," I responded, tossing it on the bed beside me as I reached for her again, caressing her with more tenderness than intensity. We'd done that already and I wanted to savor her, the way it felt when we came together as intimately as two people possibly could. She moved me in ways I wasn't prepared for but I loved every second of it.

I kissed her with purpose now, drinking in everything that made Casey the woman she was—the woman I'd always wanted—and couldn't get enough. She'd captivated me as a teen and now that she was a woman, she brought out feelings in me I wasn't used to, like possessiveness. With her fingers digging into my hair, her breath hot against my mouth, I lost myself in her. It had been a day but she was mine now and I needed her to know it.

I sheathed myself quickly and slid into her without much foreplay, but it didn't matter. She was wet, ready, and took me easily. Her hips shifted beneath mine as she clamped around me. But there was no hurry now, and our eyes met when I didn't move.

"You're beautiful," I whispered, licking her throat. "I've never loved being inside a woman this much before."

"I've never loved having someone inside me so much." Her gorgeous eyes fluttered closed and she licked her lips. "You feel so damn good. Don't move for a minute... let me feel this connection between us."

How had I ever gotten this lucky? I rested my forehead on hers and we just laid there, our bodies connected, and her fingers sought out mine. We threaded them together and sat there for a long time...minutes? Hours? I had no idea but it was the hottest thing I'd ever done, not moving inside the woman I was fucking. Just a physical connection that made me so hard it was painful.

"Now," she whispered, a hundred years later.

I started to move and our lovemaking was gradual, building to a climax that nearly shattered us both. I had to use my lips to stifle the sound as she let out a scream of pleasure. I was moving inside of her with hard, rhythmic thrusts, and she rode her second climax of the day with her voice muffled in my kisses. Her body shook as spasms overtook her, and she clutched my shoulders for dear life. Her face was cloaked in such rapture I lost every ounce of control I'd ever had, and together we rocked ourselves into another world.

9

Casey

THE NEXT TIME I OPENED MY EYES, I HAD NO CONCEPT OF WHAT TIME IT WAS. I squinted at the alarm clock next to the bed. Five thirty in the afternoon. I probably could have slept until tomorrow, but my stomach was growling, and it occurred to me I might not have much time left with Erik. Our lovemaking had been spectacular, mind-numbing, practically ethereal. But I'd been around enough to know guys like him didn't stay with girls like me, no matter how good the sex was or what sweet nothings he'd whispered while he'd been inside me.

"Where are you going?" His voice startled me, and I turned, looking over my shoulder.

"I was thinking I'd freshen up. I probably look rode hard and put away wet."

"Yeah, but I'm the one who made you look that way, so get your sweet behind back to bed."

"One minute." I was quick to use the facilities and then slid back between the sheets, resting my head on his chest. He dragged a hand through my hair, stroking it softly.

"Are you hungry?" he asked.

"Starving."

"Let's order room service."

"Okay." Relief surged through me. I had one more night with him. It probably wouldn't be enough, but after last night, I was pretty sure infinite nights wouldn't be enough. I didn't know what was going on, but it was so damn good.

"I have to move if I'm going to reach the phone," he said after a moment.

I laughed and lifted myself off of him. He got out of bed and walked to the desk where the phone was. I admired his naked torso now even more than I had earlier today, impressed with his flat stomach, tight ass and muscular arms. He was perfection in my eyes, strong, sexy and lean. Last night had been a haze of alcohol and overstimulated hormones, but I already had ideas about what I wanted to do to him next.

"Stop staring at my ass," he called over his shoulder as he waited for someone to answer the phone.

"I want to take a bite of it," I responded, grinning when he looked back at me with a devilish smile.

"I can make that happen—yes, hello, I'd like to place an order?"

He was back in bed after ordering lobster tail and champagne for two, and I curled into his arms without hesitation.

"Somehow, I didn't take you for a cuddler," he said quietly, hands back in my hair.

"I didn't take you for a hair man."

"You didn't think I'd want to run my fingers through hair as gorgeous as yours?"

I lifted my head to look into his beautiful green eyes. "I guess I never thought you'd be attracted to someone as plain as me."

"Plain?" He made a face. "What about you is plain?" He traced a line across my lips. "Your mouth is made for kissing—and at least a hundred other things I can think of."

He moved to my nose. "You have the straightest, sweetest, most perfect nose."

My eyes fluttered closed as he traced my eyelids and eyebrows. "Your eyes are as blue as the Mediterranean, and those lashes are about a mile long."

He slowly lifted my chin, forcing me to look at him. "You're the most beautiful woman I've ever known. There is no one who holds a candle to you."

I stared at him. "You're *royalty*... Like, the real thing. I'm nothing like the women in your circles. Half the time I don't have nails because of my guitar-playing, so my hands are super ugly. I haven't been to college, and I wouldn't know which fork to use at a fancy dinner so—"

Erik leaned down and pressed his lips to mine. "Do I look like I give a flying fuck about that?"

"How can you not?"

"Because that type of thing has never been important to me."

"That's not true. You take your royal duties seriously. Your father has always been so proud of you, talking about everything you do even though you're not really in line to the throne."

"I took my duties seriously because I had nothing else to do and I was still finding my way in the world. Now that I have a better idea what I want in life, I realize my royal duties—and title—mean nothing. Since I'm so far down the line of succession, I'm not ever going to be king, and technically, I've only retained my title because my uncle granted it. When my father abdicated, he released us all from those titles, but the king thought it was unbecoming for members of the royal bloodline to be without titles."

"What does all of that mean?" I asked softly.

"It means I'm just a regular guy. And I'm more than a little interested in you."

I eyed him suspiciously. "Really?"

"Before I answer that, you have to answer one question for me."

"Okay."

"Has the last twenty-four hours been as good as I think it has?"

I raised my eyebrows. "You have to ask?"

"Did you fake anything?"

"No!" I gave him a dirty look. "I was drunk, but I knew what I was doing."

"Casey, if you weren't faking, then it's not possible that you don't have the same types of feelings I have."

Oh shit. This was going in a direction I hadn't been expecting and it scared the hell out of me. I wasn't sure what direction to go with this either. I'd never been the kind of woman who played games, and Erik was too important to me to start now. As long as I was careful.

"You scare me," I admitted aloud.

"Why?"

"Because being with you would make me some kind of princess. And I don't know if I'm up to the task. I'm nothing but a musician, and even though that's all I've ever wanted to be, I don't know how I would ever fit into your world."

"You don't have to be anyone other than who you are. It may seem complicated from the outside looking in, but all that really matters is you and me. I'm not nearly as complicated—or snobby—as you may think."

I stared at him as if he'd gone crazy. "Are you sure you're not talking with your dick instead of your brain?" I asked at last.

He smiled and gently stroked my cheek with his thumb. "How can you ask that? Didn't last night show you just how much I want to be with you?"

"Last night showed me how much you wanted to *sleep* with me."

"Come on—you know better than that. With the friendship shared between our families, I would never just use you that way."

"I'm never going to be proper or regal. I know when to use manners but I can't imagine living your life or being on display for the world to criticize."

"You'd never have to."

"Why not? Like you said, the king still thinks you have a place within the family."

He took a breath. "That's what he wants, but I believe his days as king are numbered."

My eyes widened. "Why?"

"Because Limaj is going through the early stages of a revolution. A third of the country wants a religious leader to overtake the monarchy, so basically a theocracy; another third wants to be more like England, with the monarchy as figureheads only, and create a socialist government of sorts; the final third likes things as is, but they are probably the minority, more like a quarter than a third. Essentially, there is a great deal of trouble in my country, and the fact of the matter is, I'm disappointed in the direction my cousin wants to take the country when he takes over, so I want nothing to do with any of it."

"That's terrible! Aren't you upset?"

"Somewhat, but I can't change what's happening. My father and I have been working diligently to secure our personal assets. In the event of a full-scale revolution, our lives would be in danger if we returned there, so we need to be prepared for complete exile and financial independence."

"So that's why your parents have been spending more and more time in their house in Las Vegas."

"They're well aware that our days in Limaj may be numbered. If religious leaders take over, our family would probably be executed if they caught us."

"That's awful," she whispered.

"The upside to all of this is that I'm free to date the woman I've always been infatuated with."

I looked at him with a sudden new appreciation of the man he was. In the midst of what was probably the most life-altering situation he would ever be in, he was making the best of it. Although part of me wanted to be offended that he only wanted to be with me because his country was falling apart, I reminded myself that I'd never shown any interest in him whatsoever. Until last night, he'd had no idea how mutual the attraction was between us.

"But do you really even know me?" I asked after a while. "I mean, we've never dated or spent much time together—how do you know we won't be ready to kill each other after a week?"

"I don't," he admitted. "But we can find out."

"How?"

"Let's spend some time together. You don't have anything going on professionally, and I've got a plethora of events coming up we can choose to attend for fun. Come to Europe with me and I'll show you my playground as we're getting to know each other. What do you have to lose?"

I chuckled even though it wasn't really funny. "My dignity? Making a fool of myself in front of European royalty doesn't sound like all that much fun."

"You'll never make a fool of yourself with me," he whispered softly. "No matter what happens, I'll never let you fall."

I fell a little in love with him right then and there. With those gorgeous green eyes looking into mine with what seemed to be the sincerity of the world, I struggled to come up with anything as eloquent to respond with.

"Will you give me one week to prove that we could make this work?" he whispered, kissing my neck. "One week, Casey. That's all I ask. If you're not convinced we can be good together, then we'll part ways, no hard feelings."

"And if I'm pregnant?"

10

E*rik*

I WANTED TO LAUGH BUT KNEW BETTER. SHE WAS DEAD SERIOUS AND, TO BE fair, it was a serious subject. The only problem was that it wasn't a problem for me. I was already half in love with her and the thought of her carrying my baby only made me happy. I'd been enamored with her for so long, a baby would be a natural extension of my feelings. I just had to find a way to convince her of that because from any rational person's perspective, this was happening way too soon.

"I already told you—I'll never let you fall. Whether it's meeting royalty or an unplanned pregnancy, I'm not going anywhere. What can I do to convince you of that?"

She was quiet for a while, but then she traced the outline of my lips with her finger. "There's one rule if I agree."

"Name it."

"No sex. At least not for the first week."

"What?" That definitely wasn't part of the plan. Not mine, anyway.

"No sex. If you can affect me the way you did this morning all the time, then my thinking in terms of the future will be jaded. Right this second, with your body so close to mine, I would marry you just so we could do this all the time. And we both know sex isn't a good reason to be together."

"All right." I reluctantly nodded. "Agreed." I would've agreed to almost anything to keep her close.

"And it has to be real dating," she said. "You stay in one room with Sandor, I stay in another, and you arrange dinners and activities, come pick me up, etc."

"Anything else?" I asked with an indulgent smile.

"We don't start until tomorrow."

"What do you mean?"

"I'm starving and I just want to cuddle."

I pressed a light kiss to the tip of her nose. "I'm starving, too, and cuddling sounds like fun."

WE WOKE THE FOLLOWING MORNING FEELING DELIGHTFULLY REFRESHED. WE'D eaten dinner in bed, watched a movie, and then fallen into a peaceful, relaxing slumber. It had been one of the best nights of my life, as far as I was concerned, even taking into account the lack of sex. Casey was still all I wanted, and I'd been lying here dreaming up ways to win her heart for a couple of hours. It was only eight thirty, so she was in the shower and I'd called room service to order coffee, croissants, and a beautiful bouquet of white roses. I didn't know what kinds of things made her tick, but I was going to find out.

When she came out of the bathroom in a bathrobe, with her hair wrapped in a towel, I decided she was the most gorgeous woman in the world. I'd always thought she was, but seeing here like this, with no makeup and her hair wrapped up turban-style, only drove the idea home. She spotted the roses immediately and turned to me with a smile.

"They're beautiful. Thank you."

"Not as beautiful as you." I leaned down to lightly kiss her soft lips. "And you're welcome."

"What are they for?"

"Because I wanted to."

"But we're leaving today, aren't we?"

"We can bring them with us or leave them for the maids."

"You're crazy." She shook out her hair and began towel-drying it. It was long and silky, even wet, and I watched in fascination as she ran her fingers through it. "So, where are we going anyway?"

"I have to meet with our banker in Zurich, so I thought we'd start there. I've booked you for a spa day while I do boring financial things, and then we can go to dinner. The following day, we'll head to Monte Carlo. There's a party with people I think you'll enjoy, and we can stay there or head over to the south of France, whatever we feel like."

"Sounds great."

"We should pack and get ready to go."

"Okay." She smiled at me, and my heart ached with wanting her. I'd never felt like this about anyone, and it was a little strange. Sandor was probably going to give me a ration of shit the next time we were alone, but I didn't give a damn what anyone thought. I finally had the one thing I'd always wanted that had been out of my grasp, and it would take an act of war to keep me from her.

Monte Carlo was warm and sunny, and seeing Casey in a long, sleeveless sundress with a large hat on her head made me smile. She hadn't wanted me to buy her the frilly dress or the wide-brimmed hat but had given in when I asked her to do it for me. She looked stunning wearing them, her blond hair flowing out behind her as she laughed. I wished for a camera, so I could capture the moment, but she'd already ducked into a shop.

I kept forgetting she was rich in her own right and didn't need me to buy her things. I tried not to be old-fashioned like that, but something deep inside of me was anxious to take care of her, and watching her shop for herself bothered me. That was probably why I'd insisted she let me buy the dress and hat for her. I'd also picked up some jewelry that I would save for another time. There was a party this weekend that would include Anwar and perhaps even my uncle, so I would need to find her the perfect dress for the evening. The diamond necklace and earrings I'd picked up were stunning accessories that would show my family I was serious about her and make every other woman in attendance jealous.

Hopefully, Casey wouldn't balk too much when she saw them.

I wandered into the shop she'd gone into and found her with a glass of champagne in her hands, signing an autograph.

"Hey!" She gave me a sweet smile and waved but continued talking to the teenage girl as if she were the most important person in the world.

"She's actually very nice," Sandor murmured from where he stood next to me.

"She is."

"No, I mean, I hadn't expected her to be like this. She's beautiful, rich, and successful. I thought she would be a diva."

"I told you she was different."

"But you didn't know either," he protested. "You hadn't spent much time with her."

"No, but I've spent some time with her, and my parents watched her grow up. My mother would have told me if she was a spoiled diva. She would never have encouraged me to get to know her if she wasn't a good person."

"This is your mother's doing?!" Sandor looked so horrified I couldn't help but laugh.

"Have you taken a good look at Casey Hart?" I asked, cocking my head. "I know blondes aren't your thing, but do you really believe my mother had anything to do with my infatuation? She merely gave me the push I needed to do something about it."

"Your Highness. I'm so sorry, I didn't see you." The owner of the store spotted me, and I inwardly groaned. I hated being recognized when I was just out for a casual day, but it happened too often to count.

"Hello, Mrs. Safleur." I'd shopped at this boutique with my mother and sister many times, so I knew the owner.

"Is your mother here? Can I show you something?" The middle-aged woman rushed over to assist me.

"Just waiting for my friend." I motioned with my head toward Casey, and the woman's eyes widened slightly.

"Yes, of course. Can I get you something to drink?"

"We're actually leaving," Casey said, joining me and sliding her hand into mine. "Can you deliver my purchases to our hotel?"

"Of course, Ms. Hart." Mrs. Safleur smiled. "Thank you for shopping with us, and have a wonderful rest of your day." She dipped her head. "Give my regards to your mother, Your Highness."

"How many times have I asked you to call me Erik?" I asked her with an impish smile.

"I've lost count," she responded, grinning.

"Good day." I walked outside and leaned over to kiss Casey's cheek. "What did you buy?"

"It's a surprise."

"My mother and sister shop there. She sells both formalwear and lingerie."

She gave me a coy smile. "You're going to have to wait and see."

"What if I don't want to?" I asked playfully. "What if—"

"Casey! Is that you?" An attractive blonde hurried in our direction, and Sandor immediately jumped in front of her.

11

Casey

I TURNED IN SURPRISE WHEN I HEARD MY NAME. IT SOUNDED FAMILIAR, NOT like the paparazzi or a fan, and I nearly jumped when Sandor put himself between me and whomever it was. I'd almost forgotten he wasn't just Erik's good friend and cousin, but also his bodyguard.

I peeked around his shoulder and let out a breath I hadn't realized I'd been holding.

"It's okay," I said softly. "It's a friend." I stepped around him and held out my arms. "Liz! What are you doing here?"

"I live here," she responded with a grin. "Daddy's building a new hotel, and I'm overseeing the process."

"Really? I thought..." Liz was Nick's aunt, though she was only a few years older than we were. As far as I knew, she was an analyst for the CIA, and though it wasn't common knowledge, she hadn't had any part of the Kingsley family's hotel empire in all the years I'd known her.

"Hello. I'm Erik." Erik held out his hand to her.

"Elizabeth Kingsley." She paused, inclining her head. "Your Highness."

"Please. Call me Erik."

"Then you can call me Liz."

"Gladly."

Seeing him smile at Liz made something sour burn in my gut, and for the first time in my life, I was jealous. It was the oddest sensation, and I had to paste a smile on my face as I turned back to her.

"How long are you in town?" she was asking.

"I'm not sure," I said, glancing at Erik. "We're playing it by ear."

"Well, if you have time, stop by the hotel." She handed me a card. "I'd love to show you around. It's not ready to open, but we're really proud of the renovations so far."

"We will. Are you there tomorrow?"

"Every day."

"I'll see you then."

"If you come around lunchtime, I can order something in, and we can catch up."

"I'll call you in the morning," I promised.

We hugged again, and she disappeared into the crowds.

"That's Nick's aunt," I explained to Erik. "She's his father's younger sister. Nick's grandfather got remarried in his fifties and had another baby around the same time Nick's father and uncle were having children."

"She looks familiar," Erik said, frowning. "I can't place where I've seen her."

"You never met her on one of your visits to Vegas? She grew up on Long Island, but she would come around for holidays and sometimes over the summer. You probably crossed paths at one of the many family events we always attended."

He nodded. "Probably."

He had a funny look on his face, but I wasn't sure what the big deal was. Growing up, my parents, Erik's parents, and the Kingsleys had been like one big extended family. They'd shared holidays, vacations, and even parenting sometimes. Liz and Nick had grown up more like siblings or cousins since they were so close in age and she'd just been another one of the many kids we all hung out with. Nick's family owned the Kingsley Hotel empire, the largest of which was on the Las Vegas Strip. The Charleston Hotel had been around for twenty years, and Nick, the other kids and I had grown up playing hide-and-seek in its hallways, celebrating every major birthday and family event in its ballrooms, and enjoying holidays and concerts there like it was a second home.

Erik had been with us on some of those occasions, though not as often as Liz since she'd grown up in New York while he'd gone to school in Europe and only visited once in a while. It was inevitable that they'd met at some point.

"Where are we headed?" Aziz called out as we piled into the SUV Erik had rented.

"Lunch," Erik called back.

"So had you ever met Liz before?" I asked him.

He shook his head. "I'm not sure. She looks familiar but I can't place it."

"She was around in the summers while we were all growing up, but then she went to Yale and got recruited by the CIA."

"The CIA?" He looked startled. "Really?"

"She was an analyst or something in D.C. so I don't know when that changed. I guess I'll find out tomorrow."

"Interesting." He didn't seem overly concerned and conversation moved on to other things.

WE SPENT A WONDERFUL DAY SHOPPING AND TAKING IN SOME OF THE panoramic views. I'd never been here before, though I'd toured all over the world, so it was exciting to see a place I'd only read about in the past. Erik had apparently spent a lot of time here, though, because he was the perfect tour guide, pointing out landmarks and things we might like to do on another day. By the time he left me in front of my hotel suite, we'd made plans for the week, and I wondered about the wisdom of my impulsive no-sex mandate. Was I playing with fire by playing hard to get after the fact? We'd already slept together, after all.

The problem was that each time he touched me I pretty much lost my mind. He was intoxicatingly handsome, polite, richer than anyone I'd ever known—including the Kingsleys—and probably just as sweet as anyone I'd known as well. I kept trying to find fault in him and I couldn't, which was terrifying. The unprotected sex we'd had weighed heavily on me because I was nowhere near ready to have a baby, but it was like we'd both been under some kind of spell. I hadn't slept with a large number of men, but I'd had a metric shit-ton of sex. Mostly with Nick, of course, but not entirely, and I'd never, ever been careless, not even once. Erik swore that he hadn't, either, which meant something spectacular had gone on the first time we were together.

Impulsively, I grabbed the room phone and dialed his suite number. Sandor answered and I asked for Erik, feeling equal parts silly and excited.

"Hello, love. Is everything okay?" he asked when he got on the line.

"It's fine, but I was a little lonely and thought we could talk on the phone."

"On the phone?" The tone of his voice told me just how confused he was.

"Have you never dated?" I asked slowly. "Had a girlfriend whose voice you desperately wanted to hear but couldn't be with at that moment? Weren't you ever a *teenager*?"

He chuckled. "I was absolutely a teenager, but no, there's never been anyone whose voice I needed to hear so badly I wanted to spend any time on the phone with them."

"Not even now?" I asked softly.

"Perhaps now, yes. Can I call you back in five minutes? I have to use the bathroom and want to change into something comfortable."

"Deal."

I giggled to myself as I pulled off the pretty sundress he'd bought me and dug out the oversized Led Zeppelin shirt I usually slept in. I put my hair in a ponytail, washed off my makeup, brushed my teeth, and had just crawled into bed when my cell phone rang.

"This is more private than the hotel phone," he explained when I answered.

"So it is."

"Well, then...what do you want to talk about?"

"I just want to listen to your voice and ask you questions."

"Okay. You start."

"What's your favorite food?"

"Italian," he responded instantly. "You?"

"Mexican." I paused. "Do you prefer vodka, rum, or tequila?"

"Scotch." He laughed. "I'll drink tequila on occasion, but I'm not a big fan of vodka or rum. What about you?"

"I prefer bourbon, or a whiskey like Jack Daniel's. I'll drink tequila, but it tends to get me into too much trouble."

"I'm familiar with that," he said.

"Do you gamble?"

"Almost never."

"Smoke?"

"The occasional cigar."

"What's your favorite sexual position?"

He laughed. "All of them."

"Come on, we all have favorites."

"You first."

"I love being on top so I can look into a man's eyes when he's inside of me."

I heard the catch of his breath and smiled to myself.

"I'm not alone," he murmured. "So, you're going to have to guess."

"Sixty-nine?"

"Nope."

"Doggy style?"

"Nope."

"Getting a blow job?"

"That's an act, not a position." His voice dropped even lower.

"Hmmm." I thought about it for a minute. "Missionary?"

"It depends on who I'm with."

"With me?"

"Definitely."

"Why?"

"For the same reason you like your favorite."

I paused. "So you can look in my eyes?"

"And watch the look on your face at the end."

Holy hell, this guy was a dream come true. "I made a big mistake, didn't I?"

"In what?"

"My no-sex rule."

"Probably."

"We can amend the rules."

"We can, but we won't. Not for a week, anyway."

"Why a week?"

"Because that's the deal we made, and I'm nothing if not a man of my word."

I MET LIZ FOR LUNCH BY MYSELF THE NEXT DAY. ERIK MADE EXCUSES, SAYING HE had phone calls to make, and if I was honest with myself, I was happy he didn't come because something about the two of them made me feel weird. Yesterday's jealousy had passed but it had now been replaced by discomfiture, as if they had a secret. I planned to find out what it was, too, because Liz and I had essentially grown up together and it wasn't like her to be secretive about a man.

"HI." SHE LOOKED UP WHEN I ARRIVED, AND I LOOKED AROUND THE ENTRANCE to the hotel in awe.

"This is stunning."

"And it's not even finished."

"I'd love a tour."

"Of course."

Liz showed me around, pointing out where the casinos, restaurants, shops, and lobby were all going to be. It was expansive, with marble floors and crystal chandeliers. The rooms weren't fully decorated yet, but the flooring, lights, and carpets were in and the effect was stunning. I ran my hand along a carved statue, marveling in the smooth, expensive feel to not just the statue, but every inch of the building. I enjoyed luxury, but this felt over-the-top, more like a palace than a hotel. Which was ironic, considering whom I was dating.

"You're going to run this place?" I asked her once we got to what was temporarily serving as her office.

"We'll see what happens."

I cocked my head. "Does this mean you're not with the agency anymore?"

Her eyes met mine. "Noooo..." She drew out the word, which confused me even more.

"You're definitely not an analyst in D.C. anymore though."

"Definitely not."

"You can't tell me about it?"

"I can't." She seemed genuinely regretful. "I'm sorry, Casey. I honestly can't."

"Can you tell me how you know Erik?"

She smiled sadly. "I can't tell you that either."

"Liz, I'm falling in love with him, and I need to know what there is between you."

Her eyes widened. "Oh, no, nothing like that. I..." She glanced around, assuring herself we were alone. "In my capacity as an operative there have been occasions where I've mingled with the royal family. Under another name, usually a disguise. He most likely realizes he's met me as someone else but isn't sure who or when. If he's smart, he's using his time today to find out."

I sighed. "So, there's nothing romantic or sexual between you?"

"No. I swear. We've never had any personal interaction; it's all been me posing as someone else while watching members of the family or something to that affect."

"Is he a good guy?" I blurted out. "I mean, is he really as wonderful as he seems?"

"I'm not friends with him, so I can't really answer that, but I can tell you he's never been involved in anything nefarious and seems to genuinely care about the people of Limaj. He doesn't have any power, per se, but his heart is always in the right place based on the public things he says and does."

"That's my feeling too," I admitted. "I wish it didn't scare me so much."

"Love can be scary." Her voice was sympathetic, almost sad.

"Tell me about it."

"Are you hungry?"

"I could eat."

"Then you can tell me all about it over lunch." She reached for the phone and I smiled. I suddenly felt a thousand pounds lighter.

12

E*rik*

Shopping with Casey was unlike anything I'd experienced with anyone else. She had a distinct feminine side, but she didn't particularly like trying on clothes and grew bored with it relatively quickly. She tended to walk into a store, find a few things she liked, try them on, and move on. I wanted her to wear something fantastic for the party tomorrow night but felt like a bit of a hypocrite because of it. I'd spent all week telling her how I loved her just the way she was and now I wanted to change her into someone from my world. It was just for one night, but I wasn't sure how to get that across.

After we'd stopped into the third fancy dress shop, Casey took my hand and led me into a corner of the room.

"Okay, tell me exactly what tomorrow is about," she said.

"What do you mean?"

"You've been trying to get me into ball gowns and party dresses all day, so if you just tell me about the event and who's going to be there, it'll be easier for me to pick something."

"My uncle is going to be there."

"The king?" Her eyes widened. "Erik, I don't think—"

"This is why I didn't want to tell you," I interjected, cutting her off. "Look, you're beautiful, articulate, and intelligent. You know how to handle yourself, and you're going to wow everyone in the room. I love who you are but I also know that people in my circles can be jerks to newcomers, so I don't want to set you up to fail."

Her smile was full of mischief. "You know I play rock music for a living, right? I've been spoken down to, made fun of, and tossed out of expensive stores because they didn't know who I was. I can handle myself just fine. However, because I care about you, the last thing I'd ever want to do is embarrass you. Why don't you just pick out what you want me to wear?"

I hesitated. "Are you sure?"

"Absolutely. I'll try it on to make sure it fits, but you pick the dress."

"Just this once," I said softly.

She shook her head. "Don't lie. I understand the difference between you wanting to change me and wanting me to fit in. I'm an entertainer; I can play any role you need me to in public as long as you know who I am in private."

I pulled her to me, one arm circling her waist as I stared into the depths of her blue eyes. "Have I told you I'm crazy about you yet today?"

"Not yet." Her eyes twinkled.

"I'm crazy about you."

"I'm kind of crazy about you too. Now, go figure out what you want me to wear."

I ALREADY KNEW HOW BEAUTIFUL THE DRESS WAS GOING TO LOOK ON HER, BUT when I arrived at her suite to pick her up before the party, she rendered me fucking speechless. Standing there in a backless, black sequined gown with a slit up her right thigh, she blew me away for what might have been the hundredth time since we'd been together. I'd known this was the dress the moment she'd come out of the dressing room, but with her hair up in a loose but sexy chignon and her makeup flawless, I'd never seen anything as beautiful as Casey Hart. Every time I thought I couldn't love her more she threw me for a loop. I'd known allowing myself to fall for her would be crazy and complicated, but reality was even more exciting than I'd imagined. My heart beat a little too fast and the pleasure I got from looking at her was immeasurable.

"Why are you staring?" she asked in a soft voice. "Do I look okay?"

"You look..." I wasn't sure how to express what I was thinking. "You're breathtaking, Casey."

"Thank you. You look pretty hot in a tux, Your Greatness." Her cocky grin warmed my heart.

"I have a gift for you," I said, removing the velvet box from my pocket.

She took the box curiously and her eyes widened when she opened it. "Oh, my god, Erik. They're beautiful... I can't wear something like this."

"A beautiful woman can always wear diamonds. Please. I want you to have them."

She looked at me and I wished I could have read her mind in that moment. Something vulnerable flashed in her eyes, as though no one had ever given her a gift like this, but before I could decipher it, she turned her back to me so I could fasten the diamond necklace.

"Thank you," she whispered. "I've never owned anything so beautiful."

"Stunning jewels for an even more breathtaking woman."

"You're spoiling me."

"It makes me happy to spoil you."

"Then I guess it makes me happy to let you." She fastened the earrings and turned to me. "I'm ready."

"Then let's go." I took her arm and we walked to the elevator with Sandor and Aziz flanking us.

Normally it was just Sandor and me, but with Casey in the mix we'd added Aziz as a full-time bodyguard and tonight there would be a third man as our driver. I'd never felt it was necessary in the past but now that I had Casey with me, her celebrity added to my own and made us twice the targets. The paparazzi had gotten wind we were in Europe and had spotted us at our hotel, so they'd been hounding us for two days now. Casey took it in stride, but I hated it because normally I fell under the radar. Anwar and Yusef tended to get most of the attention from the press and having the tables turned was new to me.

"Sandor, you look very handsome tonight," Casey said as the four of us descended to the private parking garage.

"Thank you, Ms. Hart." He nodded, smiling at her for what might have been the first time since we'd left Las Vegas.

The drive was quick and we exited the SUV in a secret parking area, taking a private elevator up to the party. Sandor seemed nervous, and I gave him a curious stare, but he merely shook his head and focused on having my back. Casey and I exited the elevator with Sandor and Aziz behind us, while Frederick stayed with the SUV.

"Your Highness." The host of the party, a billionaire named Girard Mantha, held out his arms. "It's good to see you. Welcome."

"Thank you, my friend." I hugged him before reaching behind me for Casey's hand, drawing her forward. "Casey, this is an old friend. Girard Mantha, meet Casey Hart."

"The guitarist." Girard smiled, shaking Casey's hand. "I'm a big fan."

"Thank you." She nodded graciously.

"Let's get a drink," Girard suggested. "We need to catch up."

"Give me a few minutes," I told him. "Let me get Casey a glass of champagne and I'll find you in a little bit."

"Of course." Girard moved away, and I led Casey deeper into the room.

"Friend or foe?" she whispered in my ear.

"Girard? Neither. Pretty much only cares about business and money but he and my uncle are close."

"Speaking of which." Her eyes moved to the far end of the room where my uncle and Anwar were holding court.

"Are you ready?" I asked her. "It would be insulting for me not to approach him immediately."

"Sure." She gripped my hand a little tighter. "But I could use a drink first."

I flagged down a waiter who appeared with two glasses of champagne, and Casey took one gratefully. She downed it in a few gulps and smiled at me. "Okay, now I'm ready."

We approached the King and Crown Prince of Limaj, and for the first time in my life I was a little intimidated. Not because I was afraid of them but because I worried about how they would react to Casey. The king would be polite, of course, but Anwar was a crapshoot. He treated women like pretty annoyances to be used and tossed away. So far, he'd thwarted all of his father's attempts to get him to settle down.

"Your Majesty." I bowed my head to my uncle, who looked up with a smile.

"Erik, my boy." He got up and hugged me, something he didn't do often, so I responded in kind. "Good to see you."

"Likewise, sir." I pulled Casey forward. "May I introduce Ms. Casey Hart. Casey, King Isak of Limaj."

She dipped into a brief curtsey, bowing her head before straightening up and allowing him to take her hand. "It's a pleasure, Your Majesty."

"Casey Hart. You wrote 'Pieces of Nothing,' did you not?"

If she was surprised, she hid it well, merely smiling. "I did."

"That is my wife's favorite song. When she returns from powdering her nose, she will be pleased to make your acquaintance."

"Thank you. I'm honored to make yours."

"Well, just between us, Flawed Freedom is one of my favorite bands," he said with a wink. "I saw them on their last tour."

"I'll be sure to tell my father."

"I'm sure my brother has told him numerous times. And I must say, the news of the end of Viktim of Prey was disappointing," he continued. "Do you know what you'll do now?"

"I'm thinking about going to college," she said. "It's something I've wanted to do, and it will give me a chance to regroup and write music."

"And perhaps a little time for romance?" He smiled at me.

"Hello, cousin." Anwar joined us, his voice louder than the others as he openly looked Casey up and down. "Who have we here?"

"This is Casey Hart," I said, sliding an arm around her waist. "Casey, His Royal Highness, Prince Anwar al-Hassani."

"It's very nice to meet you, Your Highness." Casey briefly bowed her head but didn't curtsey, which made me want to kiss her.

"If you'll excuse me," King Isak said. "I have others waiting to speak to me. Casey, I hope to see you again soon. Find me later, Erik, yes?"

"Yes, sir. Thank you."

"So, where did you find this one?" Anwar asked, blatantly focused on Casey's chest.

"Casey and I have known each other since we were children," I responded easily, keeping her close to my side. "Her parents are close to mine."

"Wait, is this the one who fancies herself a musician?"

"I play five instruments," Casey said with a sweet smile. "So, I *am* a musician."

"Rock and roll isn't what I would call music." He laughed. "But I suppose everyone should learn to play something, even an instrument as crude as an electric guitar."

"Well, at least it's not a flute," I said, giving him a grin. "I mean, you were adorable performing for your father when you were twelve. You attempted something from Jethro Tull, wasn't it?"

Anwar narrowed his eyes. "If you think—"

"Hello." My aunt appeared like an angel from heaven, her perfume wafting around her like an elegant cloud, hand extended as she smiled at Casey, completely ignoring her eldest son. "I am Klara. I was so delighted to hear you were here. I enjoy your music immensely."

13

Casey

ANWAR WAS A DICK. WATCHING HIM STARE AT MY CHEST AND TALK DOWN TO me had me ready to throat-punch him, but I managed to keep my temper in check because it was obvious Erik was about to lose his. His grip on my waist had almost become painful until his aunt appeared, smiling and effectively cutting Anwar off. She was sweet, gracious, and charming, and if I'd thought I would feel uncomfortable with her, I was wrong. She led me away from the men to a small private table where we sat and chatted like old friends. She was curious about my music, my career, and my future, and she surprised me by giving her blessing for my relationship with Erik.

"Erik has always been my favorite of our nephews," she said with a mischievous smile. "We've tried for years to find the right woman for him, but nothing has ever clicked. This time, however, I see the way he looks at you."

"Oh, well..." I blushed. "I've had a crush on him for years, but I never thought he would look twice at me."

"You're beautiful and successful—why wouldn't he? Kari says you're lovely, and now that we've met, I have to agree."

"Thank you." I think I blushed again, but I wasn't sure.

"So, I heard on one of the entertainment television shows that your band has broken up. What's next for you?"

We talked music and college, as if I sat and spoke with a queen every day, drinking champagne and laughing. She was a lot like Aunt Kari, just a little older and with cleaner language since Aunt Kari cussed like a sailor.

"I've dominated enough of your time," Klara said, gracefully rising to her feet. "You and Erik should dance."

"I've enjoyed talking with you," I said, meaning it. "I hope we have the chance to do it again."

"Absolutely. Perhaps tea one day next week. I'll speak with Isak about our schedule."

"That sounds lovely. Thank you." I looked around for Erik and didn't see him, so I found my way to the ladies' room.

I'd been a little anxious when we first arrived, and meeting Anwar had been unnerving, but the king and queen had been wonderful. I'd grown up around the rich and famous, so wealth and success didn't intimidate me. Royalty, on the other hand, was different. Even though Uncle Ben and Aunt Kari had been part of my life for as long as I could remember, Uncle Ben had abdicated before I was born so I'd never seen that side of him. Erik and his sister had both been somewhat aloof, but I just assumed it was because they'd been sent off to fancy boarding schools. I'd never understood that, since Uncle Ben and Aunt Kari were so chill about everything else, but I'd never thought to ask.

Now I had all kinds of questions and I longed to be alone with Erik. Hopefully, we could leave early. I didn't mind getting dressed up and making small talk, but not when the alternative was a night of passionate fun with a guy I'd always wanted. We'd renegotiate the terms of our deal sooner rather than later because I was anxious to get naked again soon.

I touched up my lipstick and stepped into the hallway. Just as I took a step forward, a hand closed over my arm.

"Hello, Ms. Hart." Anwar's voice gave me chills, and I unconsciously jerked at my arm.

"You're hurting my arm," I whispered, holding my ground even as he tried to push me against the wall. I was at a disadvantage in my four-inch heels, but I was also a sixth-degree black belt in karate, so I wasn't afraid of him either.

"Don't put on airs with me," he hissed. "You're my cousin's current distraction, and we both know all you see in him is dollar signs."

I laughed. "You know I'm a millionaire, right? And my father's a multi-millionaire too, so…money isn't much of a pull for me."

"Then it's power." He leaned in so close I could smell the minty scent of his breath and an overabundance of aftershave. "And I can give you far more than he can."

I planted my feet and met his gaze without blinking. "You have two seconds to let go before I make a scene."

"I'm the Crown Prince of Limaj—no one will help you." He tried to move me, but I was both faster and more skilled, elbowing him in the ribs and following it up with a jab to the throat that left him gasping even though I hadn't come anywhere close to causing any damage. And all without anyone seeing, because his back was to the entrance that led back to the party.

"I'm not interested, Your Highness." I quickly walked away from him and back into the party, immediately running into Sandor.

"Are you all right?" He looked me up and down questioningly. "What is it? Did something happen?"

"No, of course not. I'm fine." I took a breath, trying to slow the staccato beating of my heart. "Do you know where Erik is?"

He looked at the red handprint on my upper arm where Anwar had been holding me. "Don't lie to me, Casey. It's my job to protect Erik, and if someone is bothering you..." His voice trailed off as Anwar came down the hallway, whispering with one of his bodyguards.

"He made a pass at me," I said slowly. "I turned him down."

"He put his hands on you." Sandor's face grew grim.

"I can take care of myself," I said firmly. "Really. There's no need to upset Erik with—"

"Upset Erik with what?" Erik stole up behind me and instantly focused on the redness of my upper arm. "Who touched you?"

I sighed. "I'm a sixth-degree black belt in karate," I repeated calmly. "I can take care of myself. I wish it hadn't been with Anwar, but he seems to think his title is a turn-on."

Erik's jaw tightened and I reached up to put my hand on his cheek. "Erik, please. Your uncle is here, and I think your aunt likes me—just let it go. Really. You said this is the only time we're going to see them, so we probably won't see Anwar again, even if we see your aunt and uncle. Let's enjoy ourselves. Okay? Please?"

He looked like he was going to protest but then let out a long breath. "Understand, if he—or anyone else—ever puts their hands on you against your will, I will handle it. The fact that you can take care of yourself is irrelevant. He's my cousin, and you're my girlfriend. The idea that he thinks—" He cut off abruptly as I wrapped my arms around his neck.

"I'm your girlfriend?" I teased, hoping to distract him. "Did I agree to this? And does this mean we're going to change the terms of our agreement now?"

He smiled indulgently. "Nice. Pressing your tits against me will work temporarily, but I won't forget. Anwar and I are going to have words at some point."

"But not tonight, right?" I pleaded.

He kissed the tip of my nose. "Not tonight."

"Dance with me?" I asked, looking into his eyes.

"Of course." He took my hand and led me to the dance floor. The music was an upbeat tango and I didn't know how, but Erik guided me effortlessly, so it was easy to follow. He was light on his feet, keeping me close to him, and I forgot all about Anwar and even my lovely conversation with Queen Klara. Erik was the only thing that mattered right now, and being close to him like this was heavenly. His body was strong and his steps confident, allowing me to follow without having to work too hard. The music was almost secondary to our movements, the way he held me, the passion sizzling just beneath the surface. I'd had no idea this type of thing existed and I knew then how important he'd already become to me.

"May I?" A deep voice brought me out of my reverie, and I looked into Anwar's dark eyes.

"Not even in your dreams," Erik said under his breath, spinning me in the other direction.

"We should leave," I whispered sadly. "I don't want to be the cause of any trouble."

"Anwar and I have never gotten along," he responded. "Nothing you're doing is causing anything. He's always been jealous of me because I'm smarter, more athletic and better looking. He knows I'm the true heir to the throne and that the only reason I'm not is because my father made a decision before I was born. He hates that and accordingly hates me. This isn't about you. I promise."

It felt like it was about me, but I merely nodded and let him lead me off the dance floor. Anwar had spoiled our evening, and I wasn't sure how to fix that.

"Erik. A word." Anwar stood in front of us, his dark eyes gleaming.

"Perhaps later," Erik said, pushing me slightly behind him.

"Now. My father wants to see you."

"Sandor." Erik called his friend's name but didn't break eye contact with his cousin. "You don't leave her side. I don't care if you have to go into the restroom with her."

"Yes, sir." Sandor immediately stood beside me.

"I'll be back." Erik pressed his lips to mine. "Don't worry."

I nodded, but there was no way in hell I wasn't going to worry.

14

E*rik*

NOW I WAS PISSED. ANWAR AND I KEPT OUR DISTANCE MOST OF THE TIME because we genuinely didn't like each other, but now that he'd put hands on Casey and then tried to cut in on our dance, he was escalating things for no reason. I wasn't afraid of my uncle, but though he was always fair, he adored his firstborn and tended to overlook many of the things Anwar did. I had a feeling this meeting wasn't going to go well, but I didn't give a shit anymore. I wasn't in line for the throne so I could afford to stand up for myself—and my woman.

We entered a private room a floor below where the party had been, and the king's guards stood outside on alert. I brushed past them and went inside, fire in my veins as I met my uncle's eyes.

"Erik. Thank you. I'm sorry to disrupt your evening, but there's been an explosion."

"An explosion?" I hadn't been expecting this, so I probably looked like a deer in the headlights as I stared at him.

"At the Parliament House. Someone got a rocket launcher close enough to take out the west side of the building."

"Casualties?" I asked automatically.

"It's Saturday night, so it was a skeleton crew, just minimal security and maintenance, but at least three that we know of."

"Shit."

Anwar pushed past me to stand next to his father. "We need to find the culprits and take harsh, immediate action. The rebels have to understand we will not tolerate this sort of violence."

"Agreed." King Isak nodded. "But we must be thorough."

"Your Majesty." One of his aides came hurrying in with a laptop. "We're getting reports from the capital." He set the computer down on the table and turned up the volume as we listened to a news report from Limaj.

"The rebels have denounced the violence," the king said thoughtfully.

"Smoke and mirrors," Anwar said. "They know what will happen when we catch them."

"Why wouldn't they take responsibility?" I asked. "They always have in the past."

"They've never been violent in the past," the king agreed.

"I think it's the religious sect," I continued. "Not the democratic rebellion. They've been escalating and—"

"Why don't you go back to your whore and leave the country to me?" Anwar growled.

"What the fuck did you call her?" I lunged at him, catching him squarely in the jaw with my fist.

"Erik." The king stepped between us, and I drew back, not even breaking a sweat.

"You asshole!" Anwar clutched his face, glaring at me.

"You want to call her another name?" I asked, narrowing my eyes. "I dare you."

"Enough." The king looked at his son with undisguised disappointment. "Why would you call the young lady a name? I met her earlier, and she's perfectly lovely. He's not ascending the throne, you are, so what do you care whom he consorts with?"

Anwar made a face. "She's beneath us, playing that vile music and drinking and carousing like a common harlot. Will you be inviting her to the castle for holidays, Father?"

"If Erik marries her at some point, I absolutely will, yes." The older man shook his head. "Regardless, we have a serious matter at hand, and the two of you are behaving like spoiled children. If you cannot work together, you can both leave."

"You don't need me here," I said, straightening my jacket. "I apologize for my behavior, Uncle." I nodded at my cousin and strode from the room. I was so tired of the pissing contests between Anwar and me. It wasn't worth hanging around, but I had to call my father anyway. He needed to be in the loop even though someone from Parliament had undoubtedly already filled him in.

It was a late night, and any hopes of getting naked fell by the wayside as I spent several hours on the phone with my father, my other cousins, and even my sister. My gut told me my soon-to-be-ex-brother-in-law, Omar, was involved in the explosion, but I needed more information. We'd discovered he was responsible for the death of Skye's maid, Saraya, because she'd been the one to tell my father what he'd done to Skye, so I already distrusted him. My uncle might not listen to me, but he would listen to my father if I put the ideas in his head, and I'd spent quite a bit of time doing just that.

I was tired and irritated the next morning, so when my uncle's name flashed on the screen of my phone, under the moniker Uncle X, I nearly choked on my coffee. He almost never called me, so this meant either my father had laid into him or some other terrible thing had happened.

"Good morning, Uncle." We were a lot more casual in private.

"Good morning, Erik." His voice held a cheerful note. "Hope I'm not disturbing you?"

"No, sir, of course not."

"Your aunt and I would like you and Casey to join us for dinner next weekend. I understand you're on holiday, but it would mean a great deal to me—to us—if you would make the trip to Limaj. Wouldn't you like to show your intended our beautiful country?"

"I've been waiting years for her to go out with me, but we're nowhere near an engagement."

"According to your father, you would marry her tomorrow if you could."

I laughed. "I would, but I don't think she's ready. And after Anwar's behavior last night, I don't know that she wants to join our family."

"I'll talk with her. Please come just for a couple of days."

I hesitated. Although I agreed that my country was beautiful, and showing her the castle and royal grounds would be a lot of fun, I was nervous about exposing her to any part of my world that would change her mind about us. Hell, about me.

"You have my word no one will do anything to upset her. Including Anwar."

"All right." I was already mentally sketching out our schedule.

"Excellent. Inform my valet of when you'll be arriving, and he'll prepare your usual suite." He paused. "You'll be sharing a suite, I assume?"

"Yes," I answered automatically. Even if she wanted to continue the no-sex rule, I knew she wouldn't want to be alone at the palace. It was huge and intimidating as hell, so I wanted her near me at all times.

"We're looking forward to it." He disconnected, and I stared at the phone for a long time before I looked at Sandor. "Looks like we're going home."

He arched a brow. "All of us?"

"The king and queen have requested Casey and I join them for dinner. I couldn't think of a way to politely decline."

"Better you than me." Sandor chuckled under his breath.

"I heard that."

"I know."

I picked Casey up, and we made the drive to Nice, since it wasn't very far. We spent the day sightseeing and talking, something we seemed to do a lot of. In the back of my mind, I kept putting off bringing up the trip to Limaj, but she was already in tune to my mannerisms and it didn't take her long to notice something was up.

"What's wrong?" she asked as we wandered through a winery just outside of the city.

"My aunt and uncle invited us for dinner."

"Oh. When?"

"Next week."

"Really?"

"I didn't know how to say no." I stopped walking and put my hands on either side of her waist. "If you're really upset about it, I'll make an excuse."

"Your aunt and uncle were lovely to me. If you think we should go, we'll go."

"Are you sure?"

"If your cousin comes near me, I can't promise I won't flatten him, but yes, I'm sure."

I chuckled, lightly kissing her before we started to walk again. "That's fair."

"Isn't there a really old monastery just outside the capital... Montgrante or something?"

I nodded, pleased that she cared enough about me to know some history about my country. "Yes, Montgrante Cathedral. It's the oldest monastery still standing in the country, though it somehow became a cathedral over the years. The current construction dates back to the 1400s, and it was originally built in 979 A.D. All that's left of that building is the stone fireplace in the back, but it's stunning. I'm sure I can arrange a private tour."

"That sounds amazing." She smiled at me, and I didn't detect even a hint of hesitation.

"The palace is memorable as well. It's not open to the public because the king and queen live there six months of the year and it's difficult to protect them with visitors all day, but as my guest, I can show you almost everything."

"I feel very special," she said softly.

"You are." I wanted to kiss her, but we'd rejoined the rest of the tour and had come to the tasting part of the event.

So far, no one had recognized either of us. I had on jeans, a Viktim of Prey T-shirt, and a Las Vegas baseball cap. Casey was in capris, a white blouse, and had her hair in a ponytail. With sunglasses on, she was almost unrecognizable, but Sandor had joined us anyway.

"I want a case of this," Casey moaned as she tasted a rosé flavored with blackberries. "It's wonderful."

I agreed with her and made a note to have a case shipped to her condo in Las Vegas.

"What do you want to do after this?" I asked her.

"Let's go sit somewhere with a view, where we can drink wine and stare into each other's eyes all afternoon," she whispered.

I smiled. "That sounds fantastic."

15

Casey

THE LAST PLACE ON EARTH I WANTED TO GO WAS THE CAPITAL CITY OF LIMAJ, but I was falling hard for Erik and was willing to do it simply because he'd asked. How often did a real live king request my presence anywhere? It had never happened before, and I knew how much Erik respected his uncle. I'd enjoyed spending time with his aunt too. So as long as Anwar didn't show up, everything would be okay. At least that's what my hope was.

As we pulled up to the palace, I didn't even try to hide my awe. It was magnificent, even more breathtaking in person than in pictures I'd seen. The whole country was beautiful, with lush flowers and lots of greenery. The mountains in the distance gave it a majestic feel reminiscent of Switzerland, but the coastline we'd passed on the way here was a lot like Greece or Turkey. I'd seen glimpses of cobblestone streets that reminded me of the United Kingdom and there was something in the air that reminded me of lavender. Maybe I was so enthralled with my new boyfriend that everything about his country captured my attention. I was charmed and curious, but now that we'd arrived at the palace, I was nervous too.

"You're sure you didn't forget to tell me anything important?" I asked him. "Things I'm supposed to say or do that you take for granted?"

He gave me a look that made my insides shiver a little, which seemed to be happening more and more often lately. "Don't worry, I'll be with you every step of the way. I told you—I'll never let you fall."

"Maybe if you say it a few more times I'll believe it," I teased.

We got out of the limousine that had been sent to pick us up, and two men immediately moved to open the gilded double doors that led inside. There were apparently two entrances. The main one was in the front of the palace and faced the street, though it was a good thousand feet behind a gate. That was where tourists congregated and took pictures. This entrance was around back and off to the side, equally fancy and guarded, but for the private use of the family and their guests.

"Welcome, Your Highness." A man in a suit smiled and shook Erik's hand.

"Good to see you, Ibrahim." Erik turned to me. "Ibrahim has been running the palace household for as long as I can remember."

"I'll have your luggage and the lady's delivered to your suite," Ibrahim said. "Will you be requiring any special services while you're with us, Your Highness?"

"I'd like American-style coffee and pastries brought to the suite each morning by nine o'clock. We won't be joining the family for breakfast."

"Yes, sir." Ibrahim disappeared back inside, and I held on to Erik's hand as we followed in that direction.

The first thing I saw was a huge double staircase that split the ornate entranceway.

"The stairway on the left leads to the guest suites," Erik told me. "The one on the right goes to the king and queen's private suites."

"Got it—left is the way I need to go if I ever get lost," I said with a smile.

"There are forty-three bedrooms and guest suites, fifty-one bathrooms, three ballrooms, five dining rooms, six gardens, and four kitchens. You'll most likely get lost often."

"Four kitchens?" I asked, letting him lead me up the stairs.

"One is for everyday meals, one is specifically for bread and pastries, one is the queen's private kitchen, and the last is only used when entertaining large crowds."

"Your aunt has her own kitchen?"

"She likes to cook, but it wouldn't be proper to have her puttering around with the help, so my uncle built her a private one about ten years ago. She loves it. Her personal chef and the cleaning crew are the only people allowed in it other than guests she invites."

"This is magnificent." I was enamored with the lush carpets, carved furniture, and stunning antiquities. I'd visited many tourist locations around the world, including Edinburgh Castle, the pyramids of Egypt, and dozens of natural wonders, but the palace here in Limaj was truly magical.

"I grew up running around here when I was on school holidays," he said. "It holds a lot of fun memories for me."

"I can't imagine living here."

Erik looked like he wanted to say something but then changed his mind, pushing a panel and revealing an elevator door.

"There's an elevator?"

He chuckled. "Several, actually. This is the one for this section of the palace. It leads to the secondary suites, which include mine and a few others. Anwar and his brothers and sisters have their suites in the primary wing on the fourth floor, where they have a bit more privacy. This floor, however, has special surprises."

"Ooooh, sounds sexy."

"Very." We stepped off the elevator and went down another set of stairs.

"Wait, we went up to go down?"

"It's all about security and privacy. Trust me." We turned a corner and came to a set of double doors. He unlocked the door, and this time when we stepped inside, my jaw fell open and stayed there.

"What..." I looked around and a little sigh of pleasure escaped me. "Is that a private pool? Like, just for you?"

He grinned. "Well, Skye would share the pool if she was here, because her suite is next door, but she's in Las Vegas." He wrapped his arms around me from behind as I stared out at the glistening water. "What do you think?"

"I'm shocked and awed," I admitted. "This is fantastic. The pool, the view, the palm trees... This takes rich to a whole new level."

"It does. I don't come often, but when I do, it's nice to indulge."

I glanced at him. "I've never even asked you—where do you live the rest of the time?"

"I have a flat about an hour from London where I spend a lot of time since that's where I went to university. If I'm traveling, I'm usually with friends or at hotels. I'm not in one place long enough to call anywhere home though."

"You sound like me. I've been on tour since I was eighteen and even though I own a condo in Vegas, I'm never there."

"Do you want a home?"

I thought about it. "I do, but I don't want to be there all the time. I want to travel, tour, explore the world, have new experiences, meet people from other cultures... But I do want somewhere to call home, somewhere I'll eventually raise a family. What about you? Do you plan to settle down in one place and be a prince without a throne, doing royal things?"

He chuckled. "Yes and no. As a member of the royal family, I like doing charity events and bringing to light important issues like world health and starvation, but since I'll never take the throne, I've also considered getting a job."

"Why?"

"Why what?" He seemed confused.

"Why would you want the drudgery of working for someone else when you can make a difference in the world with just your title and the money you already have?"

"You make a valid point. I guess it's because I'm a man and somewhere in my subconscious it feels like I should work, do more than spend the money I was simply born with."

"Working on issues that impact the entire world sounds like a fantastic job, if you ask me."

He smiled. "When you put it that way..."

A knock on the door interrupted us, and Erik went to answer it. A pretty brunette stood there smiling, and when she saw Erik, she threw her arms around him.

"You're here!" she said happily. Then she went off in an explosion of conversation in their language, which of course, I didn't understand.

"Elen, we'll catch up soon but there's someone I want you to meet." He tugged the girl forward. "Honey, this is my cousin Elen. Elen, my girlfriend, Casey Hart."

"From Viktim of Prey!" Elen's eyes twinkled. "I love, love, love your music."

"Thank you," I responded automatically.

"Elen is Sandor's younger sister," Erik said.

"Is my big brother behaving?" Elen asked, laughing.

"Sometimes," Erik quipped.

"Well, I've come to say hello and warn you."

"Warn me?" Erik frowned. "About what?"

"Anwar has been on a tear since the party in Monte Carlo. He's supposedly on his way home and not happy that you're here."

"Tough shit," Erik said. "Uncle Isak invited us."

"Well, I just wanted you to know he's being his usual asshole self. Now I have to go find my brother. Is he in his room?"

"He said something about going to visit your mother."

She wrinkled her nose. "Mother's in Brazil having a facelift."

Erik laughed. "Then your brother is undoubtedly roaming around the palace."

"I'll find him." Elen waved, calling over her shoulder, "Nice to meet you, Casey!"

Erik shut the door and grinned. "My favorite cousin other than Sandor."

"You seem close to them. Do they have any other siblings?"

"There's a boy between Sandor and Elen, Daniil, and we're all closest among the cousins."

"Who's oldest?"

"Vardan is twenty-eight, Sandor twenty-six, Daniil twenty-three, and Elen is twenty. I'm between Sandor and Daniil at twenty-four. Their mother is my father's sister, and their father is British, so they're way removed from the throne and quite happy about it."

"Is that why Sandor is your bodyguard?"

"He requested it, actually. Since he's two years older, he could have gone off to university without me and done his own thing, but he opted to wait for me so we could go together. He used those two years to do his military service and train that way."

"Is it mandatory here?"

"Yes, it's one year, for men only, either before or after university. If you do it before, and do two years, university is free. In my case, because my uncle gave me a title, as a member of the royal family, I still have to do it, but I was allowed to do it during the summers after graduating high school. I did three months after each of my four years of undergraduate. Which is why you haven't seen a lot of me the last few years during the summer."

"I don't think I knew any of that."

"For my safety and the safety of the others, I went in under an assumed name and the public wasn't made aware of what I was doing. Sandor returned with me, in a position sort of like what you might call in the U.S. the reserves, just to keep an eye on me and provide protection should anything go wrong. Higher-ups in the military knew who I was, of course, and what Sandor was doing, so they made special accommodations for both of us."

"That's pretty cool."

"I loved the military," he admitted. "It was the first and only time in my life I was treated like a regular person, and the physical part of it was both exciting and challenging."

"You look like you're in pretty good shape," I murmured, moving close to him.

He lowered his lips to mine. Lord, this man did things to me every time he touched me, and he hadn't touched me nearly enough in the last week or so. Despite that, our bodies came together naturally, and once we were skin-to-skin there was a simplistic pleasure I couldn't quite explain. Sexy and erotic, yes, but also comfortable, as if we'd been together much longer than a couple of weeks. I really liked how it felt and I was curious about his feelings about everything.

"By the way," I said, leaning back a little. "You called me your girlfriend—do I get any say in the matter?"

"You want me to ask you to go steady?"

"Maybe?" I teased.

"Just tell me what you want and I'll do my best to fulfill your needs."

"In that case, I want you to fuck the living hell out of me."

16

E*rik*

SHE DIDN'T HAVE TO ASK ME TWICE. I SCOOPED HER UP IN MY ARMS, WALKED over to the bed, and dumped her on it.

"Condoms," I said by way of explanation when I didn't join her right away.

Where the hell had I put them?

"Where are they?" she asked as I hesitated.

"No idea." I went into the bathroom, but my toiletry bag hadn't yet arrived.

Shit.

"I don't think our stuff is here yet." She laughed, getting off the bed and following me, her naked body glorious to look at.

"Crap. That means we probably shouldn't start anything either, because they'll be knocking—" Someone knocked on the door as the words left my mouth.

"Get rid of them," she whispered, nudging me.

"I'll do my best." I yanked my jeans back on as I walked to the door and opened it, expecting Ibrahim or one of the servants. Instead, Anwar stood there.

Well, this was disappointing.

"I apologize for intruding," Anwar said stiffly. "May I join you for a moment?"

"What can I do for you?" I wasn't going to let him anywhere near Casey.

"I need to apologize. Both to you and to your—to Ms. Hart."

"Say what you need to say."

"I was acting on my father's behalf, and perhaps I went too far. I merely wanted to test her, to see if she was truly devoted to you. I meant no harm."

"My uncle asked this of you?"

"He did." He took a breath. "And now he has asked me to explain and said he will also apologize tonight at dinner."

"Apology accepted." Casey's voice behind me surprised me, since I didn't know how quickly she could redress, but I merely slid an arm around her waist as she joined me. "Thank you for telling us."

"Good day." He inclined his head and moved stiffly down the hall.

I shut the door and looked at her. "Just like that you accepted his apology?"

"What was the alternative? Telling him to fuck off? That would've gone over well."

I chuckled. "It would've been amusing though."

"I've got something else in mind to amuse us," she said. "Now where the hell is our luggage?"

OUR LUGGAGE DIDN'T ARRIVE RIGHT AWAY, BUT WE HAD HALF A DOZEN VISITS from family and servants. Sandor checked in, my uncle's valet delivered a formal invitation for tonight's dinner, various cousins stopped by to say hello, and finally, someone brought the luggage. Unfortunately, it was time to start dressing for dinner, so even though it was killing me, her sexy request had to wait.

She stepped out of the dressing room in a simple, sleeveless white dress that showed off her recent tan and the curve of her delicate shoulders. She'd bought it in Monte Carlo just before we'd left for Limaj, and though it was probably a little sexier than someone else might wear to dinner at the palace, this was private and I truly didn't want her to change. There was a fine line between respect and becoming someone else, and I was in love with Casey Hart the rock star, not someone putting on an act to make my family happy. At the end of the day, my parents adored her, and they were the ones who counted. I loved and respected my aunt and uncle, but only as my aunt and uncle, not because they were the king and queen of my country.

"Are you sure this isn't too short?" she was asking me.

"It's perfect," I replied. "You're perfect."

"I don't want to embarrass you." Her eyes were filled with sincerity and a touch of insecurity.

"You won't. This is a private dinner between family. Elen and Sandor are joining us, maybe Daniil as well. It's going to be laid-back and casual, I promise. Besides, we don't have anything to prove. They already know who you are, what you do, and what our relationship is."

"What, exactly, is our relationship?" she asked quietly. "You asked me to give you a week to prove things could be good between us, but we've passed that mark and today you called me your girlfriend. I was glib about it earlier because I was trying to get in your pants, but since that didn't work, we should probably have a more serious conversation about this."

"Like I tried to say before, when your hormones took over and you tried to attack me, I'm happy to ask you to go steady or whatever else you want me to do." I laughed when she smacked my arm. She was so damn adorable. Our time together was fun, comfortable. I hadn't had anything like this with a woman before and it was nice. No, it was better than nice. Shit, who was I kidding? It was amazing and I wanted more. I wanted my family to love her like I did and for us to do everything together.

Wow. I was turning into a teenage boy.

And I didn't give a shit.

"I just mean, when we talk to your parents and stuff, are we in a relationship?"

"Absolutely. Unless you don't want to be." Wow, did I sound like a teenager or what? I'd never been like this but all I wanted was to be what she wanted. If that made any sense.

"You know I do."

"Then we are. Now let's go. We don't want to keep the king and queen waiting."

"I thought this was a casual family dinner?" She raised an eyebrow as she questioned me.

"It is—but there are limits to what the word casual means in the palace."

"What about my dress?"

"Relax about the dress. You're beautiful." I took her hand and we walked toward the elevator.

MY AUNT AND UNCLE WERE ALREADY SEATED IN THEIR PRIVATE DINING ROOM when we arrived, and I felt Casey stiffen beside me. I'd explained protocol to her, but she was still nervous, and I loved her a little more because she cared enough to want to make a good impression. I'd walked the fine line between casual and proper my whole life, so I was used to it, but this was all new to her. Hopefully, we'd be out of here in a few days and would be able to relax again.

Casey bowed her head, which was all that was required for a family dinner like this, and my uncle held out his hand to her.

"Welcome to our home, my dear. You look lovely this evening."

"Thank you, Your Majesty."

"Uncle Isak in private, eh?"

"Yes, sir. I mean, Uncle Isak."

They laughed together and I finally relaxed as I leaned over to kiss my aunt's cheek.

"Are we late?" Elen asked, joining us with Daniil and Sandor.

"Daniil!" I hadn't seen him in months, and we embraced tightly.

"Good to see you, cousin." Daniil turned to Casey, holding out his hand. "Pleasure to meet you, Ms. Hart. Elen has spent the afternoon playing your music for me and I must say I'm hooked."

"Thank you." She shook his hand. "I'm excited to know I have fans in Limaj."

"At least three," I said, chuckling.

"Four," Aunt Klara called out. "Now, shall we eat?"

We all sat down, with me next to my uncle and Casey next to my aunt. It was highly irregular for Casey and I to be separated, but my aunt dictated the seating arrangement and I didn't dare say anything. Casey gave me a frantic look, but there was nothing I could do, so I merely gave her an encouraging wink. Luckily, Elen was on her other side and I trusted Elen to guide her if she needed it, though Casey would undoubtedly be able to handle herself. I had faith in her, no matter what went on tonight.

Since the seating arrangement made me a little uneasy, I wasn't sure what else to expect. Especially knowing Anwar was in residence but so far hadn't appeared for dinner. I didn't want it to eat at me, so I broached the subject as soon as the first course was served.

"Where is Anwar tonight?" I asked my uncle quietly. "He paid us a visit earlier. I have to say, I'm a little disappointed."

I saw something I'd never seen in my uncle's eyes before: guilt. It was odd because he made life or death decisions every day and didn't bat an eyelash. Yet testing my new girlfriend made him feel guilty? I was more confused than ever.

"Anwar took my curiosity about Ms. Hart a little too seriously. I never asked him to touch or embarrass her. I merely wanted him to ask her to dance, perhaps, see how she behaved, what types of things she said. I was but looking out for you, Erik. I never wanted to hurt or embarrass either of you."

"I understand that, but you couldn't have enlisted Vardan? Or someone a little less...aggressive?"

"That was an error on my part, hence my apology. I'll apologize to Casey in private."

"Of course."

Interesting. He was backpedaling, something my uncle never did. Which meant Anwar had accosted Casey on his own, but as always, my uncle was protecting his firstborn. It irked me to no end, but this was neither the time nor the place to say something.

"So what do you think of the palace, Casey?" Elen was asking. "Isn't it amazing?"

"What I've seen so far is beautiful." Casey nodded. "I can't wait to see the rest."

"Where are you taking her tomorrow?" Aunt Klara asked me. "You should take her to the Klandar Market."

"That's a tactical nightmare," Sandor said. "It's difficult to provide protection in such an open-air arena."

"What about Olden Towne?" Daniil suggested. "There's a music shop by Timur's Café that she would probably love."

"Oh, the one with the dragon logo on the door?" I nodded. "I know the one. I've never been inside, but you're right, Casey would probably love it. The owner carves all the instruments by hand—he's brilliant."

"Sounds lovely," Casey agreed.

"And the gardens of Danalhi," Elen added. "They're stunning."

I made a mental list of all the places I wanted to show Casey in Hiskale, the country's capital and where the palace was located. We didn't have much time, though, because I didn't want to stay long. I loved my country, but Anwar's behavior worried me, and my uncle's reluctance to do anything about it was even worse. The thought of Anwar becoming king made me a little sick, and not because I wanted it for myself. "Erik?" My uncle was talking to me, and I realized I'd zoned out.

"I'm sorry, yes?"

"Would you join me in my study now that the meal is over? There's something I'd like to discuss with you."

I nodded more out of habit than any desire to meet with him, but I had manners, if nothing else. "Of course."

The table was cleared, and while everyone else went into the queen's salon for brandy and dessert, I followed my uncle to his den. He shut the door and pulled out a cigar, offering me one. I declined since I hoped to have my tongue down Casey's throat tonight but sat opposite him in a comfortable leather chair.

"First, I thought I'd update you about your sister's situation," he said without preamble.

"Situation?"

"Her maid, Saraya, was found dead on the palace steps several weeks ago. I hadn't had a chance to tell you until now."

"So Omar killed her for... what?"

"Disobeying him. Alerting my brother to the situation. Any number of reasons."

"And you're not doing anything about it?"

"What can we do since we don't know who did it or how."

"How the hell was she left on the palace steps if no one saw anything? Aren't there security cameras?" This was preposterous to me.

"Those tapes were apparently accidentally erased."

"Erased." I let out a derisive laugh. "That's rich. You know that's crap, don't you?"

"I do. Which brings me to why you're here."

"What does that mean?"

"I'd like to know what your plans are," he said in the most serious voice he'd ever used with me.

"My plans?" I was a little confused.

"You've finished six years at university and have your entire future ahead of you. What plans do you have?"

"I haven't gotten that far yet," I admitted. "I've mulled around several different options, but on the top of my list is marrying the woman in the other room. If she'll have me."

"Excellent. Klara and I agree with your parents that she's an excellent choice."

I arched a brow. "You discussed my relationship with Casey with my parents?"

"Of course. You've always been like another son to me, Erik. I care about you and want what's best for you."

"Thank you, sir."

"I've also thought a lot about having you as part of my plans to change the future of Limaj."

"I don't understand."

"You know we've been on the brink of civil war for years and though the people aren't suffering, we're not making progress as a global leader. Not even as a European leader. We've remained mostly unknown and I'd like to bring the country into the twenty-first century beyond the internet. I want women to have equal rights, our young people to want to stay and work and flourish, and for our family to be seen in a positive light around the world."

"What does that have to do with me?"

"I think you can help. You're smart, well-traveled, and you have a finger on the pulse of the international community. Your young new girlfriend is already, even at her age, a legendary musician who could bring the arts to Limaj."

"Sir, I don't think—"

"Hear me out, Erik. Please."

"Of course."

"The two of you could be part of the change here in Limaj. A strong, modern, independently wealthy woman—with the title of princess—alongside a member of Parliament."

My mouth fell open. "You want me to join Parliament?"

"I can appoint you. If you're willing."

I had a hundred things I wanted to say but he probably didn't want to hear them so I sat there trying to formulate the proper response to such an honorable offer.

"What is it, son? Talk to me. Uncle to favorite nephew. Forget my position."

"No one can ever forget your position," I said, opting for a dash of humor. "But it's nothing."

"I saw your face. This is about Anwar, yes?"

"Sir, I…" My voice trailed off. How could I tell him what a fuckwad his firstborn son and heir to the throne was?

"Go on." The look on his face warned me not to lie.

"You didn't tell Anwar to test Casey's faithfulness," I said, throwing caution to the wind. "He did it on his own and once you found out, you covered for him and made him apologize. I understand. He's your son. He'll be king someday. But the things he does are worrisome. It's not my place to say that, but you asked."

"I did indeed." He got up from the chair and walked to a small wet bar in the corner of the room. He poured two tumblers of what was most likely scotch and brought me one before sitting back down. "I've struggled for a long time with the decision of whether or not to leave the throne to Anwar. Short of having him declared incompetent or a traitor, he *will* be the next king. This is how it is and how it has always been done."

I didn't say anything, merely waited for him to make his point.

"I think he will outgrow his aggressive demeanor and learn to handle things in a more sedate manner. Once he finds a wife, has a family, I think things will change, but until then I'm hoping you will guide him."

"Guide him? Me?" I burst out laughing. "He hates me, and I don't care much for him either."

"I see this, and I would ask that you try harder, Erik. I need you. Your country needs you."

What fresh hell was this?

My country needed me?

Since when?

"I'm sorry, Uncle Isak. I love you and my country, but Anwar's policies, his stance on women's and humanitarian rights is so far opposite of my own I cannot in good faith work with him in any official capacity."

"I see."

"I'm sorry. The last thing I would ever want to do is disappoint you, but he's going to set our country back a hundred years the day he succeeds you, and I can't be part of that."

"You truly believe this?"

"With everything I am."

"Never apologize for your convictions," he responded thoughtfully. His eyes met mine and he nodded. "I appreciate your candor. You've given me a lot to think about."

17

C*asey*

Erik was with his uncle for a long time, and though I was enjoying spending time with the queen and Erik's cousins, I'd started to get a little worried by the time he finally reappeared. He was smiling, but there was a tightness around his eyes that told a different story. I rose to greet him, leaning up to chastely kiss his cheek.

"Are you okay?" I whispered.

"I'm okay." He slid his arm around me as he accepted a snifter of brandy from Sandor.

We made small talk for a while, but the king never joined us, and we left after about thirty minutes. Erik was quiet on the walk back to our elevator bay and then on the ride up. Sandor went in a different direction, wishing us good night, and Erik unlocked the door to our suite, still silent.

"What's wrong?" I asked as soon as we were alone.

"Just a weird dynamic between me, my uncle, and Anwar."

"Well, Anwar is jealous of you."

"Jealous? Why? He has everything I can't have."

"Not everything. He'll never have your striking good looks, your huge heart, and the *actual* birthright to the throne. He knows he's the second choice, so to speak. You were born to be king, not him. He got lucky because your dad fell in love with a commoner your grandfather didn't approve of and knowing that's the only reason he's the heir to the throne must grate on his ego."

"But why? Those events happened before I was born, and he was just a kid."

I shrugged. "I can't tell you why he is the way he is, but I'd be willing to bet he's jealous, plain and simple. You're not like the others. At least, no one I've met to date. You have a stately demeanor, royalty that permeates from your soul. You don't have to do anything to be a king, it's who and what you are. It's a little overwhelming sometimes."

"I overwhelm you?" he asked softly, drawing me against his chest.

"A little. But I'm getting used to it."

"I don't want to be king, Casey."

"I know, but you would still make a fantastic one, and it's written all over you, in everything you say and do. And just as an aside, your royalness is kind of hot."

"Really?" He slid his hands down my back until they rested on my ass. "How hot?"

"So hot I might need to go skinny-dipping."

"That sounds like fun. Is our no-sex mandate rescinded?"

"Absolutely."

"Thank god." He kissed me lightly. "I'm going to get condoms—you get undressed."

He didn't have to ask me twice. I stepped out of my shoes and yanked my dress over my head, tossing it on the couch. I unhooked my strapless bra and tossed it after the dress before hooking my thumbs in the sides of my panties and letting them slide to the floor.

"This is the best thing I've seen all day."

His voice made me turn, and my breath caught a little at the vision he made completely nude. I'd seen him naked before, of course, but that had been during an interlude of drunken, mindless sex. This was different. We were a couple now, and this was the first time I was getting to appreciate just how gorgeous he was. His stomach was hard and flat, the V leading down to his groin mouthwateringly sexy. His shoulders were wide, sitting atop a sculpted, hairy chest. His arms were strong and muscular, his biceps even more striking without the cover of a shirt.

I wanted to trace every inch of him with my tongue, taste the saltiness of his skin, lose myself in his touch, but there would be time for that. I'd promised him skinny-dipping and that's what we would do. In the beginning anyway. I had a feeling we'd be all over each other in short order, but I took off at a slow run and dove into the pool.

I felt the splash when Erik landed just after me and then he grabbed me, pulling me against him and lowering his mouth to mine. He tasted of brandy and moonlight, his tongue seeking mine almost desperately. We'd done a lot of kissing this past week, but not like this. Tonight's kisses were intense, powerful, as intoxicating as any I'd ever experienced. He was devouring me in ways I'd never thought possible, as if he owned me. It wasn't a bad thing, though, because being owned by Erik was the most beautiful thing ever. At this point, I'd sell my soul to the devil so Erik could own me.

We started to sink and broke apart long enough to kick back to the surface. He tugged me to a shallower part of the pool before kissing me again, his hands skimming my body as if this was the first time all over again. It felt like it too. Each touch of his fingers brought me pleasure that was far more satisfying than music, sex, or the most decadent dessert. His touch made me whole, and the heat building deep inside of me was growing more and more out of control.

One wicked finger slid between my legs and they opened of their own accord.

"I'd like to say you're wet," he murmured against my lips, "but it's kind of hard to tell in here."

I chuckled. "I'm wet, believe me."

"I can't wait to be inside of you again, baby."

"The sooner the better."

"I thought you wanted to swim."

"I want to be naked with you."

"Done." He pressed his strong chest against mine and then lifted me, so I wrapped my legs around him. Strong fingers kneaded my ass, taunting and teasing as he touched my most intimate places, fingers probing me with gentle urgency.

"I want to taste you," he whispered. He set me on the edge of the pool, standing between my legs as he slowly pushed me back.

"Oh, god." I closed my eyes as his lips traveled across my thigh, warm and sensual. He kissed a trail along the crease of my leg, my hip, my pelvis. He was like a drug because the more he touched me, the more I wanted. I'd never been this in tune to a man before and it was incredible. When his lips finally grazed my mound, I didn't even try to hide my moan.

"So beautiful," he sighed, gently pressing light kisses along my slit. He hadn't even used his tongue yet, and I was a quivering mass of need, aching for more.

The tip of his tongue touched sensitive skin, and I inhaled sharply, beyond ready for him. He took his time, licking and kissing with light, feathery strokes, his hands resting on my thighs.

"Erik..." I didn't know what I needed, but I needed more of something.

"Patience, love." His tongue grew more insistent now, flattening against me and using harder, heavier strokes that had my ass surging off the concrete to meet him. He started to tongue-fuck me and the pleasure was as exquisite as an orgasm, but I was holding back, wanting to enjoy this as long as possible.

"Erik!" I squealed when he moved down further to my back hole, working on a part of me that had never been touched.

"Easy," he whispered. "Just a tongue." He slid a finger into my vagina as he licked and kissed every inch of me, until I was practically crying for release. His lips closed around my clit and I was done, screaming his name as I bucked into his face, each wave a little stronger than the last.

When he finally lifted his head, the passion reflected there was heady. He didn't just want to fuck me—he absolutely wanted to own me, and I was one hundred percent on board with this.

He came out of the water and reached down to help me up, since my legs were still shaking uncontrollably. Lifting me in his arms, he carried me to a lounge chair and sank down with me in his lap. He'd placed some condoms on the small table beside it and quickly sheathed himself.

We didn't speak as he adjusted me so I was straddling him. One hand came up and gripped the back of my neck as he kissed me, the other gently stroking my back. He shifted his hips so his erection was between my legs, and without changing anything else, he slid into me. Slow. Thick. With purpose. I sank down, taking all of him, and we both let out sighs of pleasure. Our bodies moved in perfect unison, as if we were born to do this, and I let out another little moan as I dropped my forehead to his, letting my arms close around his neck.

"I've waited my whole life for you," I whispered.

"As have I." His eyes met mine. "I love you, Casey. I always have."

"I love you too." I hadn't planned to say it, not this soon, but it felt right, especially in this moment.

He crashed his lips to mine, fingers digging into my hips as he thrust up harder and deeper. We kissed like animals, unable to get close enough, deep enough, intense enough. Our bodies moved together, picking up speed and driving us both to the brink. Then Erik slowed down, making me cry out in frustration. He smiled, leaning in to suck on my earlobe.

"Not yet," he whispered. "I want to enjoy this."

"We can do it again," I whispered back.

"And we will." He reached out and ran his thumbs over my nipples. "You're so fucking beautiful. Watching my cock disappear inside you is fucking sexy as hell."

"Mmm." I moaned as he lifted me and slowly set me back down. He did it over and over, his eyes never leaving where our bodies were joined, until I was whimpering with frustration and need.

"You ready, baby?"

"Yes."

He thrust up and angled his hips so he hit something deep inside of me that made me cry out. His hips jerked and he licked his thumb before finding my clit. That little bit of extra pressure was all I needed and my scream tore through the night as I came again and again, rocking on his lap in utter ecstasy. His own growl was low and deep as he shot off inside of me, and we didn't stop shaking for a long time.

When I finally collapsed against him, his arms closed around me, and we didn't move at all. A light breeze made it a little chilly, but I was too content to care, basking in his warmth, his body, his love. This beautiful, incredible, gorgeous man was in love with me, and I loved him too. I didn't know what this meant in terms of the future, but I didn't care as long as he was with me.

"It's getting cold," he whispered, stirring. "Let's go inside."

"Okay." I reluctantly moved off his lap and got to my feet. He took my hand and pulled me inside where we immediately got into the shower. I rested against him, suddenly overwhelmed emotionally, and he wrapped his arms around me.

"You okay?" he asked softly.

"I'm wonderful. Everything is happening so fast, but it feels natural, like we were meant to do this."

"I know." He kissed the top of my head.

"I'm a little confused though. Like, what are we doing? Are we going back to Las Vegas? Going to continue playing all through Europe? Visiting friends? I mean, what's next?"

"What do you want to be next?"

"I have to think about my career. Maybe not right this minute, but soon."

"I'm okay with that. I don't want to change you, sweetheart. If you want to go back to Vegas and start working on music or whatever, I'm happy to go and just be with you."

"Will you be happy just hanging around Vegas while I write or record?"

"I'll be happy because I'm with you."

"You know what I mean. You've mentioned being restless, thinking about getting a real job, things like that. I don't think you're going to be truly happy following me around while I do my thing and you do nothing."

"I'm thinking about starting a charitable foundation for an issue that's important to me, but I haven't had time to sort it out. I might get a job; it just depends on what happens. Honestly, I'm not worried about it. We have the rest of our lives to think about all that stuff. Right now, I just want to be in love and have a lot of sex and follow you around like a lovesick puppy because that's what I am. And I'm not even ashamed to admit it."

"God, you're so fucking perfect it's scary," I growled, tugging his head down so I could kiss him again. I was fairly certain I would never get enough of him.

18

E*rik*

I WAS EXHAUSTED THE NEXT MORNING, BUT LAST NIGHT'S LOVEMAKING marathon was worth every lost minute of sleep. Casey fulfilled every fantasy I'd ever had, both romantic and sexual, and we'd tried half a dozen positions before we could no longer move. When the alarm went off at nine, neither of us wanted to get up, but we showered and had a light breakfast before taking off for Hiskale. We explored the gardens of Denalhi and Olden Towne before stopping for a late lunch at Timur's Café. The food was basic but delicious, and the music shop I'd told Casey about was next door, so once we were finished, we walked there.

As always in my country, I was recognized. Most people were just excited to see me, smiling and waving, but today I had a date. I was holding Casey's hand and we'd reach over to kiss now and again, so there was no doubt this was different. I'd never brought a woman home before and the people who recognized me instantly reached for their phones or nudged their companions.

"Your Highness." The owner of a candy shop I frequented was sweeping the sidewalk in front of his store and waved. "I have your favorite caramel bites."

"Oh, well then lead the way." We detoured inside and the smell of caramel was overwhelmingly delicious.

Casey sighed happily. "I love caramel—oh my god, that's almost all there is in here."

"Yes, it's his specialty." I grinned. "And wait until you taste the white chocolate wafers dipped in brandy-infused caramel."

Her eyes widened as the owner brought out a tray of delicacies. He never took money from me so I rewarded him by placing huge orders to be shipped to friends, family and even to myself when I'd been at school in London.

"This is Casey," I told him. He was one of the few who didn't speak much English in my country, but his eyes danced with excitement as he spoke to her in ridiculously broken, but discernible, English.

"Please—this is best." He pointed to different things on the tray and Casey took bites of all of them.

"Oh, god, we can't do this," she moaned in what sounded like orgasmic ecstasy. "I'll weigh a thousand pounds if we keep trying stuff."

"Good luck getting out of here without gaining at least five," I chuckled.

We sampled candy and chatted while Casey wandered around and filled a basket with things to take with her.

"How's business?" I asked the shop owner, Herman.

He made a face, shrugging. "Not so good, Your Highness. Tourists are few and far between and the locals don't indulge in sweets like mine regularly. I make a living, but the last few years have been leaner than years past."

"Why do you think that is?" I asked, frowning.

He met my gaze and then lowered his eyes. "It's a difficult time, sir."

"Tell me what you're thinking. You've known me a long time. Talk to me."

"The king, he is old-fashioned, and we worry about the direction of the country. With the religious sect becoming more powerful, people are staying home, less inclined to come downtown to shop. People are saving their money, not spending, fearing the day we have no trade with the outside world."

"Why would you think this?"

He sighed. "There is talk. Prince Anwar goes to the villages in the mountains, he stirs up trouble, talking about the west coming to take our oil. He says the only way to protect it is to keep out the west, including trade and tourism."

I frowned. I hadn't heard any such thing, but it didn't surprise me.

"This is troubling," I said. "Perhaps you misunderstood."

He shook his head. "My brother lives in such a village. Anwar has gone to the orthodox church twice, to talk with the people after services. He encourages religion and modesty for the women and sending our young men to the coast to work the oil jobs."

"And the people... are they happy about this?"

"There are some. Enough. Those in the villages are poor, they don't have the conveniences we have here in the city. They're hungry and the winters are long and cold. They believe their sons will make money and send it home to them."

"And you? What do you think?"

He looked up at me almost defiantly. "I think this will be the end of Limaj as we know it."

"Thank you for telling me. I'll look into this further."

Something deep inside of me twisted painfully even as I tried to reassure him. I didn't want this for my country or my people. Hell, I wouldn't want it for myself. How was this happening without anyone knowing about it?

"If you were our king, this wouldn't be happening," he said quietly.

I met his gaze. "This isn't possible," I responded as gently as I could.

"It is not easy, but it is possible."

"Thank you for your support. It means a lot to me." I squeezed his shoulder, but there was nothing else to say. The hoops that would have to be jumped through for me to be king were huge and difficult. I'd never even considered them.

At some point, I'd have to talk to my father about everything I'd learned, but for now, Casey had dropped more than a dozen gift boxes of different candy collections on the counter.

"All of these, please," she told Herman. "I'm eating some, giving some as gifts and bringing the rest home so I have them for a while."

I translated and Herman smiled and nodded, packing them up and chatting with her in his broken English.

Sandor took the packages to the SUV and Casey and I continued down the street. I couldn't wait for her to see the music shop, anxious to forget about what Herman had just told me and revel in showing my girl the country I loved as much as I loved her.

Casey was enchanted the moment we got to the shop, the carved dragon on the door catching her eye in addition to the gorgeous, delicately carved instruments in the window. The owner, Vicenzo, recognized Casey immediately, his face lighting up with a huge smile.

"Ms. Hart! I am humbled you have come to my little shop." His English was much better than Herman's.

"I've heard wonderful things about your work," she replied, shaking his hand.

"Your Highness." His eyes got bigger and rounder when he realized who her companion was, his cheeks reddening slightly.

"Good to meet you." I shook his hand as well, nodding. "I've been told the most amazing things about your work, and I knew Casey would want to see firsthand."

"Come." Vicenzo practically buzzed around the shop, showing Casey a plethora of instruments he'd designed, from violins to pianos to guitars.

"Your work is incredible," she whispered, fingering a flute covered with dragons etched in ivory.

"Thank you. I am honored." He bowed his head.

"An electric guitar decorated with dragon's wings that were inlaid with mother-of-pearl would be stunning," she mused. "Do you have anything like that?"

"Not at the moment," he responded. "But it can be commissioned."

"I have to think about what I want," she said. "Definitely something pink."

"Pink?" Vicenzo looked startled.

"I want something different for my next guitar, and I already have black, red, and teal guitars. I think pink is next."

"I can make this for you."

"I'll be in touch," she promised. "Once I'm back in Las Vegas and have time to figure out details."

"Of course." He handed her a business card with his personal phone number printed on the back. "Call me any time."

"Thank you." She looked around. "But now I want to browse."

She walked over to a wall with instruments and was fingering them lightly when her phone rang and she answered it with a happy smile. "Nick! I was just thinking about you... yeah, I'm at this music store in Limaj. You would not believe the custom work this guy does...no, carving... Guitars, drums, pianos, everything... oh, I don't know." She turned to Vicenzo. "Do you do bass guitars?"

"I can do anything," he nodded.

She went back to her phone call and I was all but forgotten. I hated it but reminded myself that they'd been friends forever, played in a band together and if she wanted to be with him, she could be. They could have ridden off into romantic bliss if that's what she wanted, but she obviously didn't, and I wasn't going to be the jealous guy. Well, not much anyway.

"Oh, there's these drum sticks..." She picked a pair up off a shelf. "I think

BJ would love them. Maybe as part of his birthday present...yeah? Okay, I'm going to get them... no, I don't think so. I want something custom and pink." She laughed. "Piss off, you're just jealous you don't play a pink guitar..." They talked another few minutes and then she hung up and brought the drum sticks to Vicenzo. "Can you wrap these up as a gift? They're for the drummer of my band."

"Of course." He hurried to do her bidding and she turned to me with a smile. "The band would love this place. Maybe someday I'll bring Jade."

"She would be our guest," I said graciously.

We walked out hand-in-hand and she sighed happily as she handed Sandor her bag. "I think I'm going to have a guitar made with dragons on it. I just don't know what I want yet."

"We can make this happen."

"Your Highness!" someone called out, and I instinctively pulled Casey closer to me. My fellow countrymen tended to be respectful and easygoing when they saw me out and about, but the foreign press was another story.

Sandor and Aziz flanked us, keeping the two reporters a respectful distance away, but they already had their cameras going off.

"Have you come home for good, Your Highness?"

"Is that Casey Hart?"

Casey gave a brief wave, smiling in a friendly manner but sticking close to me.

"Casey and I are on holiday," I responded, though we kept moving towards the waiting SUV. "I've brought her home to meet the family and see some of our beautiful country."

"Rumor has it that there was an altercation in Monte Carlo with His Royal Highness, Prince Anwar."

"Not at all," I said, shooing Casey into the SUV while I paused to finish my statement. "They hadn't yet met so he didn't know who she was. Once they were introduced, everything was fine. Have a good day, everyone." I got into the SUV and motioned for the driver to go.

"How did they know about me and Anwar?" Casey asked, frowning.

"There are eyes everywhere," I responded, though I was equally baffled. That had been a private party, and there were unspoken rules about taking unauthorized photos and video when royals were in attendance. My gut told me Anwar leaked the gossip to the press himself to stir things up because he didn't like the idea that Casey and I had gotten so close to his parents.

"Should we respond?"

"Nope. What I told them just now is all we're going to say. I'm sure they'll move on to something else in a day or so." At least I hoped so. We needed to get out of Limaj and go someplace where Anwar wasn't. He was starting to become a pain in my ass, and I just wanted to take my girl and get away from him.

"Okay." She rested her head on my shoulder as we made our way back to the palace.

19

E*rik*

WATCHING CASEY FALL IN LOVE WITH LIMAJ MADE ME FALL FOR HER EVEN harder. We drove to the coast and spent a few hours in the sea, getting sunburned and having a picnic on the sand. As always, I was recognized but not bothered. A few people came over to say hello, mostly older people who had sweet things to say and a few who wanted to tell Casey they were big fans. Though it made Sandor and Aziz nervous, I was never really worried around regular citizens. I wasn't sure why, but it had just always been this way.

"Do the people here approach everyone in the royal family like they know them?" Casey asked as we devoured fresh loaf of French bread, a tangy selection of cheeses, and grapes.

I shook my head. "No. I think Daniil is fairly approachable, but he doesn't spend much time here and Anwar and his brothers wouldn't be caught dead talking to the people without an agenda."

"You love your country, don't you?" she asked softly, her eyes meeting mine with loving respect.

"Of course. Don't you love yours?"

"I do, but..." She chewed the inside of her lip thoughtfully. "It's different. I'm proud to be an American, but I don't ever think of what the people of my country are doing or what's best for them or anything like that. My thoughts are purely personal—am I safe? Am I happy? Am I living a good life? And I don't mean that in a selfish way. I donate to charity and make sure I know who I'm voting for during local elections and stuff, but I kind of trust the government to take care of big stuff like trade or laws or whatever. You think of things on a different level...through the eyes of a leader."

I frowned slightly. "I guess that's true to an extent. I'm not their leader, but I do think of the people because I worry about the future for all of us. I'm blessed to be able to pick up and go anywhere I want. Most people can't and the idea that they're worried about putting food on the table is worrisome." I'd told her about my conversation with Herman at the candy shop.

"You're going to do something about it," she responded softly. "I don't know how or what, but I know it as sure as I'm sitting here that you won't sit back and let that happen."

I didn't know what to say to that, so I didn't, merely leaning over to press my lips to hers. I fell more in love with her every day.

TWO DAYS LATER, WE LEFT LIMAJ AND HEADED TO GREECE. I'D FOUND A private villa on the island of Crete where we could bask in the sun—and each other—with minimum intrusion from the press. For whatever reason, they rarely bothered me in Greece, and Casey said she loved it there, so I was looking forward to playing house for a while.

We had a gorgeous four-bedroom villa that overlooked the ocean. It was a short walk to get to the beach, but we had a pool and a hot tub that was giving me ton of fun sexual ideas. I just had to make sure Sandor went to bed early on those nights. Although it wouldn't be the first time he'd watched me have sex—hell, we'd both had sex in front of the other while we were at university—this was different. Neither of us had been in relationships then and our partners hadn't even batted an eyelash. My gut told me Casey wasn't into that kind of voyeurism and, frankly, neither was I. Not now that I'd found the woman I wanted to spend the rest of my life with.

We'd just come back from the beach when my cell phone rang, and I recognized my father's number. We hadn't spoken often since Casey and I had left Vegas and I figured he'd heard from my uncle or seen something about us in the tabloids. Either way, we didn't usually go too long without talking and I answered as Casey got into the shower.

"Hi, Dad."

"How are you, son?"

"I'm great." I sank into a chair on the patio, staring out at the beautiful view. "We're great."

"Things are good with you and Casey?"

"They are."

"That's wonderful. Your mother and I, and Casey's parents, have all been holding our collective breaths, hoping you two give us grandchildren."

"Give us a little time, would you?" I laughed. "I'm working on that."

"I'll bet you are."

We chuckled together.

"So, you took her to Limaj."

"I did."

"Your aunt and uncle liked her a great deal."

"Too bad Anwar is such a douche that it soured the experience for her."

Dad sighed. "I know, son. I wish there was a way to make Isak see it, but he doesn't."

I told him what Herman had heard as well as about the conversation my uncle and I had after dinner that night. "He said I gave him a lot to think about."

"Look, it's not like he doesn't know who and what Anwar is, but he keeps hoping he'll change, grow up, something. I put him in an untenable situation by abdicating. He wasn't raised to be the king, and Klara never planned to be a queen. They were unprepared for the responsibilities that came with it, and the kids fell to the wayside to a degree while they figured out what they were doing."

"Or, you know, Anwar is just a prick."

"That too."

"Uncle Isak asked me to be a member of Parliament, and I said no. Am I an idiot?"

"Do you want to be a member of Parliament?"

I hesitated. This was a loaded question. "For the most part, no. I don't ever want to work with or under Anwar. I don't particularly want to live in Limaj full-time, and I know for a fact Casey doesn't."

"So, what's the problem?"

"It was an honor for a twenty-four-year-old to be asked by the king." I paused. "Wasn't it?"

"It was, but you have your whole life to work in politics. Right now, you should be exploring the world—and the woman you love. You have plenty of time to take on those kinds of responsibilities. I'm relieved you said no, regardless of your reasons. You think I gave up the throne lightly?"

"No, I know you didn't."

"I don't want it for you either. The pressure is enormous, and with how unsettled our government is right now, you're better off far away."

"Well, it's not a thing since I told Uncle Isak no. Anyway, Casey and I are going to spend a few weeks here in Greece and then I suppose we'll make our way back to Vegas."

"How long are you going to wait before you propose?" My dad knew me too well sometimes.

"I don't know, but probably not long."

"Your mother sends her love, and we'll talk again soon."

"Love to everyone." I disconnected as Casey came out of the bathroom.

"Who do we love?" she asked.

"My parents."

"I have to call mine too," she said. "It's been a couple of weeks. I usually talk to my dad every other day."

"Not your mom?"

She smiled. "I talk to my mom too, but Dad and I talk music, so we talk a lot more often because I go to him for song ideas, when I'm shopping for a new instrument, when I have an equipment issue during a show... He's my go-to for everything to do with music, which was ninety-nine percent of my life before you came along. My mom and I hang out a lot when I'm home, but not as much on the phone."

"What are you going to tell them about us?" I teased, pulling her onto my lap.

"The truth? That I'm crazy in love with you and we're fucking like bunnies?"

I belted out a laugh, shaking my head. "A little too much information, no?"

"Oh, well, for a guy maybe, but my mom will flat out ask and then she and your mom will speculate, so it's easier to just give her the scoop and be done."

"If you say so." I leaned in to kiss her just as Sandor knocked on the open door.

"Erik." He held out some papers. "These arrived by courier."

"What are they?"

"Newspapers and magazines."

"And?"

"With all kinds of pictures."

20

Casey

My heart dropped to my stomach. I could only imagine what the paparazzi had on me, and they would print anything and everything now that I was dating royalty. Erik had an idea who I was and what my rock and roll lifestyle was like, but he hadn't seen much of it firsthand, and I'd had my share of wild times. I wasn't big on sex tapes or anything like that, and Nick would never betray me, but we hadn't always been alone.

"I'm going to go get dressed," I said, easing off his lap. "I'm sure whatever that is can wait until I'm wearing more than a bathrobe."

I padded into the bathroom and pulled on shorts and a T-shirt. I brushed the tangles out of my hair and blew it dry, then dabbed some mascara on my lashes. If we decided to go out, I'd add more makeup, but for now, my stomach was in knots and I didn't know what I was going to find when I rejoined Erik and Sandor.

Erik was on the phone, speaking a mile a minute in his native tongue, his free hand waving for emphasis as he shouted at someone.

"How bad?" I asked Sandor, wincing.

He grimaced, pushing one of the tabloids over to me.

Oh, hell no.

How the fuck had they gotten pictures of Erik and me making love on his private patio by the pool? Our private parts were covered with black boxes, but there was no doubt what we were doing or that it was outdoors. The photos were grainy, but there was one shot of my face that was unmistakable.

Fucking hell. This was a disaster.

Reading the accompanying article, it only got worse, talking about my partying as a rock star, my affair with hotel heir Nick Kingsley, and even my purported drug use, which wasn't true at all. I did my share of drinking, smoked the occasional cigarette, but other than a joint once in a while to help me sleep, I didn't do drugs. The other stuff, though, could be a problem. I'd been drinking long before I turned twenty-one, and Nick and I had never been shy about our sexcapades on tour. The picture of my half-naked ass hanging over a balcony while we made out at a Barcelona hotel was embarrassing to me so I couldn't even imagine what Erik thought of it.

"What is he saying?" I asked Sandor after a few minutes of listening to Erik talk in another language.

"He wants the entire palace searched and all staff questioned." Sandor paused. "He believes it was Anwar but can't say that. Ibrahim is handling the leak."

"Someone placed some kind of video camera or something in his suite," I said sadly. "That's the only way they got pictures like this."

Sandor nodded. "And either sold it to the highest bidder or gave it away to embarrass the family in general and Erik in particular."

"And me." I put my elbows on the table and rested my chin in my hands.

"He's not angry with you," Sandor said softly.

"Thanks." I watched Erik rant for a few more minutes and then went into the bedroom, shutting the door behind me as I fought off tears. I didn't know what was wrong with me, because this wasn't my first rodeo with bad press, but this was different because of Erik. I never wanted to embarrass him or have him be ashamed of me. I wasn't ashamed of anything I'd ever done, but to have it publicized like this was humiliating.

I swiped at my eyes, frustrated with myself for being so weak, and then the door opened, and Erik came in.

"Oh, baby, don't cry." He pulled me into his chest, and I melted into him, tears pouring out of me.

"I'm sorry," I sobbed. "I'm so sorry."

"Sorry? You haven't done anything wrong." He lifted my chin and swiped at my tears, but they were coming too fast.

"Casey, listen to me—none of that matters. I'm sorry they caught us like that, doing something so private, but fuck them. Really, fuck every single person behind this. They're just jealous because I have you and they don't."

"What about th-those pictures of m-me and N-nick." I couldn't even look at him.

"That was before we were together. It has nothing to do with us now."

He grabbed a tissue and gently dabbed my eyes.

"I'm not good enough for you," I whispered as a fresh bout of tears overwhelmed me.

"Oh, god, please don't ever say that." He yanked me closer, lips grazing my forehead as he held me. "I love you, Casey. This is all just background noise. Come on, you've had worse press before."

"This is about you, not me. I don't want to make you look bad."

"You know I don't give a fuck, right?" He stroked my hair until I stopped crying and got myself together.

"Wow, that hit me hard." I looked in the mirror and cringed at the mascara running down my face. "I need to clean up and—"

"You don't need to do anything but let me hold you." He kept me tightly in his arms. "I'm sorry this upset you so much, but I'm going to find out who leaked those photos of us by the pool and make sure they're punished."

"And if it was Anwar?"

"Then I'm done with him and the whole family. They can fuck right off. This isn't acceptable behavior, especially if he's going to be king. And if my uncle doesn't see that, there's nothing else I can say."

"It's still your family though," I said sadly.

"I have my parents, my sister, Vardan, Sandor, Daniil, and Elen, and now you. That's more than enough, more than a lot of people have."

"I guess that's true."

"Now, wash your face, and let's go get something to eat."

"You want to go out?" I met his eyes warily.

"I'm not hiding, and neither should you. If you really don't want to, we can stay in, but I'm not going to act like we've done anything wrong. There's a great place not far from here, and I'm dying for some fresh fish."

I didn't want to, but he was right, so I would suck it up.

"Give me a few minutes," I said.

"Hey." He called out to me as I turned back to the sink, so I gazed at him in the mirror.

"Yes?"

"You're fucking gorgeous, and I love you."

I smiled. "I fucking love you too."

. . .

THE NEXT FEW DAYS WERE QUIET. WE WENT OUT, BUT NO ONE IN GREECE seemed to care who we were or what the tabloids printed about us. We laughed with children we met on the beach, talked about fishing with the owner of the restaurant Erik loved, and strolled up and down streets lined with shops whose owners waved and smiled. Swimming in the sea every day made us lazy and deeply tanned, the outside world somehow very far away. Even Sandor was more relaxed, often joining us for a swim or a night out to listen to music. Either no one recognized us, or we simply weren't important to the inhabitants of this little town, but we enjoyed an anonymity that was refreshing enough to make us want to stay longer.

"The house is available for two more weeks," Erik said the morning after I'd mentioned how much I wanted to stay.

"Let's do that," I responded automatically. "But if we do, I want to go to town and see if I can buy that acoustic guitar I saw the other day. If we're going to be in one place for another two weeks, I need to be able to play."

"Works for me."

He got out of bed and strolled across the room to grab his shorts, so I took a moment to enjoy his glorious backside. He'd turned golden brown after a week in the sun, his Mediterranean heritage coming through with a vengeance. I was pretty tan too, though my skin burned before it turned brown and I was careful about sunscreen after growing up in Las Vegas.

"Are you staring at my ass?" he asked as he got dressed.

"Maybe." I swung my legs over the side of the bed and stood up, giving him a good view of my own naked body.

"I'm okay with that." He tossed my bathing suit at me. "Want to rent Jet Skis today?"

"Sure." I padded to the bathroom and was washing my face when I heard my phone ringing. "Who is it?" I yelled to Erik.

"Your dad."

"Would you answer and tell him I'll call him back in a few?"

"Sure."

I heard him talking in the background, then laughing and talking some more. I washed my face, brushed my teeth and put my hair in a ponytail, and they were still talking. I walked back into the bedroom and Erik looked up with a grin.

"I kept your dad on the line until you got done."

"Thanks." I leaned over, kissed him and took the phone. "Hi, Daddy."

"Hey, baby girl. Call your old man much?"

"Sorry, we've been hiding out here on Crete and it's been so nice."

"I'm glad to see the fuss about those pictures died down."

"Me too."

"Ben says it was someone new at the palace and they've been fired."

I snorted. "Yeah, right. It was Anwar, but he'll never admit it and some poor maid took the fall for him."

"We figured, but what can you do?"

"Nothing. That's why we're hanging out here in Crete. It's so peaceful. I'm going to go buy an acoustic guitar because I have so many songs in my head I can't stand it."

"When do you think you'll be back in Vegas?"

"I'm not sure. Why?"

"There's a lot going on here too. There's a singer out in New York I've had my eye on and I really wanted you to go check out his band for me... I just haven't had the energy to travel lately."

"No?" I was instantly alarmed. "Why not? You okay?"

"Yeah, just getting older, that's all."

"You're fifty-five, Daddy, not a hundred."

"Fifty-five is old when you've lived as hard as I have."

"Go to the doctor."

"I'm fine, honey, just been overdoing it lately. Don't worry."

"Let me talk to Mom."

"She's out shopping. Well, I gotta go. Love you, kiddo!" He disconnected and I blew out a frustrated breath.

"Everything okay?" Erik asked.

"My dad said he's too tired to go see this band in New York and that's not like him. Normally, he's the first one to hop on a plane. He loves to travel, especially if it involves new music, new bands, anything like that. Since the band retired, he's always looking for new projects."

"Perhaps he's got a cold or something."

"I'll call my mom at some point and see what she thinks," I said. "Anyway, is there anything to eat? I'm starving."

MY GUITAR WAS FANTASTIC. IT WAS A SIMPLE ACOUSTIC MADE BY AN UNKNOWN manufacturer and perfect for our island retreat. I'd sit on the patio at night while the sun was setting and serenade Erik, Sandor, and Aziz. I'd play classic rock favorites, my own songs, and even a few Greek staples like "Never on Sunday," which everyone knew the words to and made us all smile as we sang. We relaxed, swam in the sea, ate wonderful food, and it became our private island in a way. No one bothered us, not even when we went out, and though Aziz and Sandor stayed vigilant, we fell into a wonderful routine. Especially Erik and me. Living together came to us as easily as breathing, and for the first time as an adult, I was deeply in love.

I'd loved Nick as a teenager, but the sexual relationship we had while touring was more convenient than romantic. My first sexual partner was one of Nick's cousins, Ace Ross, and I'd given him my virginity a week or so before he'd left for the Marines. It was that broken heart that led me to Nick, and with the exception of a one-night stand in Paris once, that had been the extent of my love and dating life. Erik was different though. There was no doubt this was serious, deeply emotional, and permanent. I knew deep down there would never be anyone else for me and as wonderful as it was, it scared the hell out of me. How did you love someone this much without repercussions? What if he didn't love me the same way? What if this was a love affair for him, but not the forever kind? And how did you bring that kind of thing up? I tried not to think about it, or at least not overthink it, but it was hard.

Curling into his arms as we went to bed on our last night in Crete, a feeling of dread came over me that I couldn't explain. I told myself it was stupid, but it didn't go away, and I lay awake a long time that night.

21

Casey

Erik and Aziz went deep-sea fishing the following day, leaving me home with Sandor. I was happy to be home because I'd picked up the guitar in the morning and now I had a chance to write a few songs as Sandor puttered around the house.

I settled at a table with an umbrella next to the pool, guitar in my lap and a notebook and pen on the table beside me. I'd had some lyrics in my head for weeks, and I got them down, doodling with words and emotions and melodies.

Take it hard
Take it fast
Just tonight
Not gonna last
I'm all for love
But not with you
Show me your body
You feel it too

I NEEDED AN ELECTRIC GUITAR FOR SOMETHING THIS HARD AND EDGY, BUT I was in the groove, writing and singing under my breath, completely unaware Sandor was watching. When I finally looked up he had a smile on his face.

"I've never seen a musician actually writing a song in real-time," he said. "I apologize if that's intrusive."

I shook my head. "Nah. When I'm in the zone, nothing else exists. What do you think?" I played what I had so far.

He nodded his head to the beat. "I like it. I can almost hear the drum part, add some pounding bass..."

"I really didn't picture you as a rocker." I laughed.

"Me either." He grinned back.

I was about to play something else when my phone rang. Liz. We hadn't talked since Monte Carlo and she didn't call often, so I answered curiously. "Hey."

"How are you?"

"I'm good. How about you?"

"I'm great. I just thought I'd check in." She paused. "I saw the tabloids."

"Oh, well, you know, par for the course when you're a rocker dating a prince."

She chuckled. "I suppose there's that."

"What about you? Are you dating anyone?"

"No. Not in a while."

"How come?"

"Well..." She sighed. "After Ricky died, I threw myself into work. There really hasn't been anyone interesting enough to make me want to put my heart on the line again."

I knew her boyfriend from college had been killed in action in Iraq, but that had been several years ago now and I figured she must have moved on. "I'm sorry," I said gently. "You never talk about him and I felt weird asking."

"I try not to dwell, you know? He's gone. I'm here. But other than the occasional one-nighter, I just can't picture myself with anyone else. It's pathetic, but it's true."

"I'm so sorry."

"It's okay. So things going good with his royal hotness?"

I laughed. "Very good. I'm crazy about him. Head over heels. It's kind of ridiculous, but he makes me so happy."

"That's all that matters."

"You could find someone too, you know. You just can't look, you have to let it happen."

"I have two full-time jobs—there isn't a lot of opportunity for that."

"Two..." I let my voice trail off because I already knew one of her jobs was the kind of thing we couldn't talk about. "Well, you have to play sometimes, don't you?"

"You'd think so but there isn't much time for that. Luckily, I love my work—all of it—and I get to do some amazing things. If romance is in my future, it'll work itself. In the meantime, I'll live vicariously through you."

"Oh, well, I can tell you all kinds of good stuff."

"Ooohhh... is he good in bed?"

"Oh hell yeah." With Sandor nearby, I got up and walked into the house and our bedroom, shutting the door behind me as we talked.

AFTER MY PHONE CONVERSATION WITH LIZ, I MADE MYSELF LUNCH AND THEN went back to my song. By the time Erik got home around six thirty, "One Hard Night" had taken life and I played it for him.

"You just wrote that while I was gone?" he asked, shaking his head.

"Yeah. Why?"

"You just do that... like, write a song in an afternoon?"

"Sometimes. I mean, I get writer's block, so to speak, and it doesn't always go this smoothly, but I also haven't been writing for months between being on the road and then traveling with you, so I was ready. I can write a song a day if I'm in the groove. They're not all great, but I can do it."

He leaned over to kiss me. "You're amazing."

"It's a great song, right?" Sandor said. "It's in my head now and I can't get it out."

I laughed. "I'll play 'Never on Sunday' again and then you'll be humming that."

We laughed together and Sandor eventually wandered back into the house.

"It's been nice here," Erik said, pulling me onto his lap. "I'm really not looking forward to going home."

"Me either, but it seems like it's time."

"Yeah."

"You okay?" I asked, looking into his eyes.

"I'm wonderful. Just lazy and relaxed and wishing we could stay here forever."

"I guess we can, but I'm thinking we'll eventually get bored."

"Maybe." He got to his feet with me still in his arms. "But not likely."

I smiled as he carried me into the bedroom and kicked the door shut with his foot. I was ready to go home, but I would miss this too. Something told me our lives were about to change drastically.

22

E*rik*

The flight to Las Vegas was long and boring, and though the family plane had a private bedroom in the back, Casey fell asleep, so I was left to my own devices. Something was bothering her, but she wouldn't tell me, and I hadn't found a way to pry it out of her yet. Eventually she would break down, she always did, but she was the kind of woman who needed to work through things in her own time and her own way. I respected that, because I was the same way, but my gut told me this was about us, so I wanted her to open up. We'd gotten extremely close over the last month, and it was wonderful, but she still kept many of her emotions bottled up.

I felt her pull away sometimes, but never when it mattered. Not when we talked about ourselves or our feelings or plans for the future, not when I asked poignant questions, and certainly not in bed. Whenever I thought she might start getting on my nerves or do some trivial thing, she completely surprised me with her thoughtfulness, insight, and overall appreciation for my life, even when she didn't completely understand it. I'd never thought I'd find that in any woman, much less the one I'd been in love with most of my life. So times like now, when she did hold back, I wasn't entirely sure how to handle it. Or her.

"It's going to be hotter than balls in Vegas," Sandor said.

"You'll be fine. Believe it or not, they have AC in the U.S."

He chuckled. "Smartass."

"I haven't worked out our living arrangement yet," I told him. "So don't freak out. My hope is that we'll live at my parents' house, but you know how she is. She might be determined to live in her condo, and I don't know how we'll handle security if that's the case."

Sandor rolled his eyes. "You're the man—can't you tell her what needs to happen for safety purposes and leave it at that?"

I snorted. "Do you know Casey at all? Me pulling the me-Tarzan-you-Jane routine won't go over well. Besides, what kind of Neanderthal are you? That's not how relationships work."

"Since I haven't been in one since university, I don't think I remember how they work."

"Being my bodyguard doesn't preclude you from dating."

He shrugged. "You're always on the move. When would I have time? I make time for sex, and for now that will have to be enough."

"Sex isn't a bad thing."

Sandor grinned. "Not at all."

Casey came out of the bedroom looking refreshed and she sank into the chair next to mine.

"Hey. Sorry I fell asleep, but I didn't sleep last night."

"I know. I felt you tossing and turning. Do you want to tell me what's wrong?"

Sandor got up and moved to the other side of the plane, pulling out his headphones.

Casey sighed. "You know what they say about things that are too good to be true?"

I met her eyes in surprise. "You mean us?"

She nodded.

"Why?" I asked, frowning slightly. "I thought things have been going rather well."

"Too well." She sighed and then took a breath. "Erik, you are the most wonderful man in the world. I had a crush on you for years because you were hot and a prince and kind of mysterious, but I had no way of knowing the man you really are. Now that I do, it's mind-blowing. You're kind and giving and passionate. You like me just the way I am and seem willing to do or change anything to make me happy and to be with me."

"But?" I eyed her warily.

"Look what's already happened... I caused trouble with your cousin and the king. The press has had a field day with my history of partying, and they've already gotten pictures of us having sex. All I can see in your future is trouble. Because of me."

"You haven't been listening," I said softly, looking down at her. "I don't care about any of that shit—I really don't. The only thing the king can take from me is my title, and compared to you, that's literally nothing. You know that, don't you?"

"You have all the answers and that scares me too."

"I love you. Period. The last month has been wonderful, and there's no reason for anything to change. We'll get married, have babies and do the family thing for a while. Once the novelty has worn off and you're ready to play music again, we'll hire a nanny and take the kids on the road."

She blinked. "You'd go on tour with me?"

"Well, I assumed you'd want me to, but if that would cramp your style, I wouldn't—"

"No!" She smacked me lightly. "I meant, what would you do on tour? You'd be bored, and then—"

"Stop telling me what I'd feel and think and do. I've spent my whole bloody life being told I had to do this or that. For what, I'm still not sure. I had to have a proper education. Learn proper manners. Date certain women. Be a certain way. And for what? I'm never going to be king, and short of that, there's no reason for everything I've done other than education. For once, I'm going to do what I want, which is to marry a rock star and follow her around the world. If I get bored, I can make a few personal adjustments, but for now, that's all I want."

"The press is going to have a field day with this."

"I don't give a damn about the press," I said. "We can invite them to the wedding. I love you, we're going to be together, and I don't care who knows it."

"I'm still nervous."

"About what? Tell me each thing."

"I..." Her voice faded. "I don't know. It's just a gut feeling."

"You're scared, and honestly, so am I. There's a lot to who we are. You're rock and roll royalty, and I'm actual royalty. Our paths are going to be convoluted and disparate, but there's no one I'd rather take that journey with. Do you love me, Casey?"

"With everything I am."

"Then what else is there? You're everything to me. I've been in love with you for years. Yes, perhaps initially it was a bit of a crush, the pretty blond musician with a smokin' hot body... But I saw glimpses of the woman you were becoming, and I was both fascinated and impressed. These last few weeks have proven you're everything I thought you were and more. I love you, Casey, and I'm willing to do whatever it takes to make this work as long as you feel the same."

"I do," she whispered.

"Then let's move in together and start planning our future."

Her eyes were wet with tears as she nodded. "Okay. Yes. Let's do that."

"We have to talk about living arrangements, though."

She smiled. "I know. It's safer if we live with your parents, right? So that's what we should do."

Reason number 423,423,534 that I loved this woman.

MY PARENTS WERE SO EXCITED TO SEE US IT WAS A LITTLE EMBARRASSING. They'd prepared a suite for us in the back of their estate, where we would have privacy but was still attached so we would also have access to the rest of the house, the pool, and the kitchen. The seventeen-thousand-square-foot home was built on five acres, giving them lots of room and lots of privacy. It had ten bedrooms, three of which were suites with living areas and private bathrooms and entrances, sixteen bathrooms, a guest house for live-in help, and a five-car garage, though rumor had it my father had wanted room for ten cars and my mother had put her foot down.

The only cloud on our otherwise happy return home was my surly sister. Skye had been in a foul mood since leaving Limaj, my mother told us, and seemed to be taking it out on everyone. I planned to keep Casey far away from her for now but interaction between them was inevitable and it worried me because they'd never liked each other growing up. I had no idea why, and Casey merely said it was because my sister had always looked down her nose at her, but there had to be more to it. They were going to be sisters soon, so I planned to work on that relationship, but there was time. My only goal right now was to make Casey happy and relax a little more with everything happening between us.

My parents planned a nice dinner for all of us, including Casey's parents, the day after we arrived and there was a lot of love and laughter at the table as we ate. Skye had opted not to join us, which was fine with me, and conversation was lively as our parents grilled us within an inch of our lives.

"Can't we just start planning a wedding?" My mother pouted, playfully sticking out her lower lip.

"You will not deprive me of the romantic proposal I'm waiting for," Casey admonished her, laughing.

"What are you waiting for then?" Teal demanded of me.

"It's been, like, four minutes," I told them, laughing. "Give us a break."

"It's been a lifetime in the making," my mother said firmly. "We've known you two were meant for each other since the day you were born."

Casey shook her head. "How come no one ever told me?"

"It was written in the stars," Uncle Lucas teased. "So it was inevitable. We didn't think we had to."

Casey glanced at me. "Who are these people and what have they done with our parents?"

"We want grandchildren!" Mom and Aunt Teal spoke together and then burst out laughing.

Casey, however, didn't look amused and took a bite of her dinner instead.

That was interesting. Something else she was keeping from me. Did she not want kids? We'd talked about the subject loosely, without any details, and she'd never said anything about not wanting them. The look on her face just now told me something else, though.

We didn't have any time to talk because our parents kept the conversation moving in fifty different directions, but I kept it in the back of my mind for when we were finally alone. Casey locked herself in the bathroom when we finally got back to our room, so I got undressed and crawled into bed. I always slept naked, and Casey had started to as well, but she still spent an inordinate amount of time in the bathroom before bed. I had no idea what she did since she was already the most beautiful woman I knew, but I figured it was a woman thing.

She was taking a much longer time than usual tonight and I was just about to go check on her when she came out. She was wearing a large T-shirt, something she hadn't done since our first night in Limaj, and there was a strange look on her face.

"What's wrong?" I asked automatically, sitting up in alarm.

She looked at me, her eyes wide as she said, "I'm late."

23

Casey

I HAD NO IDEA HOW ERIK WOULD REACT TO MY NEWS, BUT HE DIDN'T BAT AN eyelash, merely reaching for me and pulling me against him on the bed.

"How late?" he asked.

"About two weeks, give or take. I don't usually pay a lot of attention because I'm really regular."

"We should buy a test."

"Yes." She shivered slightly.

"What's wrong? Are you upset?"

"Well, yeah. Aren't you?"

"Is this a trick question?" he asked slowly. "I mean, should I be? I love you. Yeah, it would've been nice to wait a little, but what's the difference? And professionally, the timing is perfect because you're between projects. It would be much worse if you were in the middle of a tour or getting ready to start one."

"That's true." I closed my eyes. "Everything is happening so fast, Erik. I'm just getting used to being in a relationship this serious, and now... What if I'm pregnant? I mean, what do we do?"

"Get married? Buy a house. Have a family. Live happily ever after?"

"Why is everything so easy for you?"

"With the exception of the physical aspect, which I can't help with unfortunately, it's easy because we love each other, we're both extremely wealthy so we can afford help, and everyone we know is going to be so damn excited. This will be a beautiful thing if you're pregnant. And if you're not, I think we should start trying as soon as we're married because you *are* in between projects."

"Are we getting married?"

"I hope so. I was planning a big romantic proposal, just as you've hinted you want, but if you're pregnant, I think we should do it immediately to avoid negativity from the press."

"Okay, one thing at a time." I shifted against him. "Tomorrow, we take a test or five. Then we'll talk about the rest."

"Deal." He kissed the top of my head. "Don't worry, baby. Remember, I'll never let you fall."

"I'm starting to believe it."

Positive.

I was kind of pissed and a little excited and incredibly scared. A baby was nowhere on my radar and this was the epitome of unplanned pregnancies. How stupid had we been? I wouldn't say that out loud, of course, because Erik was going to be stupidly happy, but I honestly hadn't thought I would get pregnant from one moment of drunken weakness. I knew it was possible, of course, but Nick and I had a condom malfunction once and I'd been fine. This was unexpected and a lot scarier for me than Erik. He'd acknowledged the physical part would be harder on me than him, of course, but that was only half the problem. Could I be a rock star with a baby? How would that work? Jade had a daughter, but it felt different somehow. Maybe because Erik was a prince. I didn't know what was going on in my head and it was confusing.

I flushed the toilet, washed my hands, and took my time coming out of the bathroom. I'd wanted to find out alone because I'd been afraid Erik would see the disappointment on my face and I didn't want him to know how scared I was. I wasn't sure why, because I trusted him implicitly, but it was something I needed to come to terms with on my own. He would be there for me, I had no doubt about that, but wrapping my head around it was another thing altogether.

He was sipping coffee on the patio when I came out and he simply held out his arms. Damn him, he knew me too well.

I climbed onto his lap and rested my head on his shoulder. "We're pregnant," I whispered.

"Are you okay?"

"No. I'm fucking terrified."

"I know. It's going to be okay though. You know I'm here and not going anywhere."

"I know."

"Our parents are going to be thrilled."

"We can't tell anyone until we're married."

"Then let's start planning a wedding."

"Okay." I was still a little shell-shocked, so it was hard to muster up enthusiasm for much of anything.

"Hey." He lifted my chin. "Tell me what I can do to make this better for you?"

"I don't know." Uh-oh, tears were threatening again, and I buried my face in his neck as they leaked out and trailed down my cheeks.

"It's okay." He held me, whispering sweet things in my ear as I got all the tears and frustration and insecurity out of my system.

After a few minutes, I sat up and wiped my face, exhausted.

"I'm going to make an appointment with my ob-gyn," I said, slowly getting to my feet. "Let's not tell anyone until I've seen her, okay?"

"Okay."

"You'll come with me?"

"Of course. I told you—I'm not going anywhere."

"Would you mind terribly if I went to my mom's today? I haven't seen much of her, and I really need to talk to her about all this."

"We're not Siamese twins," he said softly. "You're allowed to go places without me."

"I haven't really been without you in...more than a month?" I was surprised when I realized just how much time we'd spent together. "Being together is really easy."

"It is." He squeezed my hand. "Do what you need to do. I'm going to spend some time with my dad catching up on everything I've missed since we went into hiding in Crete."

THE MINUTE I SAW MY MOM, I BURST INTO TEARS ALL OVER AGAIN. AS IF SHE knew what was going on, she hugged me tightly until I could breathe again, gently stroking my hair without asking questions or saying much of anything at all. It felt good to be here in the house I'd grown up in, and though my emotions were all over the place lately, hugging my mom gave me a sense of calm again.

"Are you hungry?" she asked when I finally pulled away.

"I could eat," I admitted, sinking into a chair at the kitchen table. "Where's Dad?"

"At the studio overseeing construction."

"Okay."

"Did you and Erik have a fight?" she asked, pulling eggs out of the refrigerator. Since scrambled eggs with cheese was one of my favorite meals, she made it without even asking.

"I'm pregnant," I said.

She glanced over at me with a soft smile. "That makes me happy, but I'm guessing you not so much?"

"It's so soon! We just got together after all these years of wanting each other from a distance and now we're going to rush through everything. Engagement, wedding, buying a house, starting a family. Zero to sixty in about six weeks."

"Well, sometimes that's what happens. You love him, don't you?"

"I do. I really, really do."

"Then take a deep breath and think about all the wonderful things to come. You're going to marry this incredible man who adores you, have a beautiful baby, and then in a year or two, you'll go back to music. Deep down, that's your biggest fear, right? That you won't ever go back to music?"

I sighed. This was why I needed my mom. "Yeah."

"Erik isn't going to try to change you," she said. "That's not who he is."

"I know. I guess I'm worried about everything. My career, gaining weight, losing myself... You know what I mean?"

"I do. But with Erik at your side, you can do anything. Trust me, when you meet the right man, you become a team that can't be stopped. Just like your dad and me. Like Ben and Kari."

"You weren't pregnant when you got married."

"No, but Kari was."

"She was?"

Why hadn't I known that?

"They don't talk about it because they're still a tiny bit old-school, but yes, she was. I wasn't, because your dad and I didn't want kids. You were an accident. A happy one that became one of the best things that ever happened to us, but an accident nonetheless."

"You didn't want kids?"

I hadn't known that either.

"No. We were selfish, and you know neither of us had very good home lives growing up, so we thought we might not be equipped to be good parents."

"You were wrong about that."

She smiled as she set a plate in front of me. "I think we did okay. You're a pretty great kid."

I smiled back, and we were quiet as I ate. Being home was always my safe place, my happy place. I loved touring the world, but this was where I decompressed and regenerated. Even my condo, though I loved it, didn't relax me the way my parents' house did. I still had a room here and spent the night every so often because it was fun to come home. I wasn't sure if that was a testament to my relationship with my parents or merely that I wasn't ready to adult, but either way I was happy to be home.

"So, what's next?" My mom was asking as she put my plate and utensils in the dishwasher.

"I'm guessing you and Aunt Kari are going to plan a stupidly expensive and over-the-top wedding."

"I'm thinking mid-October," Mom said. "That gives us six weeks. We'll probably have it at the Charleston..."

I zoned out as she talked about wedding plans. If it were up to me, we would just elope, but I knew that wouldn't fly for Erik or his family. Or mine, for that matter. This was going to be the wedding of the year if our families had anything to say about it, and I was just along for the ride. Right now, all I could think about was seeing my ob-gyn in a few days. Until then, I felt like I was in a holding pattern, and it sucked.

24

E*rik*

HEARING OUR BABY'S HEARTBEAT A COUPLE OF DAYS LATER WAS THE MOST magical thing I'd ever experienced. Casey seemed enthralled as well, which was a huge relief since she'd been spectacularly depressed the last few days. I hadn't pushed her to talk or anything, but I'd been worried. Seeing her smile when we heard that fluttering beep coming out of the machine gave me hope that everything would be okay. I couldn't help if she didn't tell me what was wrong, but I understood her well enough to know she needed to work through this just like everything else in her life. I was getting used to this about her, but she'd been honest about needing a little space, so we were compromising.

"The twenty-second of May," she said as we walked out to the parking lot hand in hand. We'd come alone, in her Corvette, which she'd graciously let me drive. She'd said no one could possibly know where we were going or when, so the danger of being ambushed was minimal, and she'd insisted this had to be private. So, although my father and Sandor both nearly had heart attacks, my mother had sided with Casey and we'd made the trip without Sandor.

It was odd, because I rarely drove and had forgotten how much I enjoyed it. Casey, however, took the keys from me and moved to the driver's side.

"Hey," I protested. "What's the deal?"

"You've been driving on the wrong side of the road too long," she replied with a grin. "I nearly had a coronary on the way here."

"It was just the first few minutes," I mumbled, getting in on the passenger side.

"I'm kidding." She started the engine. "But I need to drive right now. Would you mind if we went for a ride?"

"Not at all. Where are we going?"

"I don't know, but I'm going to get on the highway and open her up."

"Really?" I didn't dare object, but I was a little nervous about it since I'd never seen her drive.

I shouldn't have worried. Like most things with Casey, she surprised me, handling the vehicle like she was born to drive it. She didn't talk, merely found her way to the interstate and headed south.

"Are we having lunch in the Mojave Desert?" I asked as she accelerated.

"We might be in L.A. before I'm hungry." She zipped around a few slower cars and didn't let up until we hit the California border. Though it made me a little nervous to be so far from Vegas without anyone knowing where we were, I figured she had a reason, and I was willing to go along with it on an emotional day like today.

"Now I'm hungry," she muttered, taking the exit ramp into a town called Baker. "I think there's a Denny's here. You game?"

I stared at her. I had no idea what Denny's was. "Um, sure."

"You've never been to Denny's, have you?" she asked, giving me a quick look.

"Don't even know what it is."

She started to laugh. "Okay, Your Greatness, time for a bit of an American education."

"Casey..." I didn't know how to voice my concerns without upsetting her. It wasn't about where we were eating, but merely the fact that no one knew where we were.

"Oh, come on, one cheap meal isn't going to kill you."

"No. It's just... No one knows where we are. If we were recognized and people got agitated..." What else was there to say?

"You think it's dangerous to stop and eat here?" She looked at me, frustration etched into her pretty features.

She pulled into the parking lot of a building with a sign that clearly said "Denny's." It looked harmless enough, so I felt a little better, but Casey was hesitant now, parking the car but not turning it off.

"You don't think it's safe?"

"I don't know," I admitted. "I don't ever go anywhere without at least Sandor. I never have, my entire life. I know it's probably strange to you, but today was literally the first time I went anywhere without some type of security, with the exception of a few classes when we were at university. It's been drilled into my head for as long as I can remember that I'm a target. Even if someone isn't gunning for me, my presence could lead to a crime of opportunity, like kidnapping because my family is wealthy."

"Fine." She put the car in reverse. "I'm sure there's a drive-thru we can hit. I have to eat."

She seemed annoyed, and I didn't blame her, but safety had to come first. Not only was my life possibly in danger, so was hers because she was with me. And she was pregnant, dammit. I hated to use that as my trump card, but I was going to worry about her, whether it upset her or not.

I grimaced when she pulled into the drive-thru lane at a McDonald's and ordered. She looked at me. "Do you want anything?"

"Sure." I told her my order and we drove to the next window. I tried to hand her some money, but she waved me off and gave the woman a twenty-dollar-bill.

We didn't talk again until we were back on the highway.

"If you're mad," I said quietly, "will you at least talk to me about it?"

"I'm not mad," she responded. "I'm frustrated. Having someone with us twenty-four seven is hard for me. I'm super independent and that feels like someone keeping tabs on me. I get the need for protection, but today was emotional, private, just for us. The idea that we can't have an impromptu, private lunch date is hard to wrap my head around."

"I know." I reached for her hand. "I'm truly sorry about that. I grew up this way, so it's just how it is for me. In time, I hope you'll get used to it. Now that there's a baby, we have to think about his or her safety as well as our own."

"I know." She stared straight ahead, eyes on the road, her burger uneaten in her lap.

"You want to pull over so you can eat? It's a long way home."

"I'm good." She popped a few fries in her mouth.

"Is this our first fight?" I asked, grabbing a few of her fries.

She smacked my hand. "No, but if you keep stealing my fries, it will be."

I laughed. Hopefully, this meant she wasn't mad anymore and we'd moved on.

. . .

When we got back to the house, my father asked me to join him in his den, so Casey headed to our room while I went to see what my father wanted. He had what looked like a velvet jeweler's case on his desk and he motioned for me to close the door, which I did.

"What's that?" I asked.

"Jewels." He opened the top. "These were some that I took with me when I abdicated, and I've been saving them for you and your sister. If you'd like one to make into an engagement ring for Casey, your mother and I would be honored."

"Wow." I stared at the stones in fascination. I'd had no idea my father had them. One in particular caught my eye and I reached for it. "That one," I said. "That's the one."

"The pink dragon." My father smiled and pulled it out of the case. "A pink diamond, both rare and exquisite. It got its name because of the fiery bursts of color, like flames from a dragon's breath. It's flawless, twelve carats, radiant cut. It would make a stunning ring."

"I'm honored to have it. Thank you. She'll love it."

"Do you know whether she wants white or yellow gold?"

"Platinum."

"I can have it set for you. I have a jeweler here that I trust."

"Can it be done soon? I want to propose sooner rather than later."

"I'll take care of it."

"Thanks, Dad."

"You're very welcome."

I hadn't even officially proposed, but my mother was in full wedding-planner mode. When we came down for dinner, she had a stack of catalogs and brochures for us. She talked nonstop while we ate, and though I expected Casey to be annoyed, she merely smiled and nodded a lot, probably more overwhelmed than annoyed since she adored my mother. My sister, on the other hand, was cranky as hell, muttering under her breath and generally being a nuisance. We hadn't had much time together since she'd left Omar, but she hadn't made any attempt to talk to me since Casey and I had moved in.

"Have you thought at all about a dress?" my mother asked Casey. "Or bridesmaids?"

"Honestly, I haven't," Casey said, "but Erik and I are going to talk about all that in the next few days. We had to find out the details about the baby first."

"Perhaps we could go dress shopping one day," my mother suggested. "Skye, would you like to join us? It would be good for you to get out of the house and—"

"Mother, I have zero interest in weddings. Especially hers."

"You mean ours," I cut in dryly.

She gave me a dirty look but didn't say anything.

"Have it your way." Our mother shrugged, going back to the brochures in front of her. "I just thought it would be a nice way to spend the day together and possibly get your mind off your troubles."

Skye rolled her eyes. "Mother, it's not really any fun to plan a wedding when I'm in the middle of a fucking divorce!"

"All right, Skye. I'm sorry I brought it up."

"No, you're not. You're just trying to rub it in because you never wanted me to marry Omar. So, go ahead—say you told me so. Go on, I know you want to."

Mom took off her reading glasses and looked at her daughter quizzically. "Skye, I understand that you've been through a terrible time, but—"

"You don't understand anything! If you did, you wouldn't ask me to help plan the wedding of a woman who's beneath us and undoubtedly going to embarrass Erik at every turn. She's never been anything but a—"

"That's enough!" My father slammed his crystal water glass down on the table with such fervor that our plates bounced. "I know your husband hurt and embarrassed you, but that's not our fault, and it's certainly not Casey's. You've done nothing but brood for weeks, and frankly, I'm over it. If you're so unhappy, by all means, go back to Limaj, go back to Omar. I don't care either way at this point."

Everyone was stunned into silence.

"I just want my life back," Skye whispered. "I don't know anyone, I don't have any privacy unless I'm locked in my room, I don't even have Saraya. Why hasn't she joined me yet? I've been trying to call her, but I can't reach her, and I need her. It's so uncivilized here... Can't I even have my maid with me?"

"Skye, Saraya can't come to you. Not now, and not ever again." My father seemed tired and I cringed when I realized that my sister didn't yet know that her lifelong companion and personal maid had been killed.

"Why on earth not? It's not as if Omar needs her in the household. She was mine to begin with and—"

"Saraya is dead," I interrupted blandly, waiting while my words sunk in. I hated to be an asshole, but she certainly hadn't hesitated to insult the woman I loved, so maybe it was time to give her a taste of her own medicine.

Skye stared at me. "What are you talking about?! How can she be dead?"

"It was Saraya who called me," my father said sadly. "After we took you from the hospital, Omar beat her until she told them whom she had called, and then she was executed."

"No." Skye stared at him. "You can't be serious. She was just an old woman…"

"An old woman who loved you very much. She died very proud that she was able to save you."

"How do you know?"

"Daniil found her. She'd been left on the steps of the palace."

"Oh god."

"She'd been badly beaten, but used her last breath to tell Daniil what had happened."

Skye's eyes welled up with tears. "Why didn't anyone tell me?"

"We thought you'd suffered enough, between the beating and the impending divorce."

"Oh my god. I'm so sorry." Skye buried her face in her hands. "I knew it. I knew he was going to do something terrible. I just didn't know who to tell."

"Who, Omar?" My father looked worried.

"He's dangerous. And so is Anwar."

25

Casey

I DIDN'T KNOW HOW WE'D WOUND UP IN THE MIDDLE OF THIS CLUSTERFUCK, but I reached for Erik's hand under the table. He looked angry, staring at his sister with an expression that told me he was going to explode. I squeezed his hand, but he was oblivious as he picked up his wine glass.

"We told you," he said. "We fucking told you he was no good, but you were determined to marry him."

Skye looked surprised to hear her brother talking to her that way, but if he noticed, Erik didn't seem to care.

"Did you really think a man from Limaj that shared your culture, religion, and general beliefs, magically appeared at your university in Paris? You didn't think that was at all coincidental?"

Skye looked shell-shocked, staring at him without saying a word.

"We all saw it, we all suspected he was using you, but you wouldn't listen to anyone. Now look what's happened."

"Erik..." My mother began.

"No, you've coddled her too long. She needs to hear the truth. She's always used her title as a crutch to be a spoiled, entitled little brat and she's not going to sit here and disrespect my future wife, the mother of my child, because she chooses to be miserable. I'm sorry. There are consequences when we make choices—and yours was to marry Omar. You're my sister, and I love you. When I heard about what he did to you, I went straight to the king and asked him what he was going to do about it. I had your back, and I always will, but you need to get over this superiority complex you have and realize that we're all equals. Our titles don't mean a fucking thing in the real world. The sooner you recognize that, the happier we'll all be. Not to mention the potential danger you've put us in, depending on how much you told Omar about our family interests. If he's in league with Anwar, he can take everything from us, Skye. Do you understand that?"

"I didn't tell him anything."

"But how much did he overhear? You've probably complained about all of us, told him about our life and what savages we are, living the good life in Las Vegas."

"I never did that." Skye blinked back tears, biting her lip as she stared at him. "If that's what you think of me—"

"I don't think anything of you except that you don't see life the way it is, only how you want it to be. And that's not how it works. If that were the case, I'd be heir to the throne, not that weasel Anwar."

There was a shocked silence as Erik's words sunk in, and while I was as surprised as everyone else by his outburst, I couldn't help but smile. So strong and proud, my prince. Ready to take his cousin to task for not doing what was right. As much as I didn't want to be a queen, the depth of Erik's emotions when it came to his country was heartwarming and a testament to the man he was. It made me fall even more in love with him.

Aunt Kari took a long drink of wine and Skye looked dumbfounded. Uncle Ben, however, smiled at his son fondly.

"If I'd known the kind of man my future son would be, I never would have abdicated," he said quietly.

"But I wouldn't be the man I am if you hadn't," Erik said. "Because you wouldn't have married Mom."

"And here we are." Uncle Ben raised his shoulders in a slight shrug.

"I'm sorry," Skye spoke up in a sad voice. "I... My life imploded the last couple of months, and I feel very lost here in Las Vegas. I don't know anyone or go anywhere, and I'm mourning the loss of my marriage. I didn't mean to hurt your feelings, Erik, or yours, Casey."

"It's okay." I gave her a faint smile. What else could I do? She was going to be my sister-in-law and it seemed like we were having some kind of intervention on her behalf.

"What I'd like to know is what you meant by you knew he was going to do something terrible," Ben said, cocking his head.

Skye made a face. "I never talked about our family because he never wanted me to talk about anything. He liked me being close by but never wanted me to say or do anything, so I listened. I'd pretend to be reading magazines and such, but I would listen, and he was always so...*angry*. About everything: money, politics, religion, education, even me. He called me a burden once, as if he'd forgotten I was in the room. When he hung up, he made light of it, said he was just talking that way because it was expected by the men in his circles, but I knew better."

"Who did he talk to? Anyone we know?"

"He's very close to Anwar. More so than anyone knows, I think."

"I knew it." Erik let out a huff. "I fucking knew it."

"And Daniil."

"*Daniil?*" The shock in the room was tangible.

Erik didn't say anything, but there was no doubt he was as startled as everyone else. Daniil had seemed so sweet, so much like Sandor and Elen, I had a hard time imagining him good friends with someone like Omar. I'd never met Skye's soon-to-be-ex-husband, but what I'd heard was enough.

"I think we're going to have to have a long talk with Sandor," Uncle Ben said after a moment.

The rest of the meal was subdued, and Erik and I escaped to our room as soon as we were finished eating. I wasn't sure what had happened at dinner, but Erik was agitated.

"What does all that mean?" I asked him once we were alone.

"It's complicated," he said, yanking off his shirt and rummaging through one of his drawers.

"What are you doing?"

"You want to go for a swim?"

"Um, sure." I changed into my bathing suit and put my hair up with a clip.

He grabbed two towels, and we made our way down the stairs and onto the patio with the pool. He kicked off his sandals and dove in without waiting for me, so I sat on a lounge chair and watched him, wondering what was going on in his head. He usually said exactly what was on his mind when it came to anything to do with Anwar, so I wanted to give him a little space tonight. He would tell me what he was thinking in his own time, and in the meantime, I was going to enjoy the last bit of light before the sun disappeared completely. We wouldn't have these long, hot days much longer so I would get my fill of them now.

I was startled awake when I realized I'd fallen asleep and Erik was carrying me up the stairs.

"What time is it?" I mumbled.

"It's only been about thirty minutes," he said. "You fell asleep while I was swimming. Seems like you're tired."

"I guess I am." I smiled. "Our baby princess is already knocking me on my butt."

"Our baby *prince* needs lots of energy to grow," he responded, setting me down on the bed.

"I'm okay," I said. "The doctor said fatigue in the first trimester is normal."

"Yeah, but since you don't have anything pressing to do, why not just get plenty of sleep?"

I yawned. "Okay, fine. But only if you come to bed with me."

"Let me take a quick shower to wash off the chlorine and I'll be right in." He kissed me and I got into bed.

THE NEXT THING I KNEW, IT WAS MORNING AND I WAS ALONE IN BED. DAMN, this pregnancy stuff wasn't for sissies. I felt great this morning, though, and while I wondered where Erik had gone, I was starving. I got dressed and cleaned up, and then hurried down to the kitchen. Hopefully, there would be breakfast in the making, or else I'd be cooking for myself. We hadn't talked about details like cooking and groceries and such, but I'd known Uncle Ben and Aunt Kari long enough to feel comfortable asking.

Luckily, Aunt Kari and Skye were in the kitchen when I arrived, and Naomi, their housekeeper, was getting something out of the oven.

"Are you hungry, dear?" Aunt Kari asked. "Erik said you fell asleep early so I figured you would be."

"I'm starving."

"I've made a breakfast casserole." Naomi greeted me with a smile. "I hope you like eggs, ham, swiss cheese, and green onions."

"Love it all," I declared happily.

"Make yourself a plate, grab some tea or coffee, and let's sit on the patio," Aunt Kari suggested. "It's beautiful out."

"Okay." I poured myself a mug of coffee and took the plate Naomi handed me, along with a napkin and utensils. The doctor had said one cup of coffee a day was okay, and I was grateful for that because I would be miserable without it. I didn't drink a lot of soda, and I was okay without alcohol, but coffee would be a lot harder. I was still getting the hang of pregnancy and it was an odd feeling, knowing I was growing a life inside of me. On the plus side, it was Erik's baby. *Our* baby. Which was incredibly cool.

Weight gain and stretch marks would be less cool, but hopefully I had youth and excellent health on my side.

"I'm sorry, what?" I realized Aunt Kari had been talking to me.

"I said, did you have a chance to look at any magazines last night? It might take time to find the perfect dress."

"No, I fell asleep. I'm sorry. Erik and I are going to sit down today to talk about all things wedding-related. Technically, he hasn't even proposed."

"Oh, he will," Aunt Kari laughed. "Trust me."

I smiled back. "I'm sure. He's a pretty romantic guy."

"Omar wasn't at all romantic," Skye murmured. "And I'm so bad at it, I never even noticed."

"You always said romance was overrated," Aunt Kari pointed out.

"I thought it was." She sighed. "Now I don't know what to think. How did I marry such a man?"

"We all make mistakes," I said carefully. I didn't interact much with Skye because we tended to butt heads, but she seemed pretty mellow today. "If he was your first love, it was a hard lesson learned."

"Who was your first love?" Skye asked, meeting my eyes curiously.

"His name was Ace." I smiled. "That was a fun but epic mistake. I was not quite seventeen, while we were recording our first album, and he was leaving for the Marines in two weeks. I fell hard and fast and was completely devastated that it was nothing but a pre-military fling for him. Luckily, the album came out not long after that, and then we went on tour, so I had a huge distraction."

"I don't foresee any huge life-changing distractions in my near future," Skye said quietly.

"Perhaps you can buy your own home, or a condominium," Kari suggested. "Spend your time decorating and reinventing yourself."

"Maybe." Skye didn't look convinced, but at least she wasn't being bitchy.

"Good morning." Erik and Uncle Ben came in and Erik dropped a kiss on the top of my head. "How'd you sleep, love?"

"Like a rock. I don't remember falling asleep or you getting up or anything."

"You'll sleep well early in your pregnancy," Aunt Kari said. "And then at the end, you won't sleep at all because you'll be uncomfortable, so enjoy it now."

"I am," I replied. "I'm just not used to it."

Erik and Uncle Ben joined us at the table, and we chatted until we'd finished eating. Then Erik and I went up to our room and he sat in a chair by the window, looking out at either the view or nothing at all. It was hard to tell by the look on his face.

"What's wrong?" I asked, dropping to my knees beside him and resting my elbows on his thighs. "Talk to me. Please. I'm not used to you keeping things in like this."

He looked down at me and smiled, running his thumb along my jaw. "I'm not keeping things in so much as turning them over in my head."

"I think you *do* want to be king," I whispered. "And the idea that you can't eats at you."

"It didn't eat at me until recently, when I realized what an absolutely incapable, impetuous, and unfit ruler he's going to be. And something almost no one knows: Uncle Isak has multiple sclerosis. He's been thinking about abdicating to Anwar for a couple of years and my father recently told me his condition is getting worse. Not many know about it, of course, because it would diminish his power and make him appear weak, but Anwar knows. And that scares me. The thought of the people of my country being ruled by him is terrifying. I don't want the job, I really don't, but it's one of those things where you don't want someone completely unqualified to have it either."

"That's understandable," I said. "Is there anything you can do?"

"Dad and I talked about it at length this morning and there really isn't."

"In a perfect world, where everything fell into place without repercussions, is there any way for the king to name you heir to the throne instead of Anwar?"

He shook his head. "Not really. King Isak, Anwar, and all of his siblings would have to abdicate first. The king could petition Parliament to vote on reinstating me as a royal heir and they would have to vote unanimously. We have a lot of weird rules about the heir to the throne in Limaj."

"But technically, from the perspective of bloodline, you are the real heir."

He chuckled. "Yes, but because of the way my father abdicated, it's a complicated mess. And remember, we're not the United Kingdom. We're a tiny eastern European country with a barely democratic government, bordering communist and theocratic countries that have had huge influences on us over the centuries. Our proximity to Turkey, Russia, and the Middle East makes us vulnerable to all kinds of attacks and rebellions, so the royal bloodline doesn't have the emphasis it would in perhaps a country like England. It's all about power and money, because of oil and trade."

I wrinkled my nose. "That sounds confusing and frustrating."

"Hence why I truly don't want to be king. However, I still care about my people and want what's best for them, which is why I'm struggling with Anwar taking over if Uncle Isak's health continues to decline."

"I'm sorry. I wish I had something intelligent to say."

"You always have something intelligent to say, and honestly, just being able to talk about it is a huge relief." He got to his feet and reached for my hands to bring me to mine. "But let's not talk about this anymore today. I have a surprise for you. Do you have a little hiking in you today? Nothing overly strenuous."

"I'm fine." I grinned. "And a hike sounds great."

"A very special hike. I'll have Naomi pack us lunch and water and give Sandor the plan. Be ready in about thirty minutes?"

"Ready for anything." I watched him go with a fond smile. I adored this man and fell more in love with him every day. My heart told me he wasn't going to sit around and let an idiot like Anwar take over without a fight, but he just didn't realize it yet. I had no idea what that would mean for our future, but I refused to worry about it. I trusted him and that was all that mattered. At least I hoped so.

26

E*rik*

We drove to the Grand Canyon, and Sandor followed a few feet behind us as we explored the West Rim. This was my first time here, though Casey said she'd come with her family a few times growing up. It was beautiful, and I took a moment to enjoy the majesty of nature before remembering the task at hand. It was going to be a beautiful backdrop to what I was about to do, and I wanted to memorize all of it. We were getting married, that was already a given, but I still wanted her to have a proposal she could remember. It wouldn't be the same as one she wasn't expecting, but I don't think she was expecting it to be today, and she definitely wouldn't be expecting this particular ring. The pink dragon was the perfect stone for her—so fiercely exotic while feminine and beautiful at the same time.

"Let's get a few pictures," Casey said, nudging me back to reality. "Will Sandor take them?"

"Of course." Sandor took Casey's camera from her and snapped a bunch of shots of us with the canyon and its view in the background.

Casey climbed up on a high, uneven rock, giving me a heart attack, as she threw her arms in the air. It was a great picture, but I couldn't wait for her to get down again, making her laugh as I grabbed her.

"Overprotective much?" she asked, leaning against me.

"A little." I looked at Sandor and gave a little nod of my head.

We were on the trail that tourists walked along to enjoy the view but it was relatively quiet here, so it seemed like the time was right.

"Hey, do you have some water?" Casey was asking.

"Just a second," Sandor hedged, looking at me.

I took her hand and dropped to one knee. This wasn't quite the backdrop —or clothing—I'd planned for this, but the view made up for a lot. The shock on her face made up for the rest.

"I know things have moved at warp speed," I said quietly, looking up into her gorgeous blue eyes. "And you're already pregnant. But I never thought you'd love me the way I loved you. Now that you do, I don't plan to ever let you go. So, in light of the enormity of my love for you, would you do me the honor of becoming my wife?"

"I, oh..." Her eyes rounded as I opened the jeweler's box. "Erik! It's *beautiful*."

"Doesn't hold a candle to you." I held out the ring.

"I... Yes." She smiled as she bit her lower lip, holding out her left hand, which I noted was shaking just a bit.

I slid the ring on, and she dropped to her knees to throw her arms around me. I'd told Sandor to take pictures but I wasn't looking to verify whether or not he was doing it because the woman I loved was kissing me like we weren't at a tourist attraction in front of a shit ton of people that had appeared out of nowhere. They were all clapping and cheering and I instinctively sensed Sandor was beginning to panic.

"We've drawn a crowd," I whispered against her mouth.

"No one knows it's us," she whispered back. But we got to our feet and I slid my arm around her as we made our way past the well-wishers that had gathered.

"I love you so much," she said softly as we moved away. "This is the most beautiful ring I've ever seen."

"It's called the Pink Dragon, and it reminded me of you the moment I saw it."

"It's huge, but I'll wear it forever."

"You'd better." I bent down to kiss her again as we continued to walk. "Because I'm going to love you forever."

"I can't wait to be your wife."

"I can't wait to be your husband."

We laughed at how cheesy we were being, but it felt too good to stop. Seeing my ring on her finger was a dream come true for me and I was going to bust my ass to be everything to her and our baby.

"One of you has been recognized," Sandor said, coming up behind us and whispering in my ear. "There are cameras. We need to go."

"Dammit." I didn't dare look but Sandor was good at his job, so I trusted what he said.

"It's fine, babe." Casey nudged me. "We're going to have all kinds of engagement sex when we get back. In fact, maybe we'll start in the back of the SUV on the way home..."

"Oh, dear god, no." Sandor groaned. "Never mind, let's stay. I'll let you two take your chances with the paparazzo..."

He was kidding but I punched him for good measure as we hurried out to the parking lot.

After several rounds of what Casey called engagement sex when we got home, she fell asleep, and I went to find Sandor. He was supposed to have gotten his brother's phone records and spoken to him as well. If Daniil was involved with Omar, we had to be very, very careful, because we were close and shared almost everything. Although I couldn't put my finger on why I had a feeling there was something bigger going on, I felt it down in my bones and I didn't want any surprises. If there was a link between Omar and Anwar, something bad was going to happen. I didn't know what or when, but I knew it was coming.

"All done with *engagement* sex?" Sandor asked as I joined him in my father's den.

"For now." I sank into a leather armchair and stretched out my legs, winking at my best friend, who rolled his eyes.

"I need a new job," Sandor muttered.

"What do you have?" Dad asked, ignoring our banter.

Sandor's hazel eyes immediately sharpened, and he opened a file. "I have three months of Daniil's home and cell records. If he's communicating with Anwar or Omar, it's through a very back channel. I've verified all of these numbers as friends, family, or businesses. Unless he's talking to them via the tailor he's been using for years or one of his university buddies, I don't know what Skye was talking about."

"Anwar isn't stupid," Dad said thoughtfully. "If he's up to something, it won't be as easy to find as phone records, but this is Daniil we're talking about. I don't believe he would be involved with anything Omar or Anwar are cooking up."

"I spoke to him after I went through his records," Sandor said. "Early this morning, before we left for the Grand Canyon. I randomly asked him how

Omar was, and his response was, 'Who?' followed by 'What are you talking about?' I know my brother quite well, and he's a shit liar and an even worse actor. There's no way he faked surprise that well. Then I told him there was a rumor that he and Omar had gotten chummy, and in light of Skye's beating, I didn't think he was on the right side of the situation. Daniil wasn't at all shocked, but he was furious. I haven't heard him use that many curse words in a long time. Personally, I think either Skye misunderstood, or Omar planted those ideas for a reason."

"To drive a wedge between us, because we're all so close," I murmured. "At the end of the day, it's us and him. Though I don't think Rafael and Yusef are necessarily on Anwar's side, I also don't think they're as aware of what's going on as they should be."

"There were always three teams, so to speak," Dad said. "Anwar, Yusef and Rafael; the girl cousins; and you, Sandor, Daniil, and Vardan. Those alliances haven't altered much over the years. I don't believe Daniil randomly switched sides, either, and that means Omar purposely fed Skye false information. Now we need to know why."

"Shit." Sandor threw the file on the desk and shook his head. "This is ridiculous. We're all blood members of the royal family. We're supposed to be united. I don't understand any of this. Is it because of power? Is that what drives people like that?"

"Power. Greed. Superiority. There are a million reasons." My father looked sad, which was rare for him, and I briefly wondered what kind of king he would have made.

A good one, no doubt, but would he have been happy without my mother? Now that I had Casey in my life, the idea of trading her for the throne, no matter how enticing, was unacceptable. I understood my father better now than I ever had before, even though the throne wasn't mine and I didn't have anything to give up. Just the thought of having to choose made me a little queasy and I quickly put it out of my mind.

"There isn't anything we can do," I said finally. "Unless we find proof that Anwar is planning something terrible, and I can't even think what that would be, Uncle Isak isn't going to give the throne to anyone else. As the firstborn, Anwar is going to ascend. The trick is whether or not we can live with him in that position."

"I'll never pledge allegiance to him," Sandor said in a tone I'd never heard him use before.

"Sandor." My father stared at him. "You can't mean that."

"I think he does." I looked at my father. "Because I won't either."

"That's treason," my father said quietly.

"I didn't say I would do him harm, I merely said I wouldn't pledge allegiance. There's a difference."

"There isn't." My father looked pissed. "It's what we do as part of the royal family."

"The times are changing," Sandor said. "It's hard to explain because you've been out of the game for a long time. You've never seen Anwar in a casual setting with his friends, with women, when he's not putting on airs for important members of the country or heads of state from other countries. He's petty, selfish, and downright mean. We've watched it for years, thinking he would grow up, take his duties seriously, but it's only gotten worse. Erik never said anything because it looks like sour grapes, the man who should have been king talking badly about the man who will be. But I was never in the running for king, nor will I ever be with his brothers ahead of me in the order, so I have nothing to lose. I won't be at his coronation, and I won't ever go back to Limaj once he ascends unless Erik asks it of me. And even then, I won't pledge my allegiance. Even if it means prison or death."

"Once Anwar is king, I won't feel safe enough to go home," I added. "Not with Casey and our child, who would be the next in line after Anwar's children based on firstborn sons of firstborn sons. My father's abdication ends with me—any children I have fall back into the order of ascension."

"How do you know it's a son?" Sandor asked, eyeing me.

"I just do." I gave him a grin. "I'm cool like that."

"This disturbs me greatly," my father said, even as Sandor and I relaxed back into our typical easy banter.

"I'm sorry, but this is a decision you made and should be familiar with," I reminded him. "You chose to abdicate for a woman. I choose to separate myself from a leader who will undoubtedly be the ruin of our country, our legacy, and our people."

"Then you should stay and fight!" my father said in a steely voice.

"You didn't. Why should I?"

27

Casey

AFTER THE FORMAL ANNOUNCEMENT OF OUR ENGAGEMENT, ERIK AND I BARELY saw each other. Between my mother and Aunt Kari, I was always on the go, dealing with preparations. Erik was involved in a lot of it, but most of it fell to me, and I was enjoying it more than I'd thought I would. I'd never been overly girlie, far too involved in my music to think about clothes and accessories, but this was different. I enjoyed dressing up and looking pretty as long as it didn't take too much effort, and since both my mother and Aunt Kari knew that, they were pulling out all the stops to make it as easy for me as possible.

The dress, however, had to be perfect and our search wasn't yielding results I was happy with. Jade was flying in to help with plans in general, and I was on my way to pick her up at the airport when my phone rang. I was surprised to see Nick's number on the screen—we hadn't spoken since that last time in Limaj—and answered quickly.

"Hey!"

"I hear you're getting married," he said without preamble.

"I'm knocked up too."

He burst out laughing. "That didn't take long."

"No, it didn't." I laughed too. We'd been friends since we were in diapers and I was glad for our camaraderie. I'd been worried he wouldn't be happy since we'd been lovers on and off for more than three years before Erik and I got together.

"Are you happy?"

"I am. Really, really happy."

"I'm glad. I've missed talking to you, but I didn't want to interrupt since you told me you guys were bouncing around Europe."

"You're one of my best friends, Nick. That's not going to change because I'm getting married."

"You sure?"

"Yes, I'm sure. I mean, obviously, we're not going to sleep together anymore, but that was never the basis for our friendship." I paused. "Was it?"

"No, silly. The basis for our friendship was causing our parents as much grief as possible through our teenage years."

"There was that."

"So tell me everything."

As much as I loved Erik, I'd been a little sequestered from my regular life since we'd gotten together, and suddenly everything poured out, from our epic vacation in Europe to seeing Liz to my worries that Erik would regret walking away from the turmoil in his country.

"Erik was born into that life," Nick pointed out. "If he's ready to walk away, he must have a good reason."

"But what if it's because of me and then he resents me for it?"

"Why would he walk away because of you?" Nick sounded genuinely confused.

"Oh, Nick, come on. I'm in a rock band. I play guitar. I never went to college. I've got manners and stuff, but I'm not the kind of girl you bring into a royal family."

"I think you're wrong, and if he loves you the way he should, he sees everything that's wonderful and perfect about you."

"Sometimes I can't figure out why he even wants to be with me. I mean, I'm pretty enough, and I'm not dumb or anything, but don't guys like him usually go for really sophisticated, educated women?"

He chuckled. "I don't think that's how love works, you know? I mean, I've never been in love—not the kind you have with Erik—but I don't think sophisticated and educated are adjectives I'm looking for in a life partner. I want someone who makes me happy, who likes me even when I'm a jerk, who understands what makes me tick. Is that what you guys have?"

I was thoughtful. "Yeah, I think it is. We're really in tune to each other's moods and needs. I mean, we've done everything at warp speed, but it feels like we've been together forever. I have zero doubts."

"Then what else do you need? And if you're really feeling insecure about it, talk to him. The worst thing you can do is keep it bottled up."

"You're right, of course."

I sighed happily on the inside. It was so good to talk to someone who understood me at this level. Erik did, of course, but Nick was different because Erik and I were still so new. Nick had known me forever and we had a bond that was more like family than friends or lovers. Our families had always been baffled because they'd been sure we would end up together, and though we'd hooked up while touring, it wasn't that kind of relationship. We were truly the best of friends and it was good to be talking again after the way we'd left things at the end of the tour.

We talked for a little longer, until Jade came running out of the airport and jumped in the car.

"Gotta go," I told him. "I'll call you soon."

"Take care, hon."

"Bye." I hung up and looked at Jade with a grin. "I have a thousand things to tell you."

"I know!" She put her sunglasses on and grinned back at me. "And I can't wait to meet your hunky royal."

I put the car in gear. "Let's do it."

WITH JADE IN TOWN, ERIK AND I HAD EVEN LESS TIME TOGETHER, BECAUSE BY the time we went to bed at night I was exhausted and usually fell right to sleep. I'd found a dress, though, as well as dresses for the bridesmaids, and by the time Jade flew back to New York four days later, I had a handle on the wedding. The wedding planner my mother and Aunt Kari hired seemed to have the details under control, and with the dress chosen, color scheme picked out, and our basic wishes sketched out for her, we could finally sit back and relax.

Today, Erik and I weren't going anywhere or doing anything. In fact, I'd arranged for breakfast to be delivered to our suite. My plans included food, sex, and just being together. Though we were living together and saw each other every day, I missed spending time together without an agenda. The wedding was taking up far too much time and with my hormones running amok, I needed his arms around me more than anything else.

"Good morning." His eyes opened sleepily as I softly kissed the underside of his jaw.

"Good morning." He reached for me. "What time is it?"

"A little after eight."

"Do we have somewhere to be?"

"Yup. Right here."

"In bed?" His eyes darkened into glittering emerald orbs, his chest rising and falling a tiny bit faster as he spoke.

"Yup. Naomi's bringing breakfast at nine, so we have time for...whatever."

"Whatever?" He pulled me on top of him, holding me firmly in place. "Is that what we're calling it?"

"We can call it whatever we want." I laughed, leaning down to meet his mouth. God, I loved the way he kissed me. Even kissing was always a spiritual experience with him. We didn't have to make love for my world to be complete; he needed only to be close to me. I kept thinking it would wear off, especially now that we were living together and navigating unfamiliar waters, but he was fantastically perfect. Maybe not literally, because no one was, but for me he came damn close.

His tongue stroked mine lovingly but with a sexy determination that made my body tremble with wanting him. He ran strong hands down my back, over the curve of my ass, the backs of my thighs, my hips...as if he couldn't get enough of me the same way I couldn't get enough of his touch. Would it always be this way? I fucking hoped so, because this man had become my world in a very short time.

He slid my top up and over my head, flinging it aside so he could lick a trail down my chest to my breasts. He took one nipple between his supple lips and sucked more gently than usual because pregnancy had made them tender and he seemed to sense exactly how much pressure was enough. A few flicks of his tongue had me squirming, and the addition of a hand in my panties gave me a lady boner. His fingers were lust-filled magic, and I wiggled out of my undies to give him better access. Jade told me she'd had zero interest in sex while she was pregnant, but that didn't seem to be the case here. In fact, I was getting impatient.

"Erik..." I protested when his lips left my chest.

"What, baby? What do you want?"

"You," I gasped. "But I don't want you—I fucking need you."

"I'll take care of that." He flipped us over, settling between my legs and sliding into me with one firm thrust.

"Shit, that's good." My eyes closed and there was nothing but us. This. Togetherness. It was corny as hell, but everything disappeared when we were together like this. This kind of intimacy transcended time and emotion and even air. I could just breathe him in as he glided in and out of me, attached in every way possible, as close to being one person as humanly possible.

"Jesus, baby, you're so fucking tight." He moved faster, and I arched my hips up to take all of him.

"Harder," I whispered. "More."

He gave me more. Hell, I'm pretty sure he gave me everything, because when my orgasm exploded out of me, I screamed like a woman possessed. He drowned my cries with his mouth, muffling his own growl of pleasure.

It took a good ten minutes for either of us to speak. That had been more than sex, and I had no words for it. Apparently, he didn't either. He was still on top of me, though, and getting heavy, so I gave a little push at his chest.

"Can we flip?"

"Sorry." He turned onto his back and I nestled into his side, my head resting in the hollow of his shoulder.

"What just happened?" I asked with a soft chuckle. "I feel like we left earth for a minute there."

"Something like that." His arms tightened. "It's always like that when we touch."

"Sometimes I worry that this has been too fast," I said. "But I can't even conceive of my life without you now."

"Nor can I."

We lay like that until my stomach growled and I realized we'd been having sex when Naomi had probably come to deliver breakfast. Oops.

"I'm sure she heard us and just kept going," he said, reading my mind. "I'll call downstairs and have her bring it back up."

"Sorry." I laughed and rolled over, getting to my feet so I could use the bathroom.

We got dressed and Erik went to get the door as I settled into one of the chairs by the window. Naomi brought in breakfast, nothing in her demeanor signifying that she'd heard our earlier passion or knew what we'd been up to. She merely smiled and poured coffee for Erik, tea for me, and departed.

"I was thinking we should start looking for a house," Erik said as he sat across from me.

"We can and we will, but I wanted to talk about something first."

"Of course. What is it?"

"I sense a restlessness in you that worries me."

"Honey, I'm fine. What are you talking about?"

"I think you're worried. About your family, your people, your country. And I'm afraid you're not doing anything about it because of me."

"What? No. I don't have any power. You know that."

"No. Listen. You have influence over your uncle. He asked you to take a role in Parliament and maybe that's something you should do... I mean, I don't want to live there full-time, and I'm definitely having my baby here in Vegas, but there's no reason you can't have a small role helping the king with whatever it is that you do as a member of Parliament."

"I said no to that offer because I didn't want to work with Anwar. That hasn't changed."

"But he's not king yet. Uncle Isak is what—fifty-five? Sixty? There are wonderful new treatments for MS, so he could be king for a long time and that means you have time to help him see the error of his ways when it comes to Anwar. I see how conflicted you are, and I hate it for you. If you want to do this, do it. I love you, Erik. And that means I love all of you, including the part of you that was born to rule, in whatever capacity you can take on based on your circumstances."

28

E*rik*

I WANTED TO THROW HER BACK ON THE BED AND RAVAGE HER AGAIN, BUT instead I got up and walked over to her, dropping to my knees beside her and putting my arm around her waist. She looked down at me with those gorgeous blue eyes of hers and just smiled, as if she could read my mind. Hell, she probably could. We were so close, so in tune to each other, it felt that way most of the time. I'd never had this with anyone else and it was part of what made us so good together. And why I loved her so much.

"You know me too well," I said softly, pressing my forehead to hers. "But I'm not torn because of you—I'm torn because of Anwar. He's not king, but he's the official heir to the throne and my uncle's right-hand man. My presence there would be frustrating to everyone, especially me. And like you said, you want to be pregnant and give birth here, so we're not going anywhere for close to a year."

"But *you* could go," she whispered. "I mean, for short trips, and not around my due date, but you could commute some. We can't be together if one of us wants to change the other. I'll always be a musician, even if I don't tour again, but I'm not going to stop being who I am. And you have to be who you are, which is a prince, with a deep love for your country and your people."

"Oh, baby." I kissed her as tenderly as I knew how, and she put her hands on either side of my face.

"I need you to be who you are, Erik. That's the man I've watched from afar for a decade, the man I let make love to me without a condom the first time we were together, and the man I want to spend the rest of my life with. I love all of you."

"I fucking worship all of you." I kissed her, hard, until we were practically tearing at each other's clothes.

"You need to eat so your stomach settles," I said, pulling away slightly. "Then if you want to go again, I'm all in."

She smiled and shook her head. "You're going to be super overprotective, aren't you?"

"Probably." I got to my feet and sat across from her, taking a sip of coffee. "So, you really think I should work with Uncle Isak in some capacity? I don't think I want to take on a formal role in Parliament. They're in session nine months of the year and often debate issues for weeks at a time. I don't want to be away from you and the baby for that long."

"Maybe you should mull it around between now and the wedding. Your uncle is coming, right?"

"Yes, he and my aunt have spoken to my parents and expressed how pleased they are for us."

"Do they know I'm pregnant?"

"I was going to ask you about that," I said thoughtfully. "I think we should keep it under wraps. First of all, miscarriages are more likely to happen in the first trimester, so I think that would be a lot easier emotionally if we don't talk about it until then. And frankly, I don't want to give my cousin any ammunition he can take to the press to make you look bad right before the wedding."

"So we tell no one?"

"No one except those who already know. How many people have you told?"

"Other than our parents? Jade and Nick are the only ones I've personally told, but I'm sure they've told people."

"I really think it would be safer all around if we asked them to keep it quiet."

"Nick might have told his parents, but he wouldn't tell anyone else, and they certainly wouldn't. I'll call Jade later, though, to make sure she doesn't call our friend Vicki. They're close and see each other all the time so I'll try to nip it in the bud."

"My father and I discussed it and we really think the less scrutiny about that the better."

"I'm fine with that. I'd kind of like to focus on my wedding and nothing else right now, you know? Thinking about the baby and finding a house and all the other stuff is kind of overwhelming."

"Then it works out perfectly." I held out my hand across the table and she set hers in it, the pink dragon on her ring finger glistening in the sunlight.

"I love seeing my ring on your finger."

"I like it too." She met my eyes and we smiled together.

Why did the simple act of smiling at each other feel so damn good?

We finished breakfast talking about our honeymoon and the desire to go somewhere warm, perhaps reminiscent of Greece. I'd already begun looking into it but pretended I hadn't so I could surprise her. She seemed to love surprises, and I was planning several for the wedding and honeymoon. I'd also found a house I thought she might like, but after her comment about feeling overwhelmed, I opted not to push it. There would be other houses, or we could build one from the ground up. I didn't care as long as she was happy and we were all safe.

"Am I going to meet the whole royal family?" she was asking me as we finished eating and somehow wound up back in bed.

"Well, my father has a brother and a sister; Isak and Edita. Edita is Sandor's mother. Her husband is Harold. He's a very distant relative of the Swedish royal family but grew up in the U.K. Isak, of course, is married to Klara, and they have Anwar, Yusef, Rafael, and Miriam. As far as I know, everyone is coming to the wedding."

"Holy shit. Are any of the cousins married?"

I nodded. "Rafael married his college sweetheart, Yolanda. She's like a third cousin or something. I don't remember the exact relationship but it's not close enough to be creepy."

She laughed. "Good to know. So they're going to mingle with...record company executives, rock stars, and all of my crazy friends and family?"

"If they want to be at my wedding, then yes, they will."

"I can't decide if I'm excited or mortified."

"Don't worry. My mother is in charge of keeping everyone in line."

"Are your other cousins more like Sandor or Anwar?"

"Vardan is pretty chill. He's probably getting married next year. His girlfriend is British, and it's been serious for a while so we think that's where it's going. And everyone except his brothers hate Anwar almost as much as I do. Yusef and Rafael are much nicer than Anwar, but very old school and rigid when it comes to rules and manners. Daniil and Elen are coming to Las Vegas early to do some sightseeing and spend time with all of us and the rest of the family will arrive shortly after them. My parents are going to have a full house the week before the wedding."

"I'm already exhausted." She sighed, nestling against me.

"You don't have to entertain anyone except for maybe one dinner because those that haven't want to meet you, but they'll be doing touristy things too, so they'll be out of our hair for the most part. Don't worry about any of that."

"When is everyone else arriving?"

"I'm not sure what Anwar's plans are, but my father is taking care of all that. He said he's having a conversation with Uncle Isak and I'm leaving it in his hands because if it were up to me, Anwar wouldn't even be coming."

"Is anyone upset we're not getting married in Limaj?"

I shook my head. "No. Uncle Isak asked about a church wedding and my father told him it was out of the question since neither of us is religious. Apparently, he let it go."

"That's good."

"Anything else on your mind about the family with regard to the wedding?"

She shook her head. "Not really."

"Good. Then we can get naked again."

"Sounds like a plan." She pulled her top off and had just tossed it on the floor when someone knocked on the door.

"Casey? Are you there? It's Skye. I have to talk to you right now. It's urgent."

29

C*asey*

I yanked my shirt back on as Erik got up and padded to the door. He opened it with a friendly but cautious smile.

"Hey, Skye. What's up?"

"Oh, thank goodness." She brushed past him and into the room. "What is this?" she asked, waving an ivory-colored piece of paper around.

"I have no idea." I looked at her in confusion.

"It's an invitation. To a ball. At..." She stopped waving whatever was in her hand and read it. "The Charleston Hotel. Some sort of masquerade ball for charity. Mother said it was your idea."

"I..." I frowned and took a second to figure out what she was talking about. "It was my idea to make the Charleston's annual charity gala a masquerade ball this year, but I don't actually have anything to do with it. The Kingsleys, my friend Nick's parents, run it."

"Why have they invited me?"

"I wouldn't know. Why didn't you ask your mom?"

"Because she said to ask you."

I did my best not to look irritated. This was undoubtedly Kari's attempt to get Skye and me to become friendly, but balls were not my forte. I'd only attended the Charleston's charity gala twice because I was usually on tour in late September and I'd quite honestly forgotten all about it. Shit. Now I was going to have to figure out a costume because my gut told me there was no way to weasel out of it, especially with Skye now involved.

"I'm not sure what your mom was thinking," I finally said. "I haven't been to one since I was eighteen because I've always been on tour. They raise a lot of money for the children's cancer center here in town and the belle of the ball is always a big deal."

"The belle of the ball?"

"There's always a beautiful, single woman, who's at least a little bit of a celebrity, who's asked to be the belle each year. I have no idea who it is this year though. I've been too busy to ask."

"I thought it was Sheridan Lyons," Erik interjected.

Skye and I both turned to stare at him in confusion.

"How do you know?" I finally asked.

"Because it was online somewhere?" He shrugged.

"Oh. Well, there you have it."

"I have no idea who she is," Skye said.

"She's a television star. I think she started with the Disney Channel and now she's twenty-one and doing feature films."

"I don't know what to do," Skye said, looking from Erik to me.

"I don't know what...you need?" I said slowly. "I mean, I think your parents always go so you won't be alone."

"Aren't we going?" Erik asked me.

"Honestly, I'd forgotten all about it until just now."

"You have to," Skye said urgently. "I mean, Mother says it would be rude not to go but..." Her voice faded. "Wait a minute, did she send me to you so we would have something in common?"

I shrugged. "I really don't know. I truly hadn't given it a thought until just now. It's going to be fun, though, and there are always lots of rich, eligible men in attendance. Wouldn't you like to dress up in a fancy dress and dance with a bunch of nameless, faceless men? You don't have to tell anyone who you are—that's the whole point of the masquerade ball."

Skye seemed thoughtful. "Oh. That does sound interesting." She turned and headed for the door. "I have to find a dress!"

And then she was gone, without even a thank you.

"At some point," Erik said, chuckling as he shut the door and locked it, "I might have to mention manners to her."

"But right now you need to come back to bed."

. . .

That afternoon, after Erik and I had more sex than two people who lived together probably should have, we were just discussing what to have for dinner when the phone rang. I answered it mindlessly, my mind on dinner.

"Hello?"

"Guess what?!" Jade's voice was loud on the other end.

"What?" I asked.

"I'm coming back to Vegas this weekend."

"You are?"

"Sheridan Lyons got married over the weekend and they asked me to be this year's belle!"

I blinked. "Oh. Wow. That's...crazy. We were just talking about the ball. I'd forgotten about it."

"You're going, right?"

"I'm guessing the answer to that is yes, since you're going to be the belle now."

"Tricia said she's got a gown and everything for me, so I just have to show up. How cool is that?"

"I guess so."

"What's wrong with you?" Jade laughed. "Why don't you sound excited?"

"My wedding is a month away, I'm pregnant and don't want anyone to find out, and my future husband's entire royal family is about to congregate in Las Vegas... I'm a little distracted, girlfriend."

"Oh, phooey. What if I bring Alyssa and we just stay in Vegas until the wedding? Frankly, Kirk's on my last nerve and I'd much rather be with you than in my big lonely house on Long Island."

"You know I'd love to have you here."

"I'll be there Wednesday. Go find a dress!" Jade disconnected and I put the phone down with a fond smile. Jade was a tall, red-headed force of nature. She had a grand presence no matter where she was or what she was doing, between her height, her long, wild hair, and her amazing voice. Men wanted her, women either loved or hated her, and her fans worshipped her. I'd loved being in a band with her and having her as one of my closest friends, but she was sometimes over-the-top with her exuberance.

"I take it we're going to this ball," Erik said, leaning against the door.

"I guess we are. You're going to need a cape."

"Excuse me?"

"A cape to go with your tuxedo. I was thinking we could do a *Phantom of the Opera* theme."

He grinned. "Whatever you want. Your wish is my command."

"Are you always going to be this easygoing?"
"I plan to try."
"I love you."
"I love you too."

The one good thing about making plans to attend the ball was spending time with Jade and Nick. BJ didn't come around much, but the three of us spent one day at my dad's new studio, checking out the final stages of interior construction, and another day hanging out at the hotel with some of Nick's family. Erik joined us that day, and for the first time everything that was happening felt real. Nick's parents, Nicky and Tricia, treated him like he was already my husband and mentioned coming to dinner one night. We ran into Nicky's brother, Matt, and he and Erik talked golf for nearly an hour while Jade and I chatted.

Though everything was casual, our social calendar got a little fuller every time we went somewhere that week, and by Saturday, we were having to tell people we'd get back to them because between our wedding, the honeymoon, and my pregnancy, we didn't want to take on too much.

As we finished getting dressed for the ball, Erik wearing a tuxedo with tails and his *Phantom of the Opera*–style mask, I decided to wear the diamonds he'd bought me in Europe. I'd never been big on diamonds and such, but because they were from Erik they were special, and everyone would be dressed to the nines tonight. Only the richest of the rich attended the Charleston's annual charity event with tickets priced at five thousand dollars per person and dances with the belle of the ball going for twenty-five thousand apiece. Ben and Kari always attended, along with the extended Kingsley family and people I had grown up with.

"Any jealous ex-boyfriends of yours I need to look out for?" Erik teased as I came out of the bathroom and stepped into my heels.

"Not a single one," I said.

"Damn, you're gorgeous." The way he looked at me made my insides shiver with excitement and I moved towards him slowly, my royal blue floor-length gown fluttering around me. It had a full skirt, something I wasn't used to at all, but Aunt Kari had said it was very princess-like and she thought Erik would love it. Based on how he was looking at me now, she'd been right, and I couldn't help but reach for him.

"Thank you. You're pretty damn gorgeous yourself."

"I won't kiss you and mess up your beautiful makeup," he said, "but I'm doing it in my head."

I laughed. "You're very gentlemanly."

"And you're very royal tonight. I can picture doing a waltz with you in the palace ballroom and having every man in the room envious of me."

"They can look all they want, but there will never be anyone for me but you."

He took my hand and brought it to his lips, kissing the back of it slowly and quite thoroughly, for a hand kiss. "Later tonight, I'm going to kiss every square inch of you, but for now, we have to go."

30

E*rik*

THE GRAND BALLROOM WITHIN THE CHARLESTON HOTEL WAS BEAUTIFUL ON A regular day, but tonight the staff had pulled out all the stops. I'd done some reading about the event and wondered why I'd never attended before. Yes, I'd spent the last four summers doing my military duty in Limaj, but this was September and even though I'd been in school, I often jetted off to this event or that one. Somehow, this hadn't been on my radar and I realized—a bit guiltily—that I'd avoided coming to Las Vegas the last few years because I'd known Casey was on tour and I wouldn't have an excuse to see her. I saw my parents in Europe often enough, so coming this far west to Vegas had been a hassle I didn't bother with unless there was the added benefit of seeing Casey.

That wouldn't be an issue anymore, of course, especially since she wanted to live here, and I wondered briefly if she liked London. We'd talked about so many things over the last seven weeks or so, but that hadn't been one of them. There were so many things I wanted to show her, share with her, and we'd been so busy lately I hadn't had a chance to ask her about any of them. There would be time, though, after the wedding. Three weeks from tonight she would become my wife, my princess, my life, and I couldn't wait.

As we walked through a gilded archway covered with a million tiny silver lights, a red carpet led us inside a lavishly decorated room. This year's color scheme appeared to be silver and some shade of lavender, from the napkins on the tables to the chandeliers, flowers, and even the waiters' cummerbunds. The Kingsleys definitely knew how to throw a party, and I was suddenly glad my face was covered, because it would afford us a modicum of privacy tonight. The types of people that attended events like these would be the richest of the rich, a who's who of billionaires and celebrities, and I'd gotten used to anonymity when I traveled.

"What are the chances of me escaping for a quickie with someone tonight?" Sandor asked under his breath, laughter in his voice as he looked around.

"Have at it. We have plenty of protection here, between my father's guards, the Kingsleys' security team, and Aziz."

"We'll see." Sandor struck a pretty regal-looking figure too tonight, in a perfectly cut tuxedo and his dirty blond hair pulled back in a ponytail. He looked much like his Swedish father, with fair coloring, and resembled Nordic royalty tonight as he walked beside me.

"I'm going to go find Jade," Casey whispered, squeezing my arm. "I'll be back in a few minutes."

"Have fun." I watched her until she disappeared around a corner.

"You're completely gone over her, aren't you?" Sandor asked.

"I am." I nodded. "She's...amazing."

"If Anwar figures out that you really love her, and she's not just a pretty piece for your arm, she's always going to be a target."

"I know." I swallowed. I didn't want to think about that shit. I'd die before I let that prick near her.

"Sandor, will you dance with me tonight?" Skye came up behind us and put a hand on his forearm.

"Of course." He smiled at her. For some reason, he was the only one of the cousins Skye truly got along with and none of us had ever understood why she avoided the rest like they had some kind of plague.

"I don't know anyone, and I think I'll die of embarrassment if not a single man asks me to dance."

I chuckled. "Not much chance of that, sis. You look stunning tonight. The men will all be clamoring to figure out who you are."

"You think?" She absently fidgeted with the gilded mask covering the top half of her face.

"Trust me."

"You're my brother, not exactly a ringing endorsement for whether or not I look attractive."

"I'm still a man, and you're still a woman. Just because there's no sexual undertone to said endorsement doesn't mean I can't see if you look nice or not. And you definitely do."

She smiled. A real smile. Probably the first one I'd seen from her since childhood, and it lit up her face, even half-covered. She looked so pretty it momentarily startled me into silence. Why didn't she do it more often?

"You're beautiful when you smile," I said quietly.

"He's right." Sandor nodded. "You should mingle with your brother and meet everyone. I, unfortunately, cannot make the introductions that Erik can."

She inhaled through her nose and blew out a breath. "Okay."

"Are you nervous?" I asked incredulously.

"Well, of course. I've never really dated. Omar was my only serious boyfriend, and now I'm in the middle of a divorce. I'm torn between hiding in the corner and dating every single man in the room."

"Perhaps we can find something in between those two, eh?" I put her hand in the crook of my arm. "Come. Let's meet some people. Do you know Nick Kingsley?"

She shook her head.

"Well, he's the heir to the Kingsley hotel empire and unattached as far as I know."

"So rich and single." She shook her head. "I'm not looking for a husband, Erik. Just maybe friends. Since I have none."

I glanced at her in confusion. "None? Like zero?"

She shrugged. "I had a couple at university, but once I started dating Omar junior year, he kept me from them. It was just us, supposedly falling in love, planning our wedding, starting our life together. Saraya was my constant companion once we were married, and other than some surface-level friendships with the wives of Omar's friends, there's been no one."

That was one of the saddest things I'd ever heard, and I shook my head. "Wow. Well, let's see what we can do about this. Okay?"

"I'll try. I'm really very shy."

"I know, but these people are close to Mother and Father and people I know as well. The community here at the Charleston Hotel, between the Kingsleys, Casey's family, and their extended families, is lovely. My time here has been limited but I know enough of them to know I like most of them and am looking forward to getting to know them better."

"I'll do my best, I'm just not sure what—" She cut off abruptly as Nick approached us.

"Hi. Welcome." He shook my hand.

"Everything looks wonderful," I told him.

"Thank you. It takes almost a year to plan these events, but my mother and Aunt Kirsten do a fantastic job."

"Nick, have you met my sister, Skye? I'm sure you knew each other as children, but it's probably been a while?"

"Years." Nick turned to her and held out his hand. "It's a pleasure, Your Highness."

"Oh, please, no." She shook his hand but was shaking her head. "Just Skye. If this is to be my home, no one here in America needs to use my title."

"Skye it is. How are you enjoying Las Vegas so far?"

"Honestly, I've been laying low, so to speak, letting the fuss die down in the aftermath of my spectacular failure of a marriage."

"Hell, we all make mistakes." He offered her his arm. "If you like, I can take you around and introduce you to people?"

She hesitated but then took his arm. "Thank you. That would be lovely."

They walked in the other direction, talking as if they were already friends and I mentally thanked Nick for taking her off my hands. As bad as I felt for her, I had a date tonight and didn't want to spend most of it chaperoning my sister.

"What just happened there?" Sandor asked in my ear. "Did you just hook your sister up with Nick Kingsley?"

"Not intentionally." I chuckled, turning as Casey came back into the room. "Keep an eye on her, will you? Just to be sure he doesn't abandon her and she actually doesn't go hide in a corner somewhere."

Sandor shook his head. "Not on my watch. She's my favorite cousin."

I rolled my eyes. "Thanks a lot."

"You're not my cousin," Sandor said, his hazel eyes growing serious. "You're my brother."

I clapped him on the shoulder as I made my way toward my future wife.

CASEY APPROACHED ME WITH A SMILE. "WELL, HELLO THERE. ARE YOU SINGLE?"

I paused, unsure what game she was playing. "Perhaps," I finally responded. "It depends on who's asking."

She giggled, something she rarely did, and it was adorable. She leaned up on her toes, as if telling me a secret. "Don't tell anyone, but I'm engaged to a future king, and he's super stuffy and snobby. I'm looking for some side action. What do you do for a living?"

Ah. So, we were engaging in some sort of play-acting. It was new to me, but I was game for anything with this woman.

"I'm a butler," I whispered back. "My liege is here this evening and I'll be shining his shoes on and off throughout the night."

Her snort of laughter was infectious, and I laughed too.

"Do you think we could steal a dance before my fiancé or your liege find us? We're in costume, after all."

"Absolutely." I took her hand and led her out to the dance floor.

"I've only recently learned to waltz," she told me. "My future mother-in-law seemed to think it was important. Do you waltz?"

"I do." The music playing was indeed a waltz and I realized what she was telling me. My mother had been teaching her to dance and she wanted to try it out in public. Her little charade was her way of pretending she was someone else, because she was nervous.

I led her around the floor and discovered she was fantastic. She moved with me effortlessly, and though I had to admit I was an excellent dancer, it wasn't because of me that she was doing so well. As a musician she had rhythm and felt the music, so even when she occasionally missed a step, she could easily mask it because it came so naturally to her.

"This is wonderful," she said softly. "I always thought these kinds of dances were antiquated and unnecessary, but I'm going to have to reassess that opinion."

I swung her around and ended the dance by dipping her. She laughed as I straightened her.

"I always thought it was boring," I admitted. "But I'm also going to have to reassess that opinion because dancing with you is anything but boring."

"We have to discuss the first dance at our wedding too."

"You want to waltz?"

"I don't know. Maybe."

"Whatever you want. Waltz, tango, stand still and sway—I'm down for anything."

"I was thinking of something more fun than that. The entire day is going to be centered on romance and eye-gazing and all that. I'd like to do something different. Maybe start out slow and traditional and then break-dance or something."

I grimaced. "I don't know if I can break-dance, but I'm down if you are."

"Hey, there's my parents. Let's go say hi! I didn't know they were coming." She tugged me by the hand in that direction and I followed amiably. My girl was a force of nature and I was happy to be swept up in her storm.

31

Casey

THE EVENING WAS WONDERFUL, FULL OF GOOD FOOD, DANCING, AND LOTS OF conversation with people I hadn't seen in ages. Jade made a beautiful belle of the ball in a sleeveless, strapless, emerald sequined gown, her long red hair swept up in a messy updo. Nick's cousin, Michael Kingsley, had danced with her several times already and I wondered if there was something going on with them, but there was no time to ask her because her dance card was full. Even at the exorbitant price of a dance, she barely had a break all evening and seemed to be having the time of her life. I was happy for her, because her life had been hard before we'd had our first hit with Viktim of Prey, so she deserved this and more.

My biggest surprise of the evening was watching Nick and Skye. They'd danced multiple times and she'd moved to his table for dinner, where they talked and laughed the whole night. She didn't seem at all his type, but maybe I didn't know him as well as I thought I did. Our relationship had always been such a strange mixture of friendship and sex, I probably didn't have any idea what he looked for in a girlfriend. As far as I knew, he'd never had a serious one. Skye seemed like an unlikely candidate, but they appeared to be getting along and I wanted nothing more than for my future sister-in-law to be happy. Or happier.

Erik had bought Sandor a dance with Jade and they were on the floor now, talking animatedly, as if they were friends. This event seemed to bring out the best in people and I enjoyed seeing it. I made a mental note to attend every year, if possible, since this had been such a memorable evening thus far. Sandor dancing with Jade might have been a highlight though. He was tall, probably six-five to her five-eleven, and he was striking in a tuxedo. I'd never really looked at him as a man before because I'd only had eyes for Erik since we'd gotten together, but women were probably going to be clamoring to find out who he was after this, and I smiled to myself just thinking about it.

"Hey, Casey." A familiar voice made me turn and it took me a moment to recognize Liz.

"Hi." I gave her a hug. "What are you doing here?"

"I try to attend every year. I didn't get in until this afternoon, though, so I didn't have time to let anyone know I was coming."

"I'm glad to see you. What's been happening? How's construction going?"

We talked about the hotel, the upcoming wedding and other random topics as I occasionally scanned the room, watching friends and family as they danced and drank. We were about to step outside to get some fresh air on the open-air patio just outside the ballroom when something caught my eye. I turned, squinting slightly as I tried to make out who was who and what was going on. Skye and a man I didn't recognize were standing by one of the ballroom exits, and he was holding her by the arm. By the looks of it, she was trying to pull away, but he wouldn't let her. He looked vaguely familiar, but also had on a mask that covered his face so I could only go on the gut feeling he was someone I knew, just not his identity.

"What are you looking at?" Liz asked, following my gaze.

"Oh, shit, shit, shit." I gripped Liz's arm. "Where's Erik? Oh my god, this is not good!"

Liz swung her gaze around and spotted Erik at the bar. "He's over there —" she began.

"Go get him. Now!" I turned and hurried over to Skye, leaving Liz confused but already moving.

"Skye!" I called out to her with a big smile. "The photographers are waiting to take a family photo of us—can you get away?"

Skye turned grateful eyes to me. "Of course," she said immediately.

"We were about to dance." Omar turned and the look he gave me was filled with hatred.

"I don't think the lady wants to dance with you." I instinctively moved closer to Skye, putting a comforting hand on her arm and squeezing lightly. I'd only seen the man in pictures before tonight, but I'd recognize him anywhere.

"The lady doesn't have a choice, unless she wants to make a scene, which I don't think she wants to do." He stepped closer to us, his smarmy gaze shooting through me like an arrow.

"Omar, please," Skye whispered softly. "Why are you here? This isn't necessary."

"Oh, but it is," he hissed under his breath. "You left me—and Limaji women do not leave their husbands. You've humiliated me and embarrassed me."

"You had a mistress," she whispered back. "Our laws do not allow for adultery!"

"The writers of those laws never had to sleep with a cold fish like you," he ground out, reaching for her again. "You will dance with me, Skye, and people are beginning to stare."

"She doesn't have to dance with you." I stepped forward. "I'm a black belt in karate, and I will take you down even if it makes a scene."

"Casey, no." Skye fearfully clutched my arm. "I'll just dance with him and—"

"What the hell is going on?" Erik's voice was low but deadly as he came up to us with Nick and Sandor right behind him like second-in-command lieutenants.

"This woman is still my wife, and I will dance with her, whether you like it or not," Omar said, his voice equally steely.

"Skye doesn't want to dance with him," I said, meeting Erik's eyes meaningfully.

"Then she won't." Nick never even looked at Skye, his eyes pasted on Omar's face. "This is my family's hotel, our event, and you weren't on the guest list. You can leave on your own, or I can have you escorted out."

"I will make the scene of all scenes if you try to keep me from my wife. Is that the kind of press you want for your precious charity event? I also paid good money for my ticket."

"Sandor, take Omar to my father and get him his money back." Nick still hadn't broken his gaze.

"So you're going to deny the children with cancer that much money just because she's being her normal selfish self?" he taunted.

"Not at all." Nick smiled but it was without mirth. "I'm going to repay that money personally. And please note, Casey and I are *both* black belts in karate—so trust me when I tell you that you won't walk out of here on your own if you don't do it in the next five seconds."

The men stared each other down until I felt sure that one was going to take a swing at the other. Skye was clutching my hand, and Erik stood next to Nick, ready to take whatever action was necessary. Finally, Omar stepped back and gave Skye a little bow.

"My apologies, Your Highness. This was obviously not meant to be tonight, but there will be another occasion, I trust." He turned to Sandor. "I understand you'll be returning my money to me?"

"Yes."

"I'll go with you," Nick said, his eyes still not leaving Omar's face, "to make sure there are no issues."

"Don't try to see my sister again," Erik finally spoke up. "The divorce will be final in a few weeks, and she never wants to see you again."

"She has no say in the matter," Omar retorted. "That's not how things work in our country."

"I don't know what country you're talking about, but women have rights in ours."

"Not for long." He walked away, his head held high, leaving us all holding our collective breaths.

"What the fuck does that mean?" I whispered worriedly.

"I don't fucking know." Erik blew out a breath. "But I need to talk to my father."

"I want to go home," Skye said in a shaky voice.

"Hang in there just a little longer," I told her. "It's going to be okay. You're safe here with us."

"I think I'm going to be sick," she whispered.

"Come on, sit down." I dragged her to the nearest table and pushed her into a chair.

"I'll get her some water." Erik motioned to a waiter as I sat beside Skye.

"Breathe," I told her. "You're okay. He can't hurt you. We're all here."

"But he came all the way to Las Vegas, to this event, to find me. How did he even know I would be here? I hadn't fully decided until a few days ago, and only our family knew."

"He was probably hedging his bets," Erik said, handing her a glass of water. "It's a huge event and you're about to be single again. It made sense that you would attend."

"What does this mean? I can't even leave the house again because he's looking for me?" Her eyes were filled with trepidation. "And what the hell was he talking about that women in our country have rights for now? He scares me."

"He scares me too," Erik said quietly.

"I wish you were going to be king," she said sadly. "He wouldn't be able to do or say those horrible things if you were."

I glanced at my fiancé and saw a muscle twitching in his cheek. He wanted to be king too. Too bad that could never happen.

32

E*rik*

THE NIGHT ENDED ON A SOUR NOTE EVEN THOUGH WE TRIED TO KEEP UP appearances in front of the other guests, who had no idea anything had happened. Omar had been given his money back and escorted from the building. Security had been told he was persona non grata at the Charleston Hotel, and though it was over, it felt far from anything even resembling over. My gut told me Omar was in cahoots with Anwar and they were up to something. Whether it was to spoil my wedding or something much worse, I had no way of knowing, but I felt it in my bones. And it scared the hell out of me.

Casey, my mother, and my sister went to bed when we got home, but my father, Sandor, Aziz, my father's security team and I sat up late into the night discussing upgrading security, security for the wedding, and our overall thoughts about what had transpired tonight. We sipped brandy and scotch until nearly dawn, exhausting every possible scenario that could go wrong and not feeling confident we were prepared for any of them.

By the time I went up to bed, it was starting to get light outside and Casey moved into my arms.

"Were you up all night?" she asked sleepily.

"I'm okay, go back to sleep."

"You're worried," she murmured.

"A little, but I don't want you to worry." I kissed the top of her head as she snuggled closer.

"I worry if you worry."

"Shhh. Our baby prince needs his rest."

"Our baby princess is giving me indigestion."

"I'm sorry. Try to rest." I felt her relax back into slumber as I held her, but sleep didn't come to me for a long time.

THE DAYS LEADING UP TO THE WEDDING WERE BUSY, BUT I'D STOPPED ENJOYING them and spent my time trying to figure out what was going on in Limaj. There were too many closed-door meetings with my father and our security teams, and that only increased as the king prepared to come to town. He'd booked the top two floors of the Charleston, and the city itself seemed to be preparing for his arrival. Traffic would be closed off on the Strip when his motorcade would arrive at the hotel and I was beginning to wonder about the wisdom of getting married here in Las Vegas. It was already a chaotic city and the addition of the royal family's arrival would add a layer of crazy I wished we didn't have to deal with.

To her credit, Casey wasn't nearly as frantic as I was. At least not that I could see. She moved through each day with a smile, taking care of each detail that came up, spending time with both her family and mine, and using the evenings to soothe me in ways I hadn't been expecting. She was so much more than a beautiful, talented musician. I'd known she was special, but not how special, how integral she'd become to my existence. Skye had begun to warm up to her after the way Casey had come to her rescue at the charity gala, which had been surprising but in a good way. I should have been having the time of my life right now, but I wasn't. Every day I woke up with a sense of dread, and I wanted to take Casey and run to a deserted island somewhere.

I'd known something was coming, but when it came it was so much worse than anything I'd been imagining. My phone rang at five thirty in the morning, ten days before the wedding and the day after the first of the family had arrived in Las Vegas to do some sightseeing before the wedding festivities started. I fumbled for the phone, getting twisted in the sheets we'd mangled during our lovemaking the night before, and finally grabbed it.

"Yes, hello?"

"It's me." Sandor sounded choked up. "You need to come down to your father's den. Now."

"What's going on?"

"Now." Sandor disconnected, and I practically levitated to my feet, trying to stay quiet so I didn't wake Casey.

I pulled on sweats and a T-shirt and slid my feet into running shoes before leaving our suite and jogging down the stairs to find the others. I knew it was bad when I spotted my mother in a robe, her hair sticking up and no makeup. She was always well put together, even first thing in the morning, so seeing her like this filled me with dread.

"What's happened?" I asked as I practically skidded into the room.

My father looked up with red-rimmed eyes. "There's been an accident. The king and queen are dead."

"Sonofabitch." Accident my ass. I knew with every fiber of my being that if the king was dead, it had not been an accident. My heart beat painfully as I began to pace. "What happened?"

"There was a meeting of the special council at the palace." My father sighed, swiping at his eyes. "Members and immediate family were called in to vote on..." He cleared his throat. "Isak wanted to award Casey the title of princess as part of your wedding present. There was to be a brief discussion and the vote. We spoke last night, I gave him my verbal vote, and he didn't expect any resistance from anyone. He'd already spoken to Anwar, who'd reluctantly agreed so everyone was called in to make it official. Anwar, Rafael, Yolanda, Yusef, Vardan, Miriam, and Daniil."

"Oh god." I fell into a chair at the thought of something happening to Daniil.

"There was a bomb." Dad took a breath. "It wiped out the east wing of the palace."

"How many?" I asked through clenched teeth.

"All but two."

"All..." I squeezed my eyes shut. "All but Anwar."

"And Daniil."

"That bastard. That no-good, conniving, piece of shit..." I let out a string of expletives in my native tongue.

"Daniil was suspicious when Anwar got up in the middle of the vote, claiming to need to use the facilities." Sandor looked as furious as I felt. "He followed him. Anwar and his two closest aides went into the safe room where the jewels are kept."

"Which is made of concrete and steel," I grunted.

"Daniil knew something was wrong and ran back to warn the others, but the bomb went off before he got there. He's banged up, but okay. I spoke to him about twenty minutes ago."

"Sonofabitch!" There was a crystal candy bowl on the table next to my chair and I flung it across the room, watching it shatter against the wall, brightly colored candies flying in every direction.

My mother approached me and leaned down to wrap her arms around me as I fought off tears. The king and queen. Vardan, whom I'd been close to. Rafael and his young wife. Studious Yusef. Innocent, oblivious Miriam. Even Miriam's husband, quiet Uncle Harold, had been in the room, even though he didn't have voting rights.

How the fuck had Anwar gotten away with this? The loss of life was unfathomable to me, and the damage to the palace was heartbreaking. The west wing. Where my suite was located. Skye's suite. A second home to me. Gone.

"Thank god Elen was already here in Vegas," my father said. "Daniil and the others were planning to leave tomorrow."

"I have to go to my brother," Sandor said. "I fear he's in danger. If Anwar's goal was to eliminate the rest of the bloodline..."

"I should go," I said automatically. "Technically, you're next in line after Anwar because of my father's abdication. I'm the logical choice because as long as you and Daniil are alive, I'm no competition to him."

"Cousin, you are his *greatest* competition," Sandor said. "He knows you are the rightful ruler, the one who should ascend the throne. I gave up my place in the succession when I took the oath of Bodyguard to the Royal Family. He also knows the people of Limaj love you and have embraced your future wife as well. His attempts to discredit her in the press fell flat, and poisoning his father's mind against her didn't work either. You are his greatest rival and it's you who has to be careful."

"Whatever he perceives as a threat has no bearing on reality," I said impatiently. "I'm not in the running unless and until every one of you is dead, and that's not happening on my watch."

"Be that as it may, where you go, I go." Sandor faced me with his arms folded across his chest.

Someone brought coffee, tea, and pastries, though no one had an appetite. We were glued to multiple televisions and websites, scouring the news for updated information even as my father had the jet prepared for a trip to Limaj. There was a lot to do, but I had to talk to Casey. Even though I'd been unconsciously preparing for something to happen, reality was jarring, and I was out of sorts. She would ground me; she always did, though we'd never gone through anything like this in our short time together.

She was in the bathroom when I got to our suite and she looked up in surprise as she came out.

"Hi. I was just going to look for you."

"Something's happened." I reached for her and pulled her onto my lap as I sank onto the edge of the bed.

"Oh no."

I told her what I knew, and the tears that filled her eyes caused my own to come to the surface. "I have to go," I whispered against her hair.

"I know." She pressed her face into the side of my neck. "Promise me you'll be back, Erik."

"I'll never leave you for long," I whispered, kissing her temple. "Come on, don't cry."

"We should cancel the wedding."

"No. Absolutely not." I pulled away slightly and lifted her chin. "I'm not letting that bastard take this away from us too."

"It'll be considered in bad taste."

"No, it won't. We'll add a special tribute to the family members we lost, maybe a photo collage or something, make it a celebration of their lives as well as the beginning of ours. We can't cancel because that's what he wants. He wants to disrupt everything, throw the royal family into turmoil and the country into chaos. I won't allow it. The people will need something as beautiful as a wedding to help them heal after such a loss."

"If we go ahead with the wedding, then we have to address why, because it really will look gauche."

"We'll hire a PR team and set up an interview for when I get back. My plan is to go and meet with Anwar. I'll pay my respects, feign interest in the funeral arrangements, perhaps even pretend to pledge my support and allegiance. I have to know what's going on, what his plans are."

"The wedding is in ten days, Erik. How are you going to do all this in ten days?"

"I don't know, but I have to try. Do you trust me?"

"Of course."

"I'm going to meet with Anwar, get a feel for what's happening, and come home."

"Be careful, Erik. He's so much more dangerous than we imagined."

"I know, but someone has to go."

"Won't people think it's strange that the whole family isn't going to mourn, plan the funeral, all that stuff?"

"Perhaps, but at this point, my concern is getting Daniil out of the country and seeing if I can find out what Anwar is planning. He's going to be king now unless we can prove that he murdered the family, and I'm probably the only one who can do that."

"He'll kill you too."

"He might try, but I'm not stupid, and both my father and I have allies within Parliament and the rest of the government."

"I don't like this." Her eyes were watery as she looked at me.

"I know." I brought her fingers to my mouth and kissed each one. "I don't either, but I have to do this. Please say you understand."

"I do." She wrapped her arms around my neck and held on for dear life.

33

Casey

Erik left for Limaj the next day, promising to be home as soon as possible. I'd had a full schedule finalizing wedding plans, but most of it was done, leaving me time to be was nervous now. Instead of dwelling on it, though, I spent the day at my condo, preparing it to be put up for sale. We weren't going to live here, after all, so why keep it? I tossed a pile of catalogs and old magazines into the recycling bin and emptied the guest bathroom medicine cabinet. My mother and the personal security guard Erik had hired had come with me and it was nice having company. I could have hired someone to do it, but I wanted to go through everything myself. Everything for the wedding was taken care of, but selling my condo, formally moving into Ben and Kari's, and packing for the honeymoon were still on the horizon.

Today was one of the last days I had left to pack up my personal belongings and get them out of the condo, so I was making the most of some very rare down time. I'd already emptied the closet in the spare room, moved all of my guitars to my dad's new recording studio, and made arrangements for a charity organization to come pick up my furniture since Erik and I wouldn't need it at Ben and Kari's and we would buy new things once we found a house. As excited as I was about marrying him, saying goodbye to my old life felt strange.

"Casey, should I just throw out everything in the refrigerator?" my mother called.

"Yes, please. Thank you." I'd slowly been picking up clothes from my condo each time I thought of something I needed, so my personal belongings were sparse. I'd packed a few boxes of picture frames, photo albums, books, and childhood memories, and my mother was going to handle the linen closet at some point, which left very little for me to do. More than anything, I was trying to keep busy so I wouldn't have a panic attack over the thought of something happening to Erik in Limaj.

"Are you all right, Ms. Hart?" My new bodyguard, Joe Westfield, was a retired Marine who'd come highly recommended.

"Just kind of stressed," I responded, smiling. I sank onto the edge of the bed and rubbed my temples.

"You're a little pale," he said quietly. "Let me get you a bottle of water."

I wanted to protest, but he was right. In fact, today was the first day I'd felt anything but sleepy with the pregnancy. I was eleven weeks along now and felt great in general, but today I'd been queasy and rundown, as if Erik had taken all my energy with him when he left this morning. It was odd to be so in tune to another human being that their absence impacted you physically, but that's how I felt.

Joe brought me a bottle of water, and I opened it gratefully. "Thank you." I took a long pull and sighed. "I guess I'm more nervous about Erik being gone than I thought."

"Don't worry. Nothing's going to happen to you on my watch, and I sent one of my men with Erik as well. Everything's going to be okay."

"Thanks for the reassurance, but we have no way of knowing what's going to happen. Anwar is crazy."

Joe nodded. "Perhaps, but I know I'll die before I let anything happen to you, and the man I sent with Erik is former Special Forces. They don't get any more badass than that." He squeezed my shoulder. "It'll be okay, kiddo."

I wanted to believe him, so I forced myself back to my feet and the task at hand.

I DIDN'T HEAR FROM ERIK UNTIL THE NEXT DAY, AND BY THE TIME HE CALLED me I was beside myself with worry.

"Where are you?" I cried when I answered the phone.

"Hello, love. I'm okay, and we have Daniil. We're at a safe house not far from the city, a place no one but my father, Sandor, and I know about. Things in Limaj are deteriorating rapidly so we're taking care not to let our guard down."

"I saw on the news there's going to be a memorial service tomorrow for everyone that was lost and that there aren't enough remains for there to be a proper funeral."

"Anwar wants to sweep this under the rug as quickly as possible to get on with his own coronation. He's an embarrassment to our family and the whole country. Parliament is in an uproar, there are protests in the streets, and when we left this morning, he was threatening to turn off access to the internet for the general public."

"Turn off access to the internet?" I echoed in shock. "Can he do that?"

"As a dictator-style monarch, he can do whatever the hell he wants once he officially takes over."

"Erik, you should leave. Get out of there."

"I'm meeting with Anwar tomorrow to get a feel for what's going on. There wasn't time to gather the government today, so Parliament and the royal assembly are meeting tomorrow at ten o'clock. Hopefully, by evening we'll be in London."

"What if he tries to set off another bomb while everyone is gathered together?"

"I think security will be tight. If he does something like that before he's officially crowned King, I think the country will implode, which doesn't bode well for his delusions. He wants money and power—he'll have neither if there's no one running anything at all."

"Oh, Erik, I'm scared."

"I know, baby, but we had to get Daniil, and I have to talk with Anwar. There's too much at stake for the people for me to just turn my back. My father has been in touch with several of our allies who are reluctant to allow Anwar to ascend the throne, so there's still a chance we can turn things around. I just don't have any answers yet. Tomorrow will tell us what we need to know."

I didn't know what to say to that, so I changed the subject. "Everyone here is kind of subdued and sad, worried about everyone, especially Daniil."

"He's hurt pretty badly, but he'll survive. We're going to move him to a hospital in London as soon as we can leave the country tomorrow."

"I love you, Erik. Please hurry home."

"I love you too, sweetheart. I'll be home as soon as I can."

. . .

WE WERE A SUBDUED, QUIET GROUP THAT EVENING AT DINNER, AND FOR THE first time I felt strangely out of place as Erik's family began to reminisce about Uncle Isak, Aunt Klara, and the others. They told funny stories about them as children, as teens, and as they grew into adulthood. No one said much about Yusef or Rafael, though they mentioned Miriam and Vardan more than once.

I had nothing to add since I'd only met Isak and Klara a couple of times and didn't know the others at all, so I excused myself after dinner and went up to our room to call my parents. I'd wanted to stay with them this week but it was a logistical nightmare security-wise, so I'd agreed to stay here.

"Hi, sweetie." My dad's voice almost brought me to tears.

"Hey, Daddy."

"What's the matter, honey?"

"I just..." I sighed. "I miss Erik, and I'm worried about him and everything is so sad with what happened in Limaj. I don't know what to do because I'd never even met most of them so it's hard for me to mourn people I don't know. Erik knew them, though, so I'm trying to be supportive, but I'm hormonal and cranky and now I think I'm gonna cry." I took a shuddery breath, trying to keep my emotions under control.

"Don't cry," he said softly. "But you can if you want to. Then you need to dry your face and keep a stiff upper lip. Erik will be back in a few days and you're going to get married and everything is going to be fine."

"Why am I having a hard time believing that anymore?"

"Because you're pregnant and hormonal. You wanna talk to your mom? 'Cause I can't really help with all the pregnancy stuff."

I chuckled. "No. I want you to tell me about the studio and all the stuff going on over there. I need a distraction."

"Oh, well, that I can do."

We talked about equipment: soundboards, amps, pedals, and specialized computer software. Running a recording studio was a lot more complicated than just playing music, and I realized I had a lot to learn if I was going to be involved.

"You're not going to have time for all this with a new baby," he said. "You should be focusing on your new family, not my retirement hobby."

"Retirement hobby? You've been talking about a studio most of my life. You finally have the time to do it, and I want to be part of it. Especially if I've got a new baby at home keeping me from being able to tour."

"You don't have a band anymore," he pointed out gently.

"Don't remind me."

"Well, you'll have plenty of opportunity to check out musicians when the studio opens in January. We've already booked our first band and I'm planning to produce a solo project for..."

We talked music for another hour, then I talked to my mother for a few minutes before begging off. Limaj was eleven hours ahead of us timewise, so it was eight in the morning there now and Erik was probably getting ready for his big meeting. I ached to hear his voice, so I grabbed the phone and dialed his number.

"Morning, love." He sounded tired, and my heart broke a little for him.

"How are you?"

"I'm okay. How about you? How's my son?"

"Your daughter is fine, sleeping peacefully right now. At least I think so."

He chuckled. "*He* is just waiting for you to fall asleep so he can start bouncing around."

"Since I haven't felt *her* move yet, I'm not sure how I'd tell."

"How long until we can find out the sex?"

"Probably another eight weeks."

"That's too long," he protested mildly. "I want to know now."

"I'm sorry?" I laughed.

"I love you, babe, but I have to go. We're getting ready to leave the safe house and head to Parliament."

"I know I've said this a hundred times, but please be careful. I don't know what I'd do if anything ever happened to you."

"I'll be okay. I've got backup, and we have plans B and C should plan A go south."

"I love you."

"I love you too. Try not to worry, okay?"

"Will you call me when it's over? Even if you wake me up?"

"We may have to move quickly, but I'll call you as soon as it's safe. I promise."

"Until later."

"Until later."

34

E*rik*

WE GOT TO PARLIAMENT HOUSE EARLY, HOPING TO CATCH SOME OF OUR known allies alone before the general meeting, but it was nerve-wracking walking into the building. I could take care of myself and Sandor was a force to be reckoned with, but neither of us could take on rocket launchers or bombs. I was wearing a bulletproof vest and we were all armed, but there was no way to predict what Anwar had up his sleeve.

"Your Highness." I turned, knowing the greeting was for me, and I was relieved to see General Martin Sarrano, an old friend and ally of my father's. He was the leader of our military, a strong, proud man who'd been a staunch supporter of Uncle Isak and his vision for Limaj.

"General." I shook his hand.

"Condolences on the loss of your uncle and the rest of your family."

"Thank you. It's a great loss for all of Limaj."

"Indeed." Our eyes met meaningfully.

"At some point, I'd like to get together," I said quietly. "Perhaps we can discuss some options for the future."

"I fear it may be too late for that," the older man responded. "But I would enjoy your company nonetheless."

We walked toward the general assembly room, and I lowered my voice.

"Talk to me," I said. "Tell me what the others are saying. How much support does Anwar have?"

"Too much," he admitted. "There are those pushing for a theocracy, including Anwar. I've heard rumors that he believes if we allow the religious sect to run the country, they'll be so busy with their Bibles and Korans they won't notice him taking all the oil and trade profits for himself."

"Can we stop this?"

"I don't know how, Your Highness," replied General Sarrano. "I fear life as we know it is about the change."

We stepped into the assembly room, and I was assaulted by a cacophony of sights and sounds. People I'd known for many years suddenly looked old, drawn, heartbroken. Everyone was speaking in hushed, whispered tones, their body language cautious, subdued. The usual energy and presence of the leaders of our government had disappeared, and the trepidation in the room was almost palpable. Many averted their eyes as I approached, while others rose to shake my hand and offer more condolences. It was an endless cycle and I was glad to finally reach my usual seat, an honorary spot to the right of where Anwar would stand when he addressed the assembly.

"I go where you go," Aziz whispered to me. "Sandor has given me strict instructions. I am not to be more than five feet from your side."

"I know." I nodded.

Because Sandor was technically next in line to the throne if you took me out of the equation, he was keeping his distance, sitting in the back of the room where he could keep an eye on everything should an attack be imminent. Our lives were in danger, we knew that, but we had to be here today. This was our last chance to delay Anwar's ascent to the throne, and though I had a feeling it was a lost cause, we had to try. Sandor, who hated all things politics and had been anxious to train as my bodyguard so he wouldn't have to think about anything but my safety, would make a far better king than Anwar. Hell, Aziz would make a better king than Anwar, and he wasn't even royalty.

I took my seat at the main table, refusing anything to drink because I didn't trust Anwar not to poison the lot of us. It was a little paranoid to think that way, but after the events of the last few days, I wouldn't put anything past him. Part of me was restless, anxious to get as far away as possible, while the rest of me wanted to fight. I couldn't explain my disparate thoughts and feelings, almost like I was two separate people. I liked anonymity, living a carefree life of leisure, and focusing on humanitarian and charitable efforts. Now that I was going to become a father, I yearned for the woman I loved and our child, picturing us in a big house and building a happy, light-hearted future.

On the other hand, I'd felt the slight tug toward the throne since childhood. If Daniil or Sandor or even Yusef had been the one to ascend, I would have been okay in my role as prince, ambassador, or something similar. But Anwar made my heart scream in agony for my people, my country, my heritage. He was an asshole with zero empathy and no heart. He would destroy my country as surely as I was breathing, and I couldn't deny the overwhelming need to stop him. It wasn't feasible, I knew this in my heart, but the feelings remained all the same.

"Good morning." Anwar strode in wearing...a ceremonial cape. The one his father wore to coronations and events of state. Holy shit, he'd lost his fucking mind because he was carrying a staff as well. My thirty-year-old, Harvard-educated, Ferrari-driving cousin was walking around like something out of a historical fiction novel.

I wasn't the only one in shock. I could see it on the faces of General Sarrano and many others, though most dipped their heads to hide their astonishment. Sandor met my gaze across the room and gave me the tiniest shake of his head. Something told us it was over, and we had to get out before it was too late.

"We gather here today to address my ascension to the throne," Anwar began without preamble. "The unexpected and extremely unfathomable deaths of my father and brothers brings me great sadness, but in order to find the perpetrators and bring them to justice, we must unite and strike back quickly and forcefully. I move that we bring a motion to the floor to vote on my ascension."

The room broke out in a chorus of discussion, shouts, and protests. I watched Anwar's face get redder and redder as he exchanged looks with his two aides, who were whispering to him furiously. I didn't know either man, which worried me, because it was usually a big deal to rise to a position like that. The fact that he'd brought in outsiders was just another nail in the coffin of my country and I didn't know what to do about it. I wanted to speak up, beg Parliament to appoint someone else—Sandor was next in line and right here—but that's not how it worked. That was probably why everyone was in a frenzy now. No matter what anyone wanted, the rules of law regarding ascension were clear, and in the current circumstances, Anwar was a shoo-in.

"Enough!" Anwar banged a gavel on the podium and raised his arms, allowing his cape to flow behind him. "We will vote. Now."

"Your Highness." Parliament's high speaker, a position comparable to the

U.S. speaker of the House, rose to his feet. "This is not the proper procedure. We must first—"

"Your Majesty." Anwar met the man's gaze. "You will address me as Your Majesty."

"Not yet," the man responded, standing up a little straighter. "We must follow the rules of assembly and the tenets of Parliament."

"Remove him." Anwar motioned to soldiers at the back of the room, and just like that, the man was forcefully pulled to the ground, handcuffed, and yanked out the back. His screams could be heard until the doors closed, and voices erupted in protest.

Anwar looked around. "Well? Who wants to be next? Do you think I'm playing games here? This is my throne, and by the end of today, I will have the votes I need." He turned to General Sarrano. "General, what say you? Do I have the confidence of the military?"

Martin looked at me helplessly, and in that moment, I knew everything was lost. He would vote for Anwar and that sick bastard would take the throne.

I had no choice but to watch in horror as each member of Parliament slowly, reluctantly, raised their hands in favor of Anwar's ascension. My blood boiled as I wondered what he had on these men and if his show of power had been enough for them to sell their souls to the devil. Had he bribed them? Threatened their families? I had no way of knowing but I couldn't watch anymore. As the vote came to an end, I motioned to Aziz and rose to my feet.

"Cousin." Anwar stood in front of me. "Come. Let us talk in private for a moment."

"I'm not sure what there is to say."

"Oh, come now. Surely you'd like to offer condolences on the loss of my parents?"

"I don't think you give two shits about your parents."

"You want to do this here?"

"Why not? You going to have me arrested as well?"

"I just might."

"Good luck with that." I wasn't afraid of this asshole, even though I probably should have been, but I was too angry and frustrated.

"You were never in the running," he hissed. "So what do you care? Go back to your life, your pretty American, before I change my mind about letting you."

"Letting me? Are you now god in addition to king?"

"Don't push me, Erik. I'll let you leave because you have no power, but you see what I can do to those who try to cross me."

"You mean like your father? Is that why you had him killed? Because he finally realized you aren't worthy of the job."

"He was sick and getting worse." Anwar shrugged. "I did him a favor."

"Yusef and Raffie weren't sick. What about Vardan? Did you just systematically eliminate all your competition?"

We were drawing a crowd now and out of the corner of my eye I saw Sandor on his phone.

"Yusef and Raffie, well, they weren't team players. The others were simply in the wrong place at the wrong time. It's unfortunate it had to go down this way."

"What the hell did you do?" I demanded, shocked and horrified. I hadn't wanted to believe it but he wasn't even attempting to deny what he'd done. "Did you seriously have your parents, siblings, and cousins killed?"

"Sometimes a leader has to take matters into his own hands," Anwar said.

"You're a murderer," I hissed, barely contained fury bubbling to the surface.

"Take care how you talk to your king," Anwar responded coldly, his dark eyes meeting mine menacingly.

"Not *my* king," I said through clenched teeth. "Never my king."

"I've been patient because we've grown up together, and your father's abdication makes you no threat, but I will not tolerate insolence."

"What are you going to do?" I shot back. "Send me to my room?"

Anwar laughed, but the sound chilled me to the bone. "You, my dear cousin, are in for a rude awakening if you think I'll allow you to blaspheme my name. I am now King of Limaj and you will bow to me, acknowledge me, and publicly proclaim your allegiance. Or else."

"Not a chance in hell."

"It would be a terrible shame if your pretty little fiancée became the victim of a fatal accident before her wedding day, wouldn't it? And then I would have to bring Skye home to face charges for leaving her husband. Sharia Law will soon be half of the land here with the Muslim contingent of our population. And I can make it so it's the half she's in."

There were no words for what I felt right now. Fury didn't begin to cover the anger raging through me like a tsunami of fire, but I kept my face neutral as I held my ground. "If you hurt Casey, there will be nowhere you can run from me. I will have the CIA, Interpol, and every mercenary in the world hunting you down until you're dead. Do *not* threaten the people I love."

"Then don't threaten *me*."

It was a stalemate that neither of us were going to win. Not today anyway, and I turned on my heel, striding from the room, Sandor and Aziz behind me.

"Heed my warning, cousin," Anwar called after me. "There are worse fates than death for your pretty American whore. She would make a lovely addition to my harem, don't you think?"

"Your harem?" I had to turn and squint slightly, wondering why no one else had said a word during our exchange. "We haven't had harems in Limaj in over a hundred years. What the hell are you talking about?"

"It was my idea." Omar stood up, smirking, and I cursed myself for not noticing him before. "I think it was a lovely tradition and it'll be fun to have a different woman in my bed every night. Especially since I'll be married to the passionless corpse that is your sister."

"Yes, but she'll give you legitimate heirs," Anwar reminded him. "And once we have her back in Limaj, she'll learn to please you or suffer the consequences."

"You're a sick fuck." I continued out the door because staying another second wouldn't end well for me and I wasn't ready to die.

"Does Casey like it in the ass?" he called after me.

I momentarily froze but didn't turn around. He was goading me, and I couldn't afford to take a swing right now, even though I wanted to more than I wanted to take my next breath. I fucking hated this prick.

WE WALKED OUT TO THE WAITING SUV AND MOTIONED FOR THE DRIVER TO GO. In the back of my mind, I wondered if Anwar would detain us, and I wasn't going to risk it. I had a lot to consider and even more to do. So much so, I didn't know what to do first. The only thing I knew for sure was that my life as I'd known it was over. Nothing was going to be the same for me or anyone close to me, and I needed to talk to my father immediately.

"Erik, what's going on?" He sounded frantic when he answered.

I told him what had happened.

"Get out of the country right now," he hissed.

"Believe me, we're going to pick up Daniil, and we should be in the air within two hours."

"Make it ninety minutes if you can."

"We're going as fast as we can."

"He actually threatened Casey and Skye?"

"I told you he was fucking crazy, and with Omar as his right-hand man, it's downright terrifying."

"What are you going to do?"

"I have a CIA contact in Monte Carlo. We're heading there tonight. I'm hoping she can help. If not, choices are limited." I didn't want to say too much on an unsecured line like this one.

"Erik, the wedding is in five days."

"I know. Believe me, I know."

"I'll take care of everyone here—you just be careful, yeah?"

"I've got Aziz, Sandor, and Daniil. We'll be fine."

"I love you, son."

"I love you too." I disconnected and stared out into the darkness.

"So, Monte Carlo?" Sandor asked.

"Yeah."

"That woman, Liz. She's CIA. You trust her?"

"I have to because right now she's the only person I can think of that may be able to help."

"Then Monte Carlo it is."

35

C^{asey}

I'D BEEN SO LUCKY AVOIDING THE PRESS UNTIL NOW, IT WAS INEVITABLE THEY would catch up to me. Leaving the shop after the final fitting for my wedding dress with my mother, Aunt Kari, and Joe, I was completely unprepared for the onslaught. Joe immediately got in front of me, but cameras were going off and I saw that they were recording everything, so I managed to calm my racing heart and get Joe to relax.

"Casey, is the wedding still on?" someone called out.

"Will you be delaying your nuptials in light of His Royal Highness's loss?"

"Is it true your fiancé endorsed the new King of Limaj?"

They were firing questions faster than I could answer them, but I was an old pro at dealing with the press and though I hated having to do it, I would handle this like I always had—with honesty and integrity, to the degree that it was safe for us.

"Please." I held up a hand. "One at a time."

"Casey, is the wedding still on?"

"Yes, it is. We discussed it as a family, with Prince Benjamin and Princess Kari, as well as Erik's cousins and extended family. Though we're grieving the loss of King Isak, Queen Klara, and the others, we refuse to let a group of terrorists ruin our special day. We believe they would want us to continue with our celebration, despite the tragedy."

"There are rumors that you and Erik have split up, which is why he hasn't been seen in Las Vegas this week, leading up to the wedding."

"Erik went to pay his respects to...the new king, and offer his condolences. He'll be home soon, and we're getting married as planned."

It went on for a few minutes, but finally Joe ushered us into the SUV and we slowly pulled out of the parking lot.

"Shit." I leaned my head back against the seat and closed my eyes. "How did they find me? The shop wasn't supposed to tell anyone."

"Probably a process of elimination. Most of the big papers have enough reporters to have them waiting at each of the bigger dress shops in town," Aunt Kari said. "It was only a matter of time."

"Did I do okay?" I asked. "I felt so stiff and formal, like I was reading from a script, even though I wasn't."

"You did fine." Mom squeezed my arm.

"I wish Erik was here." I let my head loll to the side.

"Soon," Aunt Kari whispered. "He'll be here soon."

"We can't get caught off guard like that," Joe muttered. "We need to be more careful than this, Casey. We don't know what Anwar is capable of or how far his reach is."

"I know."

"Asshole," Mom grunted from the back seat. "I've never met him, but I really hate him."

"You'd hate him more if you met him," Aunt Kari added.

"How did Isak and Klara raise such a jerk?" I wondered aloud.

"Sometimes it just happens," Aunt Kari responded.

I thought about the child inside of me, and that didn't seem possible. I already loved him or her so much, the thought of him growing up and killing me was beyond the scope of reality for me. I knew it existed in the world—hell, we'd all but witnessed it firsthand—but it didn't feel real. Somehow, I would do everything in my power to make sure I never raised a kid like that.

FRIENDS AND FAMILY STARTED TO ARRIVE IN LAS VEGAS, AND THOUGH I MISSED Erik desperately, there was no time to do anything but keep moving forward. Jade was great at distracting me from all the chaos going on, but there were so many changes happening so fast, I was struggling to keep up. Without Erik to keep me grounded, I was being pulled in too many directions when all I really wanted to do was curl up in a chair with my guitar. I hadn't played in weeks and I itched to sneak off to the studio, but there was never a free moment. If there wasn't something wedding-related to do, I felt obligated to spend time with Elen and the many friends who'd begun to arrive, but they'd been doing a lot of drinking and I felt out of place since I couldn't join them. Instead, I smiled and hugged people a lot, trying to keep up appearances and pretend I wasn't terrified for the man I loved.

"Casey, are you ready to go?" Skye stood in the doorway of our suite and I looked up from where I'd been daydreaming by the window.

"Go?"

"Remember? We're having a girls' night out?"

"Oh." I frowned. "I really don't feel up to it. I think I'll stay home."

She cocked her head. "You're the bride. Without you, there's really no point."

"Honestly, with all the death and sadness lately, I'm not feeling very bride-like."

"I know, but our mothers have planned a special evening for you, and it would be a shame to disappoint them. Besides, we need a night of fun. Come on, you look fine the way you are. It's going to be casual."

I sighed but got to my feet. "All right, let me find some shoes." I dug around for a pair of boots and pulled them on.

"Put on some lipstick; you're a bit pale."

This was new, getting a pep talk from Skye, but I did as she suggested and grabbed my purse before following her out to where Elen and Aunt Kari waited.

"Where are we going?" I asked, getting into the SUV.

"The Charleston, of course." Aunt Kari giggled.

"We have champagne!" Elen pulled out a bottle and I nearly groaned but Skye pulled out another.

"And this is sparkling water infused with grapes and pineapple," Skye said. "I think it tastes similar to champagne, but contains no alcohol."

I smiled. She was trying so hard. They all were. I was just in such a funk. My body was beginning to change now that I was twelve weeks along, and I hadn't been sleeping well without Erik. The stress of the last few weeks had been catching up to me, and I was hanging on for dear life because I didn't have much choice.

"Are you sure you're all right?" Aunt Kari asked softly. "You're quite pale."

"I'm okay." I tried to put on a brave face since so few people knew I was pregnant. "I'm not sleeping well and it's hard to be cheerful with Erik gone..."

"You mustn't let anything overpower one of the most important times of your life," Aunt Kari said softly. "I will mourn our lost family members later, when you've left on your honeymoon. For now, we're here to rejoice this wonderful event and help you celebrate. No, you must not let this ruin your wedding. I forbid it."

It was nice of her to say but not as easy to carry out because my heart was heavy, as if I had an impending sense of doom.

Once we arrived, though, it was hard to stay depressed. My mother and a plethora of friends were all waiting for me in one of the smaller ballrooms at the hotel. They'd decorated for a party, with streamers and balloons, a chocolate fountain, and shirtless waiters walking around with hors d'oeuvres. There was even a stripper pole set up in the middle of the room. I laughed when I saw it and ran to hug my mother, who was grinning at me.

"Since you didn't have a bachelorette party, we decided to put one together for you at the last minute. We thought it might get your mind off your troubles."

"Mom, you're so crazy!" I shook my head at her.

"That's what you love about me." She kissed my cheek and then moved off to greet other guests that were arriving.

It was a full house, with so many people I loved in the room, I was able to forget about my worries for a few hours. I mingled, laughing and drinking fruity sparkling water as I listened to unsolicited advice about marriage, children and even the honeymoon. I didn't blush easily, but hearing Liz's sixty-five-year-old mother talking about the new position she and her eighty-year-old husband had recently tried had me turning shades of red I couldn't even fathom. Liz was sitting next to me, and she rolled her eyes at her mother with a fond smile.

"Mom, enough. I'm going to throw caution to the wind and guess Casey won't be a virgin on her wedding night."

I laughed, nudging her with my elbow. "How did you know?"

"Oh, just a guess."

"But what fun it will be to pretend you are," Liz's mom, Melissa, said with an impish smile. "Role play is sexy and adds spice to the bedroom."

"Mo-om," Liz groaned.

"Oh, like you don't do it," Melissa shot back.

"Yeah, but I don't want to hear about you and *Dad* doing it," she said, cringing.

"Oh, what are you and Eddie doing that Liz doesn't want to hear about?" Mom asked, joining the conversation with a mischievous grin.

I looked at Liz with a put-upon sigh. "Look what you've started."

"Sorry." Liz grimaced.

Then we all laughed.

"Please tell me you're not looking for wedding night advice," Mom teased, looking at me with a funny face.

"No, I definitely am not." I laughed at her.

"Wedding nights can be so boring if you don't spice them up." Mom held out her hands, palms up. "I mean, your dad and I had already been living together for a while before we eloped, so it was just another night for us, but you know, he was a crazy rocker dude, so we were always swinging from the rafters and shit."

"Mom!" I was used to her stories about her and my father's sexcapades, but I had no idea how Erik's family would react and Elen had just joined the conversation.

"I lost my virginity in Paris," Elen said dreamily. "We're no longer together, but I still think of him fondly. He was a French artist, and his loft overlooked the city. I can't imagine a more romantic time or place to have sex for the first time."

The women all took turns talking about their first sexual experiences or wedding nights, and we were all laughing and making sweet sounds like "awwww" and "ohhhh." If it had been any other time or place, it would have been ridiculous, but it somehow felt right and the perfect way to spend an evening with special women in my life before the wedding. Especially with Erik so far away.

I started getting sleepy around midnight, and Joe brought us home. I fell asleep practically the moment my head hit the pillow and dreamt that Erik was kissing me. My heart began to beat faster and faster until I jerked awake, realizing that he was, indeed, kissing me. I gasped out his name in surprise.

"When did you get home?" I whispered in the darkness.

"Came back like I promised," he murmured. His breath was heavy with alcohol, and I squinted up at him in surprise.

"Are you okay?" I asked. "You've been drinking?"

"Yup." He kissed me again, his body heavy on mine, erection pressing against my thigh. There was no mistaking his intention, and I wouldn't have said no anyway.

"I need you," he groaned.

I sighed with contentment as he slid inside of me. This was when I felt most alive, and the week's stress melted away with his touch.

36

E*rik*

BEING INSIDE OF HER WAS THE BEST KIND OF HOMECOMING AND MY ALMOST immediate climax caught me by surprise, leaving Casey no time to reach her own. I felt like a real shit, lying there in the darkness, my body pinning her in place. My head was buried in the soft curve of her neck, and I gently pressed a kiss against the pulse beating there, letting her heartbeat penetrate my body, somehow bringing life to it again.

"I'm sorry," I whispered. "That was really inconsiderate."

"It's okay." She stroked my hair. "What's wrong?"

"Nothing." I relaxed into her as she gently pushed me over and rolled on top of me.

"Well, now that you got that out of your system, you planning on returning the favor?"

I gazed up at her lazily, that sexy smile I loved playing on her lips. "You're not too tired?"

"All I am right now is unsatisfied—are you going to leave me this way?"

"Hell no." I grabbed a fistful of her hair and pulled her face down roughly, though I kept my kisses tender.

"Are you okay?" she whispered against my lips. "You seem awfully agitated and it's not like you."

"It's been a rough week," I said softly.

"Well, you're home now, and this is going to be the best weekend of our lives."

I touched her cheek, guilt gnawing at my gut. "I can't wait."

"Would you rather not do this?" she asked. "We can go to sleep if you don't want to."

"No, I do. I really, really do." I reached up to put my hand over the tiny swell of her stomach. "He's growing."

"She is. I'm almost through the first trimester."

"Your stomach has barely changed though."

"It's coming. I think I'm going to pop, so to speak, any day now. So we need to hurry up and get married before the dress doesn't fit."

"You're going to be the most beautiful bride in the world, whether you pop or not." I was already getting hard again, just thinking about her starting to show her pregnancy and my child growing inside her.

Something I wouldn't be with her to enjoy.

"I guess you do want to go again," she murmured as my erection poked at her opening.

"Always with you." I slid into her for the second time tonight and she clamped around me, as sweet and tight as ever. I thrust up, watching her full, round breasts bounce with each stroke. I worried about hurting her, but she wouldn't let me hold back, squeezing and milking my cock in a pulsating rhythm that had us both gasping for air. I ground my hips against her, and she put her soft, warm hands on my chest for balance.

I flipped us over because I needed to be on top, in control. I ran my mouth across the curve of her shoulder and nipped at the skin. It was a primitive, baser instinct, but I suddenly felt a deep need to mark her, to make sure the whole fucking world knew she was mine. I didn't know when I would touch her again, but tonight, right now, she was mine, and I would make sure she never forgot what that felt like.

I sucked on the delicate skin of her throat until she squirmed beneath me.

"Erik, what are you doing?"

I didn't answer and didn't let up, my teeth scraping along her skin, moving to another spot and starting again. Her fingernails dug into the flesh of my back as her hips rose to meet mine, her protests dying in her throat as I shifted the angle of my cock and hit the spot that always took her where she needed to go.

"Oh god, Erik!" She convulsed around me, her body coming up off the bed as she came, wave after wave rushing through both of us. My own release was shorter this time, though no less explosive, and I pulled her as close as I could, lips still sucking on her throat.

"I'm going to kill you," she muttered, laughing in the darkness. "Why on earth would you give me a hickey two days before our wedding?"

"Think of it as a second wedding ring."

"Asshole." She dug her fingers into my hair. "Hey. Prince Caveman. Kiss me."

That I could do. So I did, over and over, until she finally gave in to exhaustion and drifted back to sleep.

I WAS UP AND OUT OF THE HOUSE A FEW HOURS LATER, THOUGH I SAT AND watched her sleep for a long time before I finally left. I knew what I had to do, and while I would do anything to keep her and the baby safe, it wasn't going to be easy. I'd begun formulating a plan, and coming home to Las Vegas had been part of it. I almost wished I hadn't, but not seeing her again hadn't been an option. I'd needed her, and according to my father she needed me too. Breaking things off would keep her safe, but the plan was complicated and had multiple levels, which was another reason why I'd come home. The problem was that Casey would never agree so I was going to have to do the hard part by not giving her a choice. Last night had been a selfish mistake, but I'd been helpless to stop myself. Not seeing her again, touching her one more time, would have been a fate worse than death.

As Sandor and I drove to the Charleston, the place where I was supposed to marry the most beautiful woman in the world in a little over twenty-four hours, I tried to focus on what I had to do, not what I wanted to do. Not what I should have been doing tomorrow. Not the woman who would undoubtedly be furious with me.

"You sure you know what you're doing?" Sandor asked as we pulled up to the private back entrance.

"I'm not sure of any goddamn thing right now," I retorted, getting out of the car and walking inside.

We got on the elevator, and I steeled myself for what was to come. No one would be happy, but what I'd seen and learned the last few days made me positive I was doing the right thing. Not for me, but for Casey and our baby. There was one piece of the puzzle that had to fall into place first, though, and my gut told me it wasn't going to be pretty.

We went to the door of Nick's suite and knocked. He opened it almost instantly with a subdued greeting and handshake. "Hey." He met my eyes warily. He wasn't stupid. He knew something serious was going on if I'd called to meet with him like this.

"There better be a good reason I hauled my ass out of bed this early," Nick said, motioning to a coffee urn. "Help yourself."

Sandor and I both got coffee and then sat across from him.

"Well, don't keep me in suspense," Nick said, assessing me carefully.

I looked at the man I was about to entrust my world to and wondered for the millionth time if I was making a mistake. Nick was Casey's oldest friend and confidante, his family as rich and powerful as mine, though in a totally different way. Their mob affiliations were kept under wraps, but they were there, and I trusted that would help keep Casey and our child alive. The Kingsleys were close to Casey's parents as well as my own, and my father assured me they were trustworthy, so here I was.

"Anwar is about to be crowned," I said quietly. "There's a rebellion trying to stop him, but they don't think they can. Not yet. My uncle had a small team in place, quietly working in the background, trying to gather intelligence about what Anwar was up to. Anwar must have found him out, which was why he had him and the others killed."

"Jesus fucking Christ," Nick muttered. "He killed his own father and brothers? That guy is batshit crazy."

"And he has me—and Casey simply by her proximity to me—in his sights. We, what's left of the royal bloodline, will never be safe with him in power. Even though it would take a literal act of Congress, so to speak, for me to ascend the throne, I'm his biggest threat. Intelligence coming from our allies in the eastern European countries is alarming."

"What does this have to do with me?"

"I can't marry her," I said, forcing my voice to remain steady even though my heart was out of control. "No one can ever know that the child she carries is mine. He will kill her while she's pregnant to keep any heir of mine from being born. If she makes it through the pregnancy, he'll stop at nothing to kill my child. I need you to marry Casey and claim my child as your own."

"Are you shitting me right now?" Nick looked as shell-shocked as I felt.

"Not even a little." I spelled out my conversation with Anwar as well as some of the details of the revolution brewing. "Until either Sandor, Daniil, or I can get a unanimous vote from Parliament that would allow one of us to challenge Anwar's place on the throne, we have to go underground. He won't rest until the bloodline is dead, and I can't just let him destroy the country I know and love."

Nick got up and started to pace. He was angry, but I sensed it wasn't at me since this wasn't my fault and he was astute enough to know that.

"She's never going to go for it," he said finally. "She'll want to stand by your side and fight."

"I know. Which is why I'm leaving before the wedding. She can't know about the plan until I'm gone."

"Jesus, Erik, do you know what that's going to do to her?" Nick faced me in frustration.

"Is the alternative better?" I asked. "Do you want her dead?"

"Of course not!" Anger exploded out of him and he pounded the side of his fist into the wall. "Dammit, Erik, how could you let this happen?"

"I would do anything to change this course of events. Believe me, this is the hardest thing I've ever had to do. You think I want to leave my woman—my son?"

"It's a girl," Nick responded absently.

I snorted. "Not hardly. There hasn't been a firstborn daughter in our family in a thousand years. I just haven't had the heart to tell her that."

He sighed. "What makes you think she'll marry me even if you do leave?"

"Because you'll make her. You'll remind her that the only real way to keep the baby safe is to make the entire world believe it's yours. Once she allows herself to mull it over, she'll do anything to protect the baby. I know her. She won't be happy, but she'll do it."

"You realize I just asked your sister out on a date, right?"

I groaned. "Shit. Well, you didn't know about the baby then, and now you have to do the right thing."

"Won't your sister know that we're full of shit?"

"Probably, but the less anyone knows, the safer it is for them. I realize what an enormous task I'm laying on you, but I don't know where else to turn. My family has the utmost respect for yours and this was actually my father's idea. He's the only other person that knows what's going on. You and Casey are close, you have a sexual history, so it's a plausible scenario that you got her pregnant before I came along, and you're truly the only person I believe can keep her safe. My goal is to overthrow Anwar, but I don't have a plan or a timeline yet, so all I can do is ask you to do me this honor."

We stared at each other for what felt like a long time. Finally, very slowly, Nick held out his hand. I shook it, and our hands remained linked for a bit longer than normal.

"I'll do anything to keep her safe," he said quietly. "But you better get your shit together and come back for her."

"You have my word."

37

Casey

THE DAY OF THE WEDDING BLOOMED BRIGHT AND CLEAR. A DESERT SUN WAS shining, but there was a cool autumn breeze. The sky was blue, clouds drifting back and forth, mimicking what was going on in my head as I stared out the window of my parents' kitchen restlessly. There were a million things to do today, but it was nowhere near time to get ready. My nail appointment was at eleven, hair at one, and makeup at two thirty. Then I would head to the Charleston and my entourage and I would get dressed in a private suite on the first floor, just next to the chapel.

"You're up early." Mom came down the stairs in bike shorts and a T-shirt. She kissed the top of my head and poured herself a cup of coffee.

"Couldn't sleep." I smiled. "Why are you up?"

"Well, it's my usual time on the exercise bike." She sat across from me. "You really are glowing, sweetheart. I can't believe you're marrying Erik today. I'm so happy and excited for you."

"Did you think you'd get a son-in-law and a grandchild all at the same time?"

She shrugged. "You know me—I go with the flow."

"What about Dad?"

"He's good—you know he adores you no matter what you do."

"Why am I so nervous?"

"Wedding day jitters are supposedly common."

"I feel sick to my stomach, like something bad is going to happen."

"Nothing bad is going to happen," Mom said softly. "Erik loves you. I'd bet my life on that."

"You are supposed to be on cloud nine today, young lady," Dad said, coming in and giving me a kiss. "I don't know what you're talking about, but it sounds serious so cut it out."

"Yes, sir," Mom and I spoke in unison.

"So, what's for breakfast?"

I threw a napkin at him. "Aren't I the blushing bride? Shouldn't you be serving me?"

"Only reason you're blushin' is 'cause you got knocked up before the weddin'." He teased me relentlessly sometimes.

I leaped out of my chair and thumped him on the back of the head with my thumb and middle finger.

"Ow!" he yelped, reaching for the dishtowel and taking a swipe at my backside.

"I guess I'm making breakfast," Mom muttered, shaking her head as she went to the refrigerator.

My dad and I chased each other around the kitchen for a few minutes and then he hugged me.

"What's wrong?" I asked him. "Now you're the one getting serious all of a sudden."

"Just seems like yesterday you were born," he said softly. "And now you're getting married and making me a grandfather. It's a lot for an old rocker to wrap his head around."

"Would you quit calling yourself old?" I demanded. "You're not old."

"Wait until you're in your fifties, then you'll see what I mean. But anyway, is anyone making breakfast?"

My mother turned and gave him a dirty look. "You ask about breakfast one more time and you'll be driving to McDonald's for it."

"Sorry, baby." He reached out and pinched her ass, making her laugh and me roll my eyes.

"You guys are definitely not old. No one old would behave like you do."

"Damn straight." He winked and poured himself a cup of coffee.

I WAS READY RIGHT AT FOUR O'CLOCK. I STOOD IN FRONT OF THE FULL-LENGTH mirror and stared at myself in disbelief. The woman in the mirror was absolutely stunning, and I had a hard time believing this day was really happening. My hair and face were coiffed and made-up to perfection, my figure still trim and sleek, and the swell of my breasts peeked out from a push-up bra while still managing to look tasteful. My gown was made of silk and lace, with a full, flowing skirt and ten-foot train. My veil hung from a diamond-encrusted tiara, on loan from Aunt Kari, and a necklace and bracelet of pink diamonds circled my throat and wrist, a gift from Uncle Ben, who said they matched my ring.

I gazed down at the diamond on my finger and sighed happily. Kari always wore fabulous jewels, but I was more of a tomboy, so I'd never thought about something so big or extravagant. I sure didn't much look like a tomboy today, though, and I resisted the urge to twirl around in my dress a few times.

"Wow, are you gorgeous or what?" Jade came bustling in, looking just as radiant as I did in the ruby-colored dress I'd chosen for the bridesmaids.

"So do you." I smiled and held out my hand. "Can you believe it's here? Can you believe this is going to happen?"

"Of course. You and Erik are meant for each other."

"I feel so..." I hesitated. "Unreal. Like I'm dreaming."

"You're not." Jade grinned. "Where's Skye, by the way? Shouldn't she be here?"

"Not sure," I said. "She was here earlier, helping me get my gown on and stuff, along with our moms and a few others, but she disappeared after she got dressed."

"Probably desperately pleading with Erik, one last time, to change his mind."

I chuckled. "Stop that—we've buried the hatchet, I think. At least I hope so. She's going to be my sister-in-law whether she likes it or not."

"I know."

"I don't want to think about anything negative," I said, looking back toward the mirror. "This is my day, and I'm going to enjoy it."

"Sweetheart, the photographer is here." Aunt Kari peeked in the door. "We need to shoot the bridal party now, before the men arrive."

"All right." I moved outside with Jade beside me.

"Are you gonna be bummin' if I go sneak a smoke?" Jade whispered.

"Yes, but go ahead and do it anyway." We snuck the occasional cigarette on tour. It was our private thing.

"Thanks." Jade wandered off, motioning to Vicki, who was standing around taking pictures.

"Are you all right, love?" Kari slipped her arm around my waist. "You shouldn't overdo it, you know."

"I'm fine. I'll probably need a little rest and a snack between the pictures and the ceremony."

"Casey!" a voice called out from the courtyard, and I turned to see Tabby hurrying toward me, also resplendent in her bridesmaid gown. Tabby had been the band's tour manager until she and BJ had gotten married, which was when Lance took over. Although we weren't as close now that Tabby and BJ were so settled, I'd wanted her to be in the wedding party.

"Tabby, you look beautiful!" I grinned.

"Look at you!" Tabby's blue eyes grew round. "You really are glowing! Are you pregnant?!"

I flushed but shook my head. "I'm just so happy!"

"Well, you look it."

"Casey!" My name was being called by a dozen people, and I hurried to greet guests who had arrived early to watch the picture-taking process.

It took an hour for the pictures to be taken, and then all of us returned to the suite beside the chapel. I disappeared into the bathroom and touched up my makeup. Then I found a bottle of water and sank into a chair, kicking off my shoes.

"You all right?" Mom asked, kneeling beside me.

"I'm fine, just resting now, while I can."

"It's going to be a long night, so don't hesitate to take little breaks."

"I won't. I promise."

"You want me to get everyone out of here for a few minutes so you can relax before the ceremony? There's just fifteen minutes."

"That would be awesome, Mom."

"All right." Mom squeezed my hand. "I'm so proud of you, honey—and you're going to be the most beautiful bride ever. I mean it."

"Thanks, Mom. I love you."

"I love you too." Mom made short work of dispersing the lurking bridal party, and soon I was alone with my thoughts.

I gazed out at the Las Vegas Strip that I'd always loved and smiled to myself. Hopefully, Erik would someday love it the way I did, and I'd do everything in my power to make him happy and to share the best parts of my life with him.

There was movement by the door, and I glanced up, startled out of my thoughts. "Sandor." I stood up quickly, slipping my shoes back on. "What are you doing here?"

He looked uncomfortable and quietly cleared his throat. "You look—unbelievable. I can't put it into words."

"What's wrong?"

He cleared his throat again. That's when I noticed he wasn't in his tuxedo, and my stomach dropped. I knew something bad was coming.

"He's not coming, is he?" I asked in a shaky voice.

He shook his head. "He, um, he sent this." He motioned to a large, rectangular box I hadn't noticed before.

"Are you kidding me right now? He sent me a package and didn't even have the balls to talk to me personally?"

"He's not breaking up with you, sweetheart. He's trying to save your life. Anwar…"

I swallowed back tears as bile rose in my throat. *Damn him.* I should have known he would do something like this. I should have known his showing up in our bed drunk in the middle of the night two days before the wedding was some kind of goodbye.

"Listen to me." I pulled my beautiful engagement ring off my finger and held it out. "You take this to him. You take it to him and tell him he has to come back and put it on my finger again or I won't wear it. We can and will fight that bastard. I'm not willing to give up everything I love because one lunatic hates us. I won't. I refuse. Tell him that."

"Casey, I can't—" he began.

"Instead of staying to protect me—*us*—he's leaving me to handle it on my own?"

"No. He's leaving it to me to handle." Nick stood in the doorway and I whirled around in frustration.

"What in the ever-loving fuck are you talking about, Kingsley?"

"Sandor, will you shut the door and give us some privacy?" he asked.

"No, don't shut the fucking door," I snapped. "Take the ring back to him and tell him what I said. Do you understand?"

We stared at each other until Sandor finally looked away. He obviously had no experience with a hormonal, pregnant, jilted bride on her wedding day. I would not, could not, back down. Not for something so important.

"Casey, he can't do that."

"Damn all of you!" I hissed angrily. "Take the fucking ring."

Sandor took it reluctantly and backed out of the room, shutting the door behind him.

"Open the box, Casey." Nick folded his arms across his chest.

The look he gave me brooked no argument and though I was on the verge of exploding, I took a deep breath. I had to think about the baby because I was overheating and my heart rate felt high. I was a little clammy too, which wasn't good. I sank into the nearest chair and took a few breaths.

"Could you get me some water?"

Nick grabbed a bottle and opened it, kneeling beside me. "It's going to be okay. Trust me. Open the box."

I looked in that direction suspiciously. What the hell was it?

"Would you bring it to me, please?"

He did as I asked and laid it at my feet.

"I'll give you some privacy," was all he said.

Then I was alone with a weird-looking box and my stupid wedding dress. With a sigh, I put down my water and gingerly sat on the floor next to the box. It wasn't that heavy, so I angled it to where I could open it and fidgeted with the top.

I had a pair of scissors in what we'd called my wedding emergency kit and I used them to cut through the packing tape. I slowly slid off the top and froze. The tears came before I could brace myself and my fingers shook as I gently lifted the most beautiful guitar I'd ever seen out of the box. A folded piece of paper fluttered to the ground and I reached for it, tears blurring my vision as I tried to read it:

My BEAUTIFUL BRIDE,

Right now I know you're heartbroken and angry, but please know I love you. Yesterday, today, and forever—you are my love, my light, my hope for the future. I'd never willingly leave you, but I also have to protect you. Anwar is crazy and he's going to do everything in his power to eliminate every possible blood heir to the throne, which means me. And my son that's growing inside of you. I know you don't believe me, but it's a boy. We haven't had a girl born first in a thousand years...ask my father. But even if it's a girl, she's still in danger. As are you. This was the only way to save you.

In the meantime, my wedding gift to you—another pink dragon for my beautiful pink dragon. I wish I could have seen your face when you got this, but I hope you love it and will think of me each time you play it. Vicenzo swears it's the greatest thing he's ever created and I agree.

Trust in my love. Trust that I'll be back for you. Trust that I'll never let you fall.
Erik

LAYING THE NOTE DOWN NEXT TO ME, I LIFTED THE GUITAR OUT OF THE BOX and stared at it in wonder. It was everything I could have wanted in an electric guitar. When I put the embroidered strap with my name on it over my head and let the body rest against mine, it fit me like an extension of my torso. When I ran my fingers down the neck, the frets seemed to meld with the tips of my fingers and I plucked out a basic melody, testing the sound. It was so beautiful, I was startled enough to have to pause, taking a moment to tune the strings. I wanted to hear it sing for me because I already knew it would.

I had an almost psychic connection with my guitars. I knew within seconds of picking one up whether or not I would be able to play it well. Most of the time, the answer was a resounding no, but not today. This one, this gorgeous, handmade pink guitar inlaid with a dragon carved from ivory, was going to be special. Not only because Erik had given it to me, but because it was the most magical thing I'd ever held in my hands.

38

E*rik*

I'd always loved Monte Carlo, but today I hated it. My wedding day. The day I was breaking the heart of the woman I loved. I was halfway across the world from her, and Sandor had undoubtedly gone to her and given her my gift and the letter by now. It was four in the morning here, but I'd been up all night, and since Las Vegas was nine hours behind us, it was still my fucking wedding day there.

I itched to reach out, call my father or Nick or even Sandor, anyone who knew what was going on, but that wouldn't get me anything. It was done. I'd made the hardest decision of my life to protect my woman and my unborn child, and now I had to live with it.

I twirled the empty snifter of brandy in my right hand absently, just for something to do, and heard movement behind me.

"Brooding isn't going to help," Daniil said. "You've done what's necessary."

"Knowing I did the right thing doesn't help either."

"It should." Daniil sat across from me. He was still pale and bruised but on the mend. We were staying here at the Charleston in Monte Carlo, in Liz's private suites. She was in Vegas for the wedding, of course, hiding her own involvement in what I was doing. She'd hated being a part of it, but as a

CIA operative, she understood what I was doing and why. She had to go, though, even if it was just for perception. She and Casey were friends, and her presence was expected. She'd been pissed when she left, but we were safe and sequestered in the hotel. It wasn't open for business, and since her private suite was finished, workers didn't wander up to this floor. She'd left us well-stocked with food and water, and we had an internet connection, so here we sat in our luxurious prison.

"Erik?" Daniil spoke my name and I realized I'd dozed off. I was going on no sleep for almost forty-eight hours and my body was demanding I rest.

"I guess I'm going to take a nap," I said, getting to my feet. "Will you be all right on your own?"

"I'm fine." He waved me off.

I WOKE TO SOMEONE SHAKING ME AND I ROLLED OVER IN FRUSTRATION. "WHAT is it?" I hissed, trying to focus.

"You've been asleep all day." Daniil looked down at me. "And we have company."

I sat up and stared at Sandor, who looked rougher than I felt. "Hey. You're back. What's going on?"

"She's pissed." He dug something out of his pocket and tossed it at me.

I raised a hand to catch it instinctively and winced when I realized what it was. Her ring. Fuck. She'd given him the ring and told him to bring it back to me. Not to my father, whom it truly belonged to, but to me. Yeah, my little vixen was more than pissed.

"We did this for a reason."

"She doesn't care. She says she'd rather be dead than live without you."

"She's hormonal and hurt," I said, trying to make light of her emotions. I didn't, I never would, but I had to pretend in front of Sandor and Daniil.

"She's hurt, upset."

"What about the guitar?" I asked. "Did she like it?"

"She was in tears, so I'm guessing yes."

"Sonofabitch."

"You did this to protect her. It's not like you don't love her."

"I fucking worship her," I muttered, rubbing my hands down my face. This was such a clusterfuck. I wanted to fly straight to Limaj and pound my fist into Anwar's smug face over and over until there was nothing left but a bloody pulp. I could almost feel the blood oozing onto my hands as I hit him, see the skin of his face splitting as I continued to hit him. It was a satisfying fantasy, but not satisfying enough and I got to my feet in frustration.

"She said she wants to fight together, that leaving her alone isn't what you promised."

"Why are you telling me this?" I demanded.

"Because she shoved this ring in my chest and glared at me until I promised I would," Sandor growled back.

We glared at each other until I finally backed down because arguing served no purpose. This wasn't either of our faults, but somehow, I was the one in Anwar's crosshairs. Deep down, I knew it was because I was the only one who could take the throne from him and he obviously knew it too.

"What are you thinking?" Sandor asked finally.

"Get Nick on the phone for me, will you?" I finally asked. "I need to know if she's okay."

He nodded and got on the phone, handing it to me a minute later.

"She's hanging on by a thread," Nick said when he answered. "The press is having a field day with this bullshit."

"As we intended."

"Yeah, but I don't know about the wisdom of leaving her at the altar. I mean, she knows you didn't dump her, but the rest of the world doesn't, and the headlines are pretty ugly."

"The uglier the headlines, the more believable it will be to Anwar." I'd said that to myself repeatedly as we'd planned this, because I hated what I was doing to her.

"Yeah, well, she's furious, pregnant, and hurting." Nick sounded frustrated. "And she doesn't want to talk to me at all."

"You have to make her."

"I will eventually, but right now she's holed up at her dad's house not talking to anyone."

I was upset about the whole situation, but that was so like Casey I couldn't help but smile. She really was a fiery little dragon. "Keep me posted, would you?"

"Of course."

I put the phone down and looked at Sandor. "Why don't you go get some rest? I have phone calls to make."

"Call Casey," Sandor muttered, leaving the room.

"I agree," Daniil called over his shoulder.

"You guys are not helpful," I yelled after them. I didn't know what to do. I'd done the right thing, I was sure of it, but Casey had taken the anger path instead of the heartbroken one, and I hadn't anticipated that. With her hormones out of control and a full house at the wedding, I'd figured she'd fall apart. That had been dumb on my part. The woman I loved was no shrinking violet, which made everything that much harder.

My Casey, the love of my life, would not give up on us so easily. Our love wasn't a fleeting affair or a casual tryst; we were soulmates, the loves of each other's lives. She would fight for me. For us. For our child. It was the most beautiful thing in the world, but also the most dangerous. Why didn't she understand that? Anwar was ruthless and wouldn't hesitate to kill her. As it was, I was worried about him getting to Skye, and who knew what Omar would do if he did. Seeing him at the ball had been jarring and caught all of us by surprise. Casey had to know how dangerous this was.

The best solution would be to eliminate Anwar, but that was no easy feat. I would need an army, probably the whole military, and the support of people who were probably very confused right now. Even if it was possible, it wasn't a quick fix. I didn't have a plan, the finances, or the backing to forge a coup like that, even with my father's help.

I was truly at a loss and there wasn't a damn thing I could do about it.

39

Casey

I HID OUT AT MY PARENTS' HOUSE FOR TWO DAYS. THEY BABIED ME AND WE ATE too much, talked too much and I cried far too much. My parents, Erik's parents, and Nick and his parents knew what was going on, of course, but no one else did and that didn't make it any easier. The press was on a tear, speculating about what I'd done, what was going on, and where Erik was. I tried to keep up with what the media was saying but I was overtired and overwhelmed. Unfortunately, I couldn't stay here any longer. For the charade to work, for people to believe I'd been jilted and was having another man's baby, I had to move in with Nick. Marry Nick. Pretend I was in love with Nick.

It was jarring, so utterly different from the life I'd been planning the last two months, I had no idea what to do first. I'd barely spoken to him, though it wasn't Nick I was angry with. Hell, he was trying to help, protect both me and my baby. I was just so angry at the world, at Anwar, at fate. This wasn't even a little bit fair and I desperately needed Erik. He was the only thing that would calm me right now but there was no way to reach him and it didn't help that I was worried about him as well.

"Are you ready to go?" Dad poked his head into my room and I smiled faintly.

"Ready as I'll ever be." I lumbered to my feet as though I weighed a thousand pounds. It wasn't just my body that felt heavy, but my entire being. Without Erik, I wasn't functioning properly and the light had gone out of my life. The only thing that brought me even the slightest bit of pleasure was my new guitar—aptly named The Pink Dragon. It and the accompanying letter hadn't been out of my sight since I'd gotten them and I'd read the letter at least two dozen times.

Trust in my love. Trust that I'll be back for you. Trust that I'll never let you fall.

Those words had become my mantra and I repeated them as often as I needed to get through the next hour, minute, or second. Time ran together right now.

"As far as I can tell," Joe said as I got to the bottom of the stairs, "no one has any idea you're here so they shouldn't see you leave either." He and a group of carefully selected men had been tasked with my safety, and though I was frustrated that Erik had made all these decisions without me, I would do whatever was necessary to protect our baby. Our son.

It was funny that I almost believed it was a boy now, just because he'd said so, and I thought about that as I followed Joe out to the waiting limousine. It had been sent from the Charleston to collect me and I hugged my parents tightly before getting in.

"It's going to be okay," Mom whispered. "You'll see. Just keep your chin up."

"You got this, honey." Dad hugged me next.

"I love you guys," I said tearfully.

Then I got into the limo and closed my eyes.

NICK WAS WAITING WHEN WE ARRIVED AT THE PRIVATE ENTRANCE, QUICKLY taking my hand and leading me up to his suite of rooms. He'd begun renovating them after we got back from the tour last summer since he was planning to live here full-time and wanted more than a hotel room as a home, despite the fact that it had been an exceptionally nice hotel room. His parents had taken the entire floor beneath the penthouse, making it into a home almost like any other, with multiple bedrooms, bathrooms, a kitchen and more. Nick now had the penthouse floor and had begun creating something similar. He loved the Charleston and planned to live here forever. It probably wouldn't have been my first choice, but I'd grown up running around here so it felt a little like home, despite the changes he was making.

"It'll have four bedrooms, four bathrooms, a kitchen, a hot tub and a workout room," he told me as he showed me around. "Right now, the only rooms that are finished are my room—the master bedroom and bath—and the main living area. Everything else is in progress. It's a little noisy during the day, but they're gone by six and don't come in until nine. I can delay that if you want to sleep later..." His voice trailed off, his eyes watching me intently.

"It's fine," I responded numbly.

"You okay?" Nick gently touched my shoulder.

"Just tired. I want to lie down, I think."

"Do you need me to get you anything?"

"No." I walked slowly to his—our—bedroom, looking around without seeing anything. Joe's men had moved most of my personal belongings over here yesterday, and I had my own closet in the guest room, but my toiletries and such were now mingled with his in the master bathroom. It was such an odd feeling, I wasn't sure what to do. I was supposed to be sharing a life with Erik now, building a home, starting our family... not living here with my best friend, pretending that this was normal.

I forced the thoughts from my mind and concentrated on washing my face, brushing my hair and pulling an oversized sweatshirt over my yoga pants.

I was staring at the ceiling when Nick came in and lay beside me on the bed. "You're not okay, are you?"

"No, not really."

"What can I do, Casey? I'm trying to protect you—you know that, don't you?"

"I do, and I appreciate it. I'm just a little more heartbroken than usual today. I miss him so much." Tears filled my eyes and I swiped at them angrily.

"I know." He leaned over and kissed my forehead. "But I have a surprise for you. Hang tight."

He disappeared and then came back a minute later, holding out his phone.

"I don't want to talk to anyone," I murmured.

"You do. Trust me." He wiggled the phone in front of me. "Take it."

I scowled but did as he asked, speaking into it gingerly. "Yes? Hello?"

"Hello, love."

Erik.

Tears squeezed out of my eyes before I could stop them and everything I'd thought I would say if I had a chance disappeared. I was overwhelmed with emotion and couldn't come up with a single word.

"Come on, don't cry." His voice soothed me as it always did. "I love you, Casey, and I'm working on coming home. Please don't cry."

"How could you leave me?" I cried, sobbing.

"I'm coming back." He sounded strong, determined. "I'll never leave you, never. Trust me, baby. You know me. You know you're my everything."

"I miss you," I whispered.

"I know. I miss you too. But I'm coming back. I don't know how long it'll take or what I have to do to protect all of us, but I will. Please tell me you believe in me and that you'll wait for me."

"Of course I'll wait for you." I sniffled and fumbled for a tissue. "Forever. Longer, if necessary."

"But I need you to marry Nick, sweetheart. It has to be the performance of a lifetime. You have to marry him, be seen with him, hold his hand, kiss him in public—show the whole world that I was nothing but a tryst to you."

"Erik." My heart squeezed in agony. I liked Nick. Hell, I loved him, but I wasn't in love with him. How was I going to pull this off?

"It's going to be hard, for both of us, but we have to do this. Our baby, our lives, depend on it."

"This sucks ass," I muttered.

He chuckled. "Believe me, I know."

"But what are you going to do?"

"I'm in hiding, gathering intelligence and working with a group we're calling the anti-rebellion to take the country back. I have to have a lot of support, though, and that's going to take time. Anwar will have to screw up a few times before I can count on that kind of backing, so you have to hang in there for me."

"You'll call and check in, right? I have to hear your voice, Erik, or I can't do this."

"Whenever I can get to a secure line. I promise."

"I'm so scared. How can I have this baby without you?"

"You'll have Nick and your family, your friends... You'll do it because you're my strong, brave dragon queen and you're going to kick ass and take names, just as you've always done."

"Dragon queen?"

"Yup. By the way, I'm pissed you gave back the ring."

"I won't wear it until you put it back on my finger."

"And I'm going to do that as soon as I possibly can."

"I love you, Erik."

"I love you too. I have to go, but I'll call soon. I'll try to call once a week, but if I can't, don't panic. I'll call as soon as I can."

"Say it," I whispered.

"I love you." His words were like a balm on my tattered soul.

"And?"

"I'm coming back."

"Promise."

"I fucking swear."

"Be careful."

"Always."

He disconnected and I hugged the phone to my chest, keeping the sound of his voice in my head, my heart. He was okay. He loved me. He was coming back.

Trust in my love. Trust that I'll be back for you. Trust that I'll never let you fall.

I stood up and blew my nose, straightening my spine. Fuck Anwar and his bullshit. I wouldn't let him beat me. Not physically, not emotionally, not in any way. I was tougher than this and we would show him who was boss.

I walked into the living room and Nick looked up with a smile.

"Feel better?"

"I do. Thank you." I went and sat next to him.

He reached for my hand and I locked my fingers with his, relying on a lifetime of friendship to boost the strength I was struggling to find on my own.

"So?" he asked.

"Are you sure you're up for this? It's asking an awful lot of you, Nick."

"Which part? Marrying you?"

"All of it. Getting married, having a baby, making that fucker Anwar believe what we need him to believe."

"This isn't hard for me, really. I already know and like you. We've been as intimate as two people could be, so no one is going to be freaking out about getting dressed in front of the other or sharing a bed—and I'm not talking about sex. Day to day, this is no different than being on tour. Minus the music."

"And the sex."

He chuckled. "I'm good. Really. I mean, we'd have to revisit that if this was going to be forever, but until Erik comes back, I'm not some sixteen-year-old who just got his dick sucked for the first time."

I smiled. "Okay then. Tomorrow, we make it legal and I take back my life."

"It won't be forever," he said gently. "You'll see. And it'll be fun. We can run around the hotel like we used to, except, you know, less drunk... play music, maybe you can even take some classes with me since you want to go back to school. It'll go fast, Casey. Wait and see."

I nodded. I didn't know if I believed it, but I had to pretend or I wouldn't survive this.

Trust in my love. Trust that I'll be back for you. Trust that I'll never let you fall.

Get ready for NOWHERE LEFT TO RUN, book 2 of The Royal Trilogy—preorder here!

If you enjoyed Nowhere Left to Fall, please consider leaving a review at your retailer of choice.

COMING SOON

Nowhere Left to Run — Book 2 of The Royal Trilogy

I have nowhere left to run...
I'll never love another the way I loved him. He might have been a prince, but to me he was just Erik. The father of my child. The man whose love was so fierce, it's like it never left me.

Some days I swear I can still feel his presence surrounding me, until I'm reminded that our love song is over.

Moving on is the hardest thing I've ever had to do.

Hollow without him, the music that's been pouring out of my soul is the only way to ease the ache.

It will never replace the love of my life, but for my baby's sake, I have to try.

Every tragic lyric, every minor chord, proves that I can't outrun his ghost or the truth... my heart beats only for him.

Nowhere Left to Hide - the exciting conclusion to The Nowhere Trilogy!

We have nowhere left to hide...

Erik
Loving her from the shadows shattered my heart.
Watching her move on nearly destroyed me.

COMING SOON

I let them both go, knowing it was the only way to keep them safe.

Now the threat is back and there's only one way to protect them: Come back from the dead.

It's time to claim what's mine.

My woman. My kingdom. My life.

Casey

The only man I ever truly loved died to protect us, and nothing will ever be the same.

I've spent the last decade becoming someone else, forcing myself to let go of the past.

The past won't let go of me.

The life I've rebuilt is crashing down around me.

I thought it was over, but fate isn't finished with me yet.

Made in United States
Orlando, FL
02 April 2023